TO WEAR A DEMON CROWN

Madeleine Eliot

Copyright © 2023 Madeleine Eliot

All rights reserved

The characters and events portrayed in this book are fictitious. Any similarity to real persons, living or dead, is coincidental and not intended by the author.

No part of this book may be reproduced, or stored in a retrieval system, or transmitted in any form or by any means, electronic, mechanical, photocopying, recording, or otherwise, without express written permission of the publisher.

Cover design by: Madeleine Eliot
instagram.com/madeleineeliotwrites

Map design by: Lindsey Staton
instagram.com/honeyy.fae

Portrait designs by: Kaja McDonald
instagram.com/bookishaveril

Edited by Aurora Culver, A. Linda Farmer, Kelsey McCullar, Jenessa Ren, Kimberly Sathmary, Lindsey Staton, Heidi Torr, and E.F. Watson

Proofreading and copyediting by Megan Brown, Maggie LeMmon, Brook McNabb, Cait Millrod, Abigail Myles, Christina Routhier, Dakshayani Shankar, Caressa Slater, Jess White, and Brenda Vann

Printed in the United States of America

To those who have loved and lost and carry on.

Blessed be my feet that walk in the path of the Lord and Lady.
Blessed be my knees that kneel at the sacred altar.
Blessed be my heart that beats to the drum of compassion.
Blessed be my lips that they may speak the truth.
Blessed be my eyes that see the path of spirit.
May the love of the Lord and Lady surround and guide me through life and this day.
So mote it be.

WICCAN DAILY PRAYER

CONTENTS

Title Page
Copyright
Dedication
Epigraph
Expanded Map of the Darklands
Pronunciation Guide
The Empress   1
Chapter 1   3
Chapter 2   16
Chapter 3   26
Chapter 4   36
Chapter 5   47
Chapter 6   60
Chapter 7   71
Chapter 8   82
Chapter 9   92
Chapter 10   102
Chapter 11   111
Chapter 12   121
Chapter 13   131
Chapter 14   143

Chapter 15	155
The World	165
Chapter 16	167
Chapter 17	179
Chapter 18	189
Chapter 19	198
Chapter 20	208
Chapter 21	218
Chapter 22	230
Chapter 23	241
Chapter 24	252
Chapter 25	264
Chapter 26	275
Chapter 27	289
Chapter 28	300
Chapter 29	310
Chapter 30	318
Epilogue	333
Coming October 13	339
Acknowledgements	341
About The Author	343
More Books by Madeleine Eliot	345

EXPANDED MAP OF THE DARKLANDS

PRONUNCIATION GUIDE

Akela: Ah-KEE-lah

Beltane: BELL-tain

Brigid: BRIDGE-id

Carnon: KAR-non

Cernunnos: Ser-NOON-owz

Cerridwen: KARE-uh-dwen

Demon: DEE-mon

Daemon: DAY-mon

Elara: Ehh-LAR-uhh

Herne: HURN

Imbolc: IM-blk

Lughnasadh: Loo-NAH-sah

Mabon: MAY-bin

Ostara: Oh-STAR-ah

Oneiros: Oh-NEE-rowz

Samhain: SAH-when

Scathanna: Ska-THAN-nah

Tyr: TEER

Yule: YOOL

THE EMPRESS

Part 1

MADELEINE ELIOT

Chapter 1

"You've got to be fucking kidding me!" I shouted, fear making my pulse race as the wall of flame surrounded me on all sides. "This is barbaric!"

"Try it again," Carnon commanded, deaf to my complaints. "Control your fear and focus, Red."

"It's hard to focus when I'm about to be incinerated for the fifth fucking time today," I gritted out, pulling on that spark of sun inside me, so different from the life and death magic I was almost able to wield with perfect accuracy. I could barely make out the sky with all of the smoke, and I coughed as the heat stung my eyes and nose.

We had been at this for more than a month, Carnon spending at least two hours with me each day to hone my demonic gifts and perfect my witch gifts, which could now be powered by demonic intention.

My magic and abilities had grown. Whether it was from living in the Darklands for long enough, or from the magic of our mating bond, I couldn't be sure. Within two weeks of our disastrous trip to Ostara, I was withering and healing trees, whole forests, and even a very unwilling Lucifer. He had been grateful to stay behind in Oneiros when we left for the Court of Sun a few days ago.

We had then moved on to testing my witch magic, and I was now able to cast most simple spells with intention alone, building an altar in my mind instead of on the ground before me. My witch magic still required a cost, but I could pay it with energy, or with some of my demon magic, or with something that was naturally consumed by the magic anyway.

Now, Carnon wanted to explore and master the other gifts my father had given me.

I had used the fire first when my rage at Mama's death had consumed me, and I'd nearly burned the Covenstead to the ground. I had done it again a few hours after her death, and once more two weeks ago, when Carnon had pushed me into rage and anger during a training session that had pulled the fire from me.

Carnon had tried to be patient and supportive, but he wanted me to talk about how I felt. About the grief and loss that felt like they were carving a permanent hole where my heart had been. More often than not, I responded in anger, only to apologize and melt into a puddle of tears a few hours later.

If he was getting annoyed at my grieving process, he

didn't show it. He loved me emotionally and physically with the same passion he had always shown me. But I still felt that emptiness and anger, which made it hard to love him back as well as he deserved, and even more difficult to control the fire.

Being in the Court of Sun for the last two days had brought the fire magic out even more. Something about being in the place where the magic originated brought it simmering to the surface of my skin.

The problem was putting the fire out. Once I could summon the fire at will, Carnon wanted me to learn to smother it.

It wasn't going well.

"Focus, Red," Carnon shouted from outside the wall of fire. "Calm your anger. Let it go."

"Again, it's hard to be calm under these circumstances," I grumbled, gritting my teeth against the heat. An ember landed on my arm, burning the skin with a hiss. I brushed it off, sending my healing magic to the spot with barely a thought as I tried to focus on the fire.

"Please be careful," Cerridwen shouted nervously from the edge of the ring Carnon had marked on the ground for our practice.

"And please don't melt the palace," Brigid agreed, glancing anxiously at the building of gold and glass that marked the seat of power in her Court.

I rolled my eyes, sweat dripping down me as the heat of the fire blazed. I hadn't been able to smother the fire a single time yet, and I was exhausted from tapping into my magic all morning.

I took a deep breath, trying to force calm, cooling darkness into my mind, like the shadows I had seen

Carnon summon a hundred times since he first showed them to me. My focus slipped as I remembered the shadows and fire around me as the Crone had opened Mama's throat. Anger surged and the wall of flames exploded.

"Shit!" Carnon shouted, dousing the courtyard in shadow. Cerridwen and Brigid had both screamed in panic, and Herne was swearing colorfully as Carnon undid my mistake.

Smoke rose gently from the singed stones beneath my feet, and I looked up to see my mate scowling at me. A normal person would quake at the ferocity of his stare, but all it did was fan the flames of anger in my blood.

"What the fuck was that, Elara?" he growled, reaching out to grab my shoulder.

I dodged away. "Fire, obviously," I snapped, storming to the edge of the courtyard and snatching up a water skin. I gulped the water down as Carnon stalked toward me again.

"You could have burned us all alive," he barked, pushing the water skin out of my hands and gesturing to our friends, who were watching with expressions ranging from mild to acute panic. Carnon gripped my shoulders and shook me gently. "Gods above, Elara."

"But I didn't," I snarled, trying to pull away. His grip on my shoulders was too firm, not bruising but certainly not gentle. "And clearly, I can't do this. Now let me go."

"No," Carnon replied, glaring down at me. He was breathing heavily, we both were, and I saw something heated flash behind the anger in his green, slitted eyes. A spark of desire lit me as he glared down at me, my fearsome mate never failing to ignite my passions. *Not the time, Elara.* He took a deep breath, the anger cooling and the gentle, patient teacher returning.

I felt a twinge of disappointment.

"I can't help you control the fire if you won't manage your anger, Red," he said gently, cupping my face with his hands. I tried to turn away, feeling some of my anger fade into embarrassment.

"Look at me," Carnon said, turning my face back toward his. His eyes softened when they looked into mine, and he stroked a thumb over my cheekbone. "Anger serves a purpose, Red, but it will eat you alive if you let it. I need you *not* to let it."

I swallowed, my heart catching at his words. For the past month I had felt only anger or gaping, endless emptiness at the death of my mother. Anger seemed the safer of the two emotions, something I could channel into my magic or into desire that could be sated by Carnon. But it was putting a strain on both of us.

"I know," I said quietly, holding his gaze. "I'm just..."

"I know," Carnon murmured. "I'm sorry I couldn't save her."

His expression was so somber, so weighed down with guilt that I couldn't stand it. I wanted to say something to reassure him, to remind him that I didn't blame him for Mama's death, but the words just wouldn't come. They never seemed to come.

I had tried, the day she died, to bring her back. Hours after she passed, once the first wave of grief and hollowness abated and I could think a little more clearly, I became convinced I could revive her. I had saved that baby, and so I could save Mama. Cerridwen had placed her body in a spare room after we had returned, and I spent half of that first day of grief attempting to bring her back.

Even when my magic returned, she remained lifeless. Carnon had tried with me, both of us draining our magic a second time to no avail. He didn't have a satisfactory explanation for me. Brigid suspected that her soul had already passed on into the arms of the Goddess, whereas the babe hadn't been ready to go.

It was brutally unfair. What was the point of this magic if I couldn't use it to save the person I loved most in this world? My rage had begun to consume me then, and it had taken Carnon cocooning me in shadow to prevent me from burning the palace to ash.

I sighed, without the words of forgiveness I knew my mate needed. I was angry, at myself and at him and at the Goddess. But I knew it wasn't his fault. When I sensed the others approaching us from behind, I lifted on my toes to press a kiss to his cheek. "I'll try harder," I whispered.

He caught my lips in a quick, fierce kiss as I pulled away. I wound my arms around his neck, letting him pull me closer as one of his hands traced my curves, moving lower and lower.

Sex was simple. Far easier than talking or feelings or words. The fire and passion of our claiming had yet to dim, even after more than a month had passed. It was easier to get swept away by those passions than to deal with the hurt and the guilt, and I let out a little moan as Carnon squeezed my backside.

A gruff voice behind us groaned, "Get a room," and the spell was broken. I pulled away, flushed from the heat of my mate now, rather than the fire.

"We have a room," Carnon replied, looking over my

head at Herne, Lord of Beasts and his oldest friend. He begrudgingly loosened his grip on me as I took a step away. "It was you who insisted we leave it this morning."

Brigid coughed with embarrassment behind us and I shot her an apologetic grimace. The Lady of Sun was one of the four Daemon Lords who ruled the Darklands and advised the Demon King, and she had suggested this visit almost a month ago. While she claimed it was because she thought her libraries might hold answers about my magic, I knew the real reason was that, in those first days after Mama's death, she was worried about me.

"Maybe a change of scene will help," she had suggested as she took tea with me and Cerridwen on one of those interminably long afternoons filled with aching empty sadness. "The sea and the sun and the sand is…" she glanced at my mate's sister, looking for assistance. Cerridwen just shrugged and sipped her tea. "Rejuvenating," she finished brightly.

"You can't keep to your rooms until Lughnasadh," Herne growled, earning a poke in the ribs from Cerridwen as he reminded us that we had an audience. "What? It's true."

"You've forgotten what it's like to be newly mated," Cerridwen said, giving her mate an annoyed look. "Let them have their fun."

"Herne is right, I'm afraid," Carnon sighed, holding me away from him a little. "We have a great deal to do while we are here, and so far we've accomplished none of it."

"We only just arrived the day before yesterday," I argued, taking another swig of water to cool the combined heat of my fire magic and the warm sun.

"You needed time to rest," Brigid agreed, smiling amiably. She looked like she was manifested entirely from sunshine here, her golden hair and skin glowing brightly in the morning light.

"Lest you have forgotten, mate," Carnon said, giving me a wry smile, "we are supposed to be researching your father and your magic and these varying prophecies Brigid found. Not to mention the history of the Bloodwood and a way to defeat your grandmother."

"I haven't forgotten," I snapped, my anger constantly bubbling at the surface of every interaction. Cerridwen raised a concerned brow at me, and I sighed, taking a calming breath. "Training me to use my magic is also important. Perhaps more important than searching through dusty old books for information that might not even be there."

"Those books might hold answers we need, Elara," Carnon argued, crossing his arms and studying me. "And you've already trained enough today, unless you're determined to wither some of Brigid's staff or set the whole palace ablaze."

Brigid let out a little cry of protest at these suggestions, and I sighed.

"I want to master the flames," I argued, mirroring his stance. "I need to master them, or I'll have no hope of killing the Crone."

Carnon pursed his lips, noticing my use of her title. She had stopped being my grandmother when she murdered my mother, and I refused to call her 'my' anything. The memory of my mother's blood spilling over my hands haunted me nightly, and Carnon suspected that my hatred for the Crone was the reason I couldn't control my fire.

It killed me not to know what she was up to. I was desperate in the first few weeks after Mama's death to enchant another mirror and tear her limb from limb. But we had been more unprepared than we realized last time, and Carnon cautioned patience.

"I wish that Tyr and Scathanna had agreed to lift the ultimatum we set last month," Brigid said regretfully. She took my arm gently in hers and led me from the courtyard, clearly hoping to dissuade me from more magic practice. Carnon, Cerridwen, and Herne fell in behind us. "Especially since Herne and I no longer support it."

The ultimatum had been to bring the Crone's head to the Daemon Lords as proof of my loyalty. They had refused to allow Carnon to name me Queen until I completed the task. I shuddered.

"And we should never have requested it anyway," Brigid continued firmly, misinterpreting my shudder as fear over facing the Crone again. "I shouldn't have let Scathanna bully me into agreeing."

"It's fine," I said gently, patting her hand as we reentered the palace. It was a monument of glass and gold, beautiful in the sunshine of this court. Technically, the palace belonged to the royal family, but Brigid and every Lord of Sun before her lived in the palace as its steward. If there was any place we might learn more about my father, it was here, where he once served as this Court's Lord. "I doubt Scathanna will ever accept me as her queen."

"Herne and I need to collect the latest news from the border," Carnon said, catching my arm. The witches had been attacking the wards to the Darklands for weeks now, and the fact that they were tied to Carnon's life and will was keeping them steady, for now at least. Carnon looked me up and down, then frowned, as if what he saw was worrisome. "Will you be alright without me for an hour or two?"

I gave him my most withering stare. "It's a library, Carnon," I said dryly, "not a battlefield. I think we'll be fine."

His frown lifted as he leaned forward to kiss my cheek. "I love that smart mouth of yours," he murmured, giving me a second kiss on the lips. He paused, sweeping a thumb over my cheek before adding, "I'll come find it and you when we're done to debrief. No setting fire to the library."

He jumped back lithely before I could swat him away, smirking as he waved. Herne rolled his eyes as if our romance personally offended. I knew this wasn't the case, since Herne had given me something of a begrudging blessing before we had completed the claiming, but Herne always looked like he disapproved of everything. He planted a kiss on Cerridwen's cheek before following his king. She was the only person he liked unequivocally.

I let Cerridwen take one of my arms while Brigid took the other, and we turned away toward wherever this massive library was.

"Are you truly well, Elara?" Brigid asked, glancing around quickly before pinning me with bright blue eyes. "You seem…better?"

"I am," I said, smiling at her, though noting the question in her tone. "Not…" I swallowed, the memory of Mama's blood hot on my hands flooding me for a moment. "Not perfect. But better. I'm…angry still."

"I think that's to be expected," Cerridwen said lightly, giving my arm a squeeze. "It was months before my parents' deaths stopped haunting me every moment. You'll get there in time."

I winced. I often forgot that Carnon and Cerridwen had lost their parents too. I wondered if Carnon had felt as broken as I still did. He had been only five when they had been murdered by some unknown demons hoping to take advantage of his status as the next Demon King, or dethrone him. They had never found out who was behind the plot.

"Where's Akela?" Brigid asked suddenly, noticing the absence of my furry shadow. He and Artemis, the strix who was bonded to Carnon for life, had joined us on this trip as always, and Akela was rarely separated from me. He seemed to have decided that he was my personal guard-wolf, and I didn't mind his near constant company.

"Probably hunting," I said, realizing I hadn't seen him since the night before. "He certainly needs the nourishment after running the whole way from Oneiros."

"I'll have the cook send up some raw steaks when he returns," Brigid said, looking utterly thrilled at the idea of serving my wolf raw meat.

"Let me change before we go," I said, entering our rooms and gesturing to the sitting area. "I'm sweaty and I smell like a bonfire."

Our rooms looked out onto the distant sea, a glimmering blue jewel against the horizon. I pulled off my dirty leathers and replaced them with a comfortable skirt and blouse, the weather too warm to make trousers comfortable.

"How old is this library again?" I asked, rebraiding my copper hair as I returned to the sitting room. Brigid, in her white sleeveless gown of finest silk, looked like a true queen in this palace. I had chosen comfort over finery with simple bodices and skirts or trousers. I didn't really need all the pockets any more, since I could cast my witch magic by intention, but a good witch is always prepared, and I preferred to be armed with chalk and crystals just in case. Cerridwen favored leathers while on duty, as she was technically serving as my personal guard while we were in the Court of Sun.

"At least two thousand years," Brigid answered, gesturing for us to follow her from our rooms. "And there are over a million books. I've already asked the scholars to pull a few that might be useful to you."

"Based on how our research has gone so far, I'm not that hopeful. And King Alaunus," I added, still feeling like my father's name was foreign on my tongue. "He studied there?"

"He did," Brigid confirmed, giving me a knowing smile. "I believe he wrote several of the books of prophecy himself."

Demons from the Court of the Sun generally had two sets of powers: fire and sight. I had clearly inherited fire, but Carnon and I had been unable to discover if I had the power of sight or prophecy as well. Brigid had some skill at it, but aside from some conveniently arranged tea leaves, I hadn't felt anything prophetic about myself or had any visions like my father had.

Brigid led us through several golden halls and passages until we came to a set of huge golden doors.

"Why are all libraries housed behind giant doors?" I mused, remembering the moonstone doors that concealed the royal library in the palace in Oneiros.

"Because scholars are pretentious," Cerridwen replied. Brigid shushed us as she pressed her hands to the doors. They must be spelled to open at her touch, because the gilded panels swung forward on a phantom breeze.

I gasped.

"Welcome to the largest library in the world," Brigid beamed.

Chapter 2

"This is a *few* books?" I asked, looking in horror at the piles and piles of books that had been neatly stacked by the scholars for our perusal.

We were in a private reading room, one of a hundred that could be found throughout the massive library. The room was richly appointed, the gold walls inset with brightly colored glass that afforded a view of the stacks beyond. Thousands and thousands of books were shelved on bookcases of deep mahogany, each labeled with tiny golden plaques that indicated some filing system known only to the scholars who maintained the library. Every few yards, squashy armchairs and loveseats sat nestled into little alcoves and curtained-off rooms, the furniture comfortable enough for a lengthy period of reading.

When Brigid said the scholars had pulled a few books, I pictured the stacks that Carnon pulled from his royal library. But there were at least a hundred tomes stacked to the ceiling in the tiny reading room. All were bound in leather and in various stages of aging and decay, with ponderous and utterly dull titles like, *The Compendium of Demon Magicks*, and *Prophesy of the Sun, Volume XVII*.

"I *did* ask them to control themselves," Brigid said with a wince. "The scholars can be a little zealous. But we will help you go through them all!"

Cerridwen gave me a wide-eyed expression of panic, followed by a sigh of resignation when my only response was a single raised eyebrow. "Of course we will," she agreed unenthusiastically.

I laughed at her failure to disguise her misery and sighed too, flopping into the nearest armchair and pulling the closest stack of books to me. "What are the policies on wine and macarons in the library?"

"I'm fairly certain it's a strong no," Brigid replied, grimacing apologetically. "But maybe I can have refreshments sent to an empty reading room?"

I waved her off, groaning resignedly over my macaron-less future. No one made them as well as Pierre, anyway.

"I thought you should also have this," Brigid said, taking the armchair closest to mine. She held out a little leather book, one I had seen before when she had shared the prophecies she thought might be about me. "It's my research. I've taken notes on a lot of the prophecies, and I wrote down where they came from, so we can easily find the books if we need to. I also recorded our old tarot readings, just in case we need to reference them."

I took the book from her, marveling as I flipped through a few of the pages. I found the two prophecies she had already shared with me, as well as several other jotted down notes and theories.

"Thank you," I said, feeling a little overwhelmed at her kindness. "You didn't need to do that."

"It was no problem," Brigid replied brightly. "I love research."

I smiled at her clearly not-feigned enthusiasm, so different from Cerridwen. "Can I see this one?" I asked, pointing to the title of a book Brigid had written next to a prophecy I had heard before.

It was one that King Alaunus had made ten years ago, that Brigid had shared with me before Mama's death: *A sacrifice of blood will keep her safe until the Demon King can claim her.* Brigid believed that I was *her*, although I had no idea what the sacrifice of blood meant.

It was also this prophecy that convinced Brigid that Alaunus was my father, although Carnon had already suggested this. My mother had confirmed it as she died, and a large part of me ached to know him in a way I never had before.

When it had just been me and Mama, it hadn't really mattered to me who my father was. No witch was raised by her father, and asking about him made Mama sad, so I let the mystery be. Now that I had lost her, I felt a drive to learn more about the man—or male, I supposed, since he was a demon—who had sired me. My mother's mate, who had somehow found her across realms.

Rather like how Carnon had found me across realms, I supposed. The parallels between our relationships were not lost on me. Maybe Brigid's prophecy had been about my parents, rather than me and Carnon: two beings from opposing worlds coming together for the first time in a thousand years. Even more reason to read the prophecy in full.

"I'll go ask the librarians to hunt it down," Brigid agreed, giving me an encouraging smile. "And anything else Alaunus recorded here. There might be something meaningful for you in them."

Cerridwen raised a brow at me as Brigid left. She had plopped down into the loveseat across the low work table, and it looked like she had flipped open whatever book was nearest to her in an attempt to look studious.

"Do you think that prophecy is about you?" she asked, flipping a page that she clearly hadn't read. "Seers can see the past, too. Maybe it was about someone else."

"Could be," I conceded, turning to the other prophecy Brigid had shared. "But it's written in the future tense, so chances are it's not about the past."

"What do you think the sacrifice was?" Cerridwen asked, giving me a sympathetic look. I knew she was thinking about my mother.

"Not Mama," I snapped. Cerridwen looked so abashed that I immediately felt guilty for my sharpness. "Sorry," I winced, softening my tone. "This was ten years ago, and I was already with the Demon King when the Crone murdered her. She wasn't a sacrifice."

She nodded, pursing her lips as she turned back to her book, and I turned back to mine. Gods, I needed to get my anger under control.

Despite this thought, I was ready to tear out my hair in frustration when Carnon found us two hours later. Straining my eyes over the tiny, ancient text in the moldering tomes had led to very little progress, other than all three of us becoming snappish with each other. I was hungry, and my head ached from reading about long dead Demon Kings and politics.

There were very few mentions of witches in anything we had combed through so far, but Brigid said we had mostly been reading the newer texts. We'd have to dig into thousand-year-old books and manuscripts to get to witch-demon history. The shining sun outside the huge windows convinced me that it should wait for another day.

Brigid hadn't been able to locate any of the books of prophecy with Alaunus' records. I thought this was strange, since a former Lord and King's work should probably be both protected and studied, but she assured me that the library was huge, and that the scholars would keep looking.

"Is there a chance his records were destroyed?" I asked, slamming my last book in frustration. Carnon raised a brow at me as he sauntered into our reading room, Herne glowering behind him. "Sorry," I added, giving Brigid an apologetic wince. "Working on the anger."

"No," she said, seeming unfazed by my outburst and apology. She frowned thoughtfully, chewing on her lower lip. "Nothing is destroyed in this library. It's more likely he concealed them somewhere."

"No luck, Red?" Carnon asked, dropping a kiss on my head before flopping down on the couch next to Cerridwen. She shoved her brother away irritably and he gave her an impish grin. "You're all in such a lovely mood."

"You would be too if you'd spent two hours uselessly

pouring through dusty old books," she snapped.

Herne grunted, a sound somewhere between a laugh and a groan, and I looked at Cerridwen's mate. "You don't look happy either. The news is bad?" I turned back to Carnon, whose signature smirk had fallen away.

"It's not great," he conceded with a sigh. "Is this room secure, Brigid?"

"I think so," she replied, hesitantly. "It's really only the scholars and us down here."

Carnon nodded, seeming wary still, and leaned forward on his knees, his hands clasped as he looked at each of us in turn. "Scathanna's casters never arrived at the border."

"What?" cried Brigid and Cerridwen as one. Herne nodded with a grimace, and only I seemed to not understand the importance of this. I remembered that Carnon had ordered casters, who could direct magic outward offensively, from the courts to the border when the witches had first begun attacking, but perhaps there was an innocent explanation for their absence.

"Maybe they were delayed?" I asked, trying to read the dark look between Herne and Carnon.

"They were not delayed," Herne growled, his fist clenched so hard on the back of the loveseat behind Cerridwen that I heard the upholstery creaking.

"Tyr's casters arrived, few as they are," Carnon added. He nodded toward the Lady of Sun. "And Brigid's. Shadow should have arrived before either."

"So what does that mean?" I asked. "I thought the witches couldn't get past your wards?"

"They can't," Carnon agreed. "And from what I understand, your grandmother cannot enter or destroy the Bloodwood. At least, that's the history I was told."

"Then why is it a problem if Scathanna's casters haven't arrived?" I asked.

"It means she didn't send them," Brigid explained quietly.

"It means she's a fucking treasonous bitch," Herne corrected angrily.

"We already knew that," Carnon said, giving his friend a warning glance to cool his fury. My mate turned back to me, looking suddenly exhausted. "But it's likely she is defying my orders long enough to either blatantly usurp me or at least weaken my position as king."

"So what does that mean?" I asked, feeling like I really should have read up on demonic politics more. If I was going to be part of this court, then I should actually know what I was doing as its queen.

"It means I'll have to summon her to court, and it's a lot of pomp and paperwork and time wasting," Carnon groaned, flopping back on the loveseat and scrubbing his hands over his face. "And she'll deny any wrongdoing and there won't be anything I can damn well do about it until she breaks the official deadline I'll have to set."

"Sounds like you don't have a lot of power as the Demon King," I quipped, tilting my head to study him.

He sat up, brows raised in derision. "Welcome to the party, Red," he said. "I told you already that no ruler rules alone. It's all politics and nonsense."

"How many casters did Tyr send?" Brigid asked, pulling Carnon from his ire.

"Only twenty," he replied, "but that's not surprising. Blood has never been rife with casters. Offensive blood magic is supposed to be quite challenging. Most don't bother learning it."

"So with my casters, we have what? Two hundred?" she asked, tilting her head to study her king. "That should be enough to defend the wards."

"It should," Carnon agreed, "if we are only defending them from the witches."

"What does that mean?" Cerridwen asked, looking alarmed. She glanced between her brother and her mate, who shared a look of grim certainty.

"Later," Carnon interrupted, stopping Herne as he opened his mouth to reply. "The shadows may have ears, and I don't feel like going on a spider hunt right now. Let's bathe and change and regroup at sundown in our rooms. Brigid, can you send dinner there for us?"

Brigid nodded and Carnon stood, brooking no argument from either of the Lords or his sister as he held out a hand to me. I took it, letting him pull me out of the reading room and through the golden hallways of the library.

Late afternoon had painted the walls a rose gold hue, but I didn't have time to admire the glittering stacks or glass dome above us as Carnon set a swift pace for our chambers. He kept my hand firmly clasped in his until we were through the doors and he had warded them against entry.

Brigid had explained when we arrived that the King's suite was always kept prepared, in case the monarch visited. Our rooms were spacious and beautiful. Painted frescos of flowers and fruits and sunshine decorated the high, arched ceiling, and the windows looked out onto a sparkling, azure sea some miles away. The bedroom adjoined an elegant sitting and private dining room, and the spacious private bathing chamber had a tub that rivaled Carnon's back in Oneiros. Cerridwen and Herne were staying in a separate guest suite, so we were gloriously and mercifully alone each night.

Before I could ask him what he had meant, Carnon whirled on me and crushed me in a fierce kiss. While I was no longer a stranger to his tempestuous demonstrations of affection, it caught me off guard, and I stumbled backward until my back hit the golden door.

"Gods," I gasped, pushing him off me a little so I could get a breath in. He had bitten my lip a little harder than usual, and I touched it gingerly. "What was that for?"

"No reason," Carnon murmured, replacing my fingers with his on my lip. "Sorry for that." I felt a momentary tingle, and a flash of bright light told me he had used his healing magic on it. Before I could ask him what had gotten into him, he was kissing me again, his forked tongue twining with mine as one hand slid up my thigh to cup my rear.

"Carnon," I moaned, hating myself for pushing him off me again. "Tell me what's going on."

He sighed, dropping his forehead to mine and shaking his head slightly. "I didn't want to bring you into a war, Red," he said. "And that is exactly what I'm afraid is about to happen."

"I thought you were always at war with the witches," I argued, flattening my palms on his chest and wishing for bare, golden skin beneath instead of his usual black tunic.

"This is different," he said, pulling back to look at me. His serpentine eyes glinted emerald between us, and for just a moment, they flashed wholly green.

"Why are you angry?" I whispered, running my

hands in soothing strokes down his chest. Now that I was paying attention to it, I could feel him practically vibrating with rage. It was a wonder he had kept a leash on it while we were with the others. No wonder he had wanted to be alone.

"Because," he said, pursing his lips and studying my face intently. "If Scathanna didn't send her casters to defend the wards, it means she intends to attack them instead."

Chapter 3

Dinner was a quiet affair, held on the balcony of our room overlooking the sea. Carnon and Herne shared their suspicions with Brigid and Cerridwen, and the evening passed in quiet contemplation of how to proceed.

"Can you even *be* overthrown?" I asked, nodding toward Artemis, who was perched on the balcony rail. She looked at me with the strix-equivalent of a raised brow, as if to ask me, *Are you serious?*

"Technically, no," Carnon replied, sipping his wine thoughtfully and feeding chunks of steak to Akela, who had returned while we bathed. He sat between our chairs, alternately eating the bites of steak and resting his huge, furry head on my knee. "If I die, the Horned God will send a strix to guard a new king."

"It won't come down to that," Herne growled darkly. Cerridwen put a soothing hand on his arm.

"I'd also prefer that," Carnon agreed wryly, "and it's likely that Scathanna would keep me alive and imprisoned, rather than kill me and have to deal with a new king."

"She couldn't possibly win against you and the other three Lords," I argued, scratching Akela's head for comfort. "Could she?"

"No," Herne growled. "But we don't know where Tyr's true loyalty lies. If he were persuaded to stand against Carnon, the two of them could pose a serious threat."

"This is all speculation though," Brigid argued, looking plaintively at us all. "It could all just be a misunderstanding. Perhaps Scathanna's casters were simply delayed."

"You have been Daemon Lord of Sun for only a few years, Lady Brigid," Carnon said, smiling wanly. "You have no idea what Scathanna is truly capable of."

"Has she done something like this before?" I asked, surprised that she could still be a lord if she had opposed a previous king in the same way.

Herne nodded, looking grim. "Two hundred years ago. She opposed Alaunus when he outlawed blood magic against mortals in the Darklands. Most of demonkind understood the law to be for the good of all of us, since mortal dreams power our magic. Too many mortals were fleeing the Court of Shadows and Blood, and Alaunus overruled the Lords and imposed protections for mortals in those courts. Including Scathanna's."

"He gave Scathanna and Tyr's father, the Lord of

Blood at the time, a choice: uphold the law or die. They agreed, but you can imagine Scathanna's displeasure when Alaunus later outlawed the unwilling theft of blood. Scathanna viewed it as a betrayal of what makes us demons."

"And Tyr's father?" I asked. "How did he take it?"

Carnon shrugged. "He was already dead by then. Tyr killed him and seized the Court some time before that. Shortly after we moved to the Court of Beasts." He glanced at Cerridwen, and I understood that he meant after his parents had died. He went on without mentioning it. "Tyr was more willing than his sire to fall in line, or at least to make a show of trying."

I shuddered at the bloodthirstiness of the Daemon Lords.

"Can you not just get rid of Scathanna then?" I asked. I didn't love the idea of Carnon killing anyone, but if Scathanna was actively opposing him and looking to enslave mortals through blood magic, it might be the only choice.

Carnon shook his head. "Not without hard evidence of treason. The Horned God demands it. I can't do anything unless she actually acts against me."

"Failing to follow an order isn't enough to prove she's looking to usurp you?" I asked, raising my brows in disbelief.

This time, Herne answered. "The position of Daemon Lord is as sacred as that of the King. Our families were chosen to lead by the Horned God himself. Killing one of us without the God's blessing is heresy. And probably also a death sentence."

"Like I said," Carnon added, stretching his arms above his head ostentatiously. "Being King isn't all it's cracked up to be." He turned to Herne and Brigid, tilting his head in question. "Your advice?"

"Bring Scathanna to court and question her publicly," Herne said unfeelingly.

"Maybe visit her court in person?" Brigid suggested, glancing warily at Herne. "If you're looking to prevent a war, surely courtesy is the best path forward."

Herne scoffed at this, but Carnon studied Brigid thoughtfully and drummed his fingers on the table. "And you?" he asked, turning to me.

"Me what?" I asked, frowning at him.

Carnon smiled, both warm and somehow mischievous. "What does my Queen suggest?"

"I'm not your Queen," I argued. "Not until the Lords agree to crown me at least."

"You are my Queen, with or without a crown," Carnon argued, his gaze going a bit molten as he looked at me. "I value your counsel. What do *you* think I should do?"

I looked around the table at my friends. Family, I realized. Brigid may not technically be related, but she was almost as close to me as Cerridwen at this point, and she smiled at me encouragingly as I took a breath.

"I think I agree with Herne," I said finally, giving Brigid an apologetic wince. "Calling Scathanna to court may put her on the defensive, but you need a show of power. Calling the Lords to you shows her that you are still in control, especially if Brigid and Herne agree to the summons."

"Agreed," Carnon said, as if my advice settled the matter. "I'll send Scathanna the summons tonight. We will return to Oneiros in three days, after the feast for Lughnasadh. Will you be able to join us?" he added, turning to Brigid. I realized he was asking, rather than ordering her to Oneiros, and it reminded me that Carnon truly hated the power games he was forced to play with Scathanna.

Brigid nodded. "Of course. That should be enough time to get through the majority of the books the scholars pulled. I can bring anything you want to examine further with me." She smiled warmly, reaching over and giving my hand a squeeze, a silent acknowledgement that she didn't blame me for siding with Herne.

Herne was looking slightly less surly than usual as we disbanded, the decision having gone in his favor. Cerridwen hugged me goodnight as she left with her mate, and Brigid did the same before leaving for her own quarters. She assured us that she would speak with the scholars about searching for more of Alaunus' work and packaging books we needed to transport to the royal library.

I poured myself a second glass of bloodberry wine, my limit before I started spouting uncontrolled truth, and headed for the balcony rail, watching the dark ocean and listening to the waves crashing as Carnon bid everyone goodnight.

"Cheers," Carnon said, stepping to my side and clinking his glass against mine. He took a long drink and leaned over the balcony rail, cutting a striking figure in all black as he looked out at the sea. I silently admired the planes of his handsome face and the glint of moonlight on his horns for a moment before turning back to the water as well.

"Is it always like this?" I asked, sipping the sweet wine and enjoying the burst of bubbles across my tongue. "Being King?"

"More often than not," Carnon answered, sighing deeply. "I wouldn't wish the job on my worst enemy."

"Do you hate it?" I asked, frowning at the exhaustion in his voice. Carnon had always seemed dedicated to his role, despite its difficulties. Perhaps the threat of looming war was making him reevaluate his sense of duty.

"No," he said eventually, turning to look at me steadily. "I don't hate it. Not all the time at least. I want to do the job well. It's just…" He sighed again, turning back to the dark sea. "It's a lot of pressure. To bear the responsibility for all of demonkind. To try to uphold the laws of the Horned God faithfully."

"You bear it well," I said, earning a dark chuckle from my mate.

"That's a pretty lie, Red," he crooned, giving me a wicked look. "But I love your pretty lies."

"It's not a lie," I argued, turning into him a bit as a chill breeze lifted my hair and made me shiver. "And *you're* one to gripe about lying," I added with a playful nudge.

Carnon chuckled again, throwing an arm around me and pulling me close. He dropped a chaste kiss atop my head and sighed into me. "If only it was just you and me in this infernal palace, and not a whole host of servants and my Daemon Lords." He trailed kisses down the side of my face to my ear, and then to the crook of my neck. More shivers ran down my arms at the feel of his lips on my skin. He whispered, "Think how loudly I could make you scream for me."

"An audience has never stopped you before," I gasped, pressing my body closer to his as his arm tightened around my waist.

"Hmm," he hummed, pointed fangs scraping against my throat in a way that was far more sensual than it should be. "You make an excellent point as always, my Queen." I shuddered as he moved to the other side of my throat. "Are you well, Elara?" he asked, speaking into my neck. "Truly?"

"I'd be better if you got on with it right now," I groaned as his tongue flicked over my pounding pulse.

He pulled away, eliciting a little whine from me that made him laugh darkly. His face sobered almost immediately. "Answer the question, Red," he commanded, looking at me seriously. "You've been through a lot. How are you coping?"

"I don't want to talk about that right now," I argued, pushing aside the pain of grief that flashed through me and trying to bury it beneath desire. I pushed closer to him, fumbling at the laces of his trousers.

"You never want to talk about it," Carnon admonished, clasping my hands to still them. He frowned down at me, and I felt a growing irritation at his refusal to just give me what I wanted. "Talk to me, Red."

"I said I don't want to talk about it," I retorted, scowling at him. "I want to do more *enjoyable* things."

"Elara—"

"Stop!" I snapped, pulling back from him. "Just stop. I told you I *don't* want to talk about it."

"You *need* to talk about it, Red," Carnon insisted, closing the distance between us again. He put down his wine glass and took my face in both hands. "Your anger and grief are going to consume you if you don't. It's no wonder you can't quell the fire magic."

"I can't quell it because you annoy me," I snarled, trying to step back further and finding myself trapped between Carnon and the balcony rail. "It's impossible to not be angry around you."

"Such pretty lies," Carnon crooned, stroking a thumb over my cheekbone. He dropped his forehead to mine. "Let me in, Red. Let me help you."

"If you don't want my body tonight, then this conversation is over," I said, trying to push him away from me again.

He yielded a step this time, frowning at me sadly. "Gods above, you know I do," he said, his voice so full of sympathy that it drained all of the desire from me. "But I want more than just your body, Red. You know that. I want all of you, heart and mind and soul. And you're keeping them from me."

I had no good reply to this. No way to deny it or twist the accusation on him, or prove him wrong. I tried to walk around him, to simply leave and end this conversation that way, but he had me trapped again in an instant.

"Don't walk away from me, Elara," he growled, his hands returning to my face. "Just...give me something. Anything. Tell me you love me or you hate me or you blame me. Tell me you're raging inside, because I can *see* it, even if you try to hide it. That fire burns in you like it's fueled by rage alone."

"Stop," I pleaded, trying to push past him again to no avail. The careful wall I had built around my grief was going to crack under his questioning, and I didn't want him to see that. I wasn't ready to feel the pain and loss again the way I had after that first week, when I'd chosen to bury the feelings under a drive for revenge.

"Never," he argued, kissing me tenderly in a way I both loved and hated at that moment. "I will never stop pushing you or fighting for you or loving you fiercely."

"Please," I whispered, a tear sliding down my cheek as the dam cracked and the pain welled up in me. He wiped the tear away.

"I lost my parents before I was old enough to really understand that loss," he said quietly, brushing away more tears with his thumbs. "You're allowed to grieve."

"I don't have *time* to grieve," I argued, swiping angrily at my face. "I need to kill her. I want her to suffer." The words sounded more bitter than I had intended them to, but Carnon smiled at me in triumph as if I had finally given him what he wanted.

"She will, Red," he assured me, kissing me fiercely this time, one arm wrapping around my waist to pull me into him. Desire sparked again, despite the tears that continued to fall, as he said against my lips, "I will make sure she feels every moment of agony she has caused you, my love."

Our joining was fierce and ragged after that, my soul as exposed as my body as he tore the gown from me and ran calloused thumbs over every inch of my freckled skin. We barely made it to the bed as I pulled at him frantically. I ripped at his laces and shirt in my eagerness to remove them, the fire of desire rekindled in that strange way of demon mates.

He pulled me down onto him, his tongue teasing mine and making heat pool between my thighs in a way that had me scrabbling to get closer to him. I slid onto him roughly, gasping as he thrust into me, the angle deep and consuming as he captured my mouth with his and swallowed my moans and cries of pleasure.

I cried my release so loudly that I was sure the whole golden city heard, but I didn't care as Carnon's hand and tongue and cock took me over that edge again and again, obliterating the grief for a few blissful hours and replacing it with pure, boneless ecstasy.

We ended in a sweaty tangle of limbs, the moon high in the night sky casting us in silver shadows. I ran a finger over the intricate tattoos on Carnon's chest as he stroked my hair and placed tender kisses to my freckled shoulders.

"I love you, Elara," Carnon mumbled against my brow as he pulled me down to rest on his chest. He held me tightly to him, his lips trailing a line of kisses over my forehead. "Don't shut me out."

I swallowed, a knot of emotion rising again in my throat at his words and his love. I couldn't reply in kind, the words lodging in my throat and choking me as I tried to make the promise to him.

He sighed, as if he knew exactly what I was struggling with. "At least, if you do shut me out, Red," he amended, stroking a strong hand over my bare backside and shifting to look down at me, "let me back in again."

I met his eyes, emeralds in the light of the moon, and nodded. "I'll try."

Chapter 4

Carnon joined Brigid and me in the library the next day while Herne and Cerridwen took a morning off. I was hopeful that we would be able to make some progress with our research, but by lunch, I had learned absolutely nothing useful. I became so irritated with the books that I accidentally set one ablaze, to the absolute horror of the scholars.

"It's fine," Brigid said soothingly, patting the rather singed but not irreversibly damaged book. "The scholars can probably replace the cover. Why don't we take a break and have some tea?"

"I am so sorry," I said for the tenth time as Carnon led me out of the library.

He chuckled and gave my hand a little squeeze. "Maybe we should plan on training before researching each day. Work off your temper before letting you into a building with precious, flammable objects."

"Careful, or I'll turn my temper on you," I teased, internally lamenting my lack of control over the flames. "Did you find anything useful?"

"Nothing that answers any of our questions," he replied, sighing and squeezing my hand again. "We will find something, Red."

"The scholars think they've tracked down some more books of prophecy," Brigid chimed in, giving my shoulder a reassuring nudge. "Maybe something of Alaunus' is written in them."

As she was speaking, Brigid's voice went suddenly distant. I blinked, trying to clear the fog that had invaded my brain, and felt myself sway.

"Elara?" Carnon asked in alarm, his voice also sounding far away.

I blinked again, but when my vision cleared it wasn't Carnon or Brigid or any of my friends I saw in the golden hallway outside the library. It was a different man.

He was tall, with hair a warm, golden brown and eyes a blazing blue. He wore finery like Carnon's, and a crown with metal twisted into the shape of horns. He hurried down the hallway toward me, something held tightly in his arms. I threw my hands out to stop him from careening into me, and he was suddenly gone, his face replaced by Carnon's wide-eyed, panicked expression.

"Gods, Red," he breathed, giving me a little shake. "What's wrong?"

"Sorry," I said, feeling suddenly dizzy and a little sick. "I don't...."

My knees buckled and Carnon caught me, lowering

me to the ground gently.

"Fuck," he murmured, pouring his healing magic into me. "What the hell—"

"What did you see?" Brigid interrupted, kneeling down next to me.

"See?" Carnon snapped, the panic making his eyes flash wholly green.

"You saw something, yes?" she pressed, taking my hand. "A vision?"

I shook my head, uncertain what exactly had happened. There was probably no point in hiding anything from Brigid though, so I paused, then nodded.

"The dizziness is common with new seers," Brigid explained, more to Carnon than to me. He let out a breath he must have been holding for several long moments, nodding as if understanding were dawning on him. I wished it were dawning on me a little, too.

"I'm not a seer," I protested weakly, letting Carnon and Brigid haul me to my feet, where I swayed again.

Carnon hoisted me up into his arms like a rag doll. "I believe you might be," he said, striding toward our rooms with a purposeful gait. "It makes sense that you'd inherit both of your father's gifts. It's possible being in his court is drawing it out of you."

"I'll send for tea," Brigid said, running off down another corridor to alert the servants. She shouted back at us, "Make her drink some water!"

"Will you never stop causing trouble, Red?" Carnon teased, pushing backwards through the doors of our bedroom and settling me gingerly on the couch. "Do you need healing?"

"I'm fine, you overgrown serpent," I said, pushing his hand from my brow.

He smirked, looking both relieved and wickedly amused. "Now I believe you. Don't move."

He left and returned a moment later with a glass of water, just as Brigid entered our room. Cerridwen and Herne were in tow, and my friend rushed over to me, placing her hands on my brow.

"Are you alright?" she asked, almost as panicked as her brother had sounded.

"She's just peachy now," Carnon replied sarcastically, giving Cerridwen a wry smile. "Sarcastic as usual. Sit down, Cerridwen, so she can tell us what happened."

"It's really not a big deal," I mumbled, sipping the water. "Just a little dizziness."

A servant entered with a tea tray, and another with a huge plate of macarons, and I let Brigid serve me tea while Carnon plied me with sweet deliciousness. They were not as good as Pierre's, but still better than no macarons.

"Now tell us what you saw," Brigid said, once everyone was settled with tea.

I looked around at several sets of raised eyebrows, including Herne's, then I sighed and put down my teacup. "Just a man," I replied. "Brown hair, blue eyes. He was walking in the hallway toward me."

"That's it?" Herne growled, looking as though it had been a waste of time summoning him. Honestly, it really had.

"That's it," I replied, taking another sip of tea. "Your voices went all distant, then I saw the man, and then he was gone."

"Is there anything else you can tell us about him?" Carnon pressed. He was sitting next to me, his arm around my shoulders squeezing a bit more tightly than necessary. "What he was wearing or doing, perhaps?"

I shrugged, taking a bite of macaron. "He was dressed well," I replied, my mouth full of macaron in a very undignified way. I felt uncomfortable with the attention of all of my friends focused on me. "He was holding something, but I couldn't see what it was. Oh, and he was wearing a crown."

"Alaunus?" Cerridwen asked, turning to Carnon with wide eyes.

He nodded once. "That would be my guess."

I swallowed, mouth going a bit dry. "I saw my father?"

"It makes sense, for your gift to manifest that way," Brigid said, patting my hand reassuringly. "Most seers begin with visions of the past, and most with familiar people or places."

"Alaunus is not familiar to me, though," I said, feeling a pang of hurt despite the truth of this. I had never known my father, and he was anything but familiar.

"Your heart knows him. Your soul," Brigid said. I raised my brows at her in disbelief, and Carnon chuckled.

"Do you not believe you have a soul, Red?" he teased, caressing a thumb over the bare skin of my arm.

"Not one that remembers people I've never met," I replied, furrowing my brows as I took another macaron from the plate. I lifted my teacup, draining the contents.

"Wait," Brigid said, holding out her hand expectantly. "Let me see."

"The teacup?" I asked, passing it to her. I knew Brigid had minor gifts in divination, and she believed in the power of tarot cards and tea leaves, but I wasn't convinced the few times I had seen something in the leaves wasn't just coincidence.

"It's called tasseography," she explained, turning my cup this way and that as she examined the pattern of the leaves at the bottom. "The symbols or images formed by the leaves can mean something to someone with sight." She frowned, holding the empty cup out to me. "What do you see?"

We leaned in as one, peering at the tea leaves in the bottom of the cup. Truthfully, I saw a soggy mess, but I tried to find discernible shapes in the lumpy remains.

"A cross?" I suggested, the words coming out more as a question than an answer. "And maybe an insect?"

"A spider," Carnon growled, looking darkly at the teacup.

"That's what I thought, too," Brigid said, worry etched into the lines of her face.

"Well, what does that mean?" I asked, sitting back as everyone exchanged concerned looks.

"The cross means danger," Brigid explained. "Trouble or upheaval."

"And I think we all know what the spider means," Carnon added.

※ ※ ※

Brigid agreed to teach me the basics of tasseography and tarot to see if they would help me harness the gift of sight that both she and Carnon were convinced I possessed.

I wasn't sure that a lucky drawing of tarot cards and a few prescient tea leaves were really enough to qualify me as a seer. The dizzy spell could have been stress or fatigue, and maybe it wasn't my father I had seen. But they were convinced, and I supposed it wouldn't hurt to test their theory.

"Training, divination practice, and research," I grumbled at Carnon after everyone else had departed. He had insisted I rest, but the others had returned to the library to search for any of Alaunus' records. Akela had taken up watch at the foot of the sofa on which I was reclined, his snores indicating that he was having an afternoon nap. "When will I have time to sleep or eat?"

"You can eat between books," Carnon joked, earning a poke in the ribs from my foot, which was resting on his lap. He turned over the report he had been reading and pinned me with a glare. A wicked gleam in his eye told me he was the opposite of angry. "Ow. Not very queenly behavior, my love." He trailed a long finger delicately across the arch of my foot, making me hiss and pull it off his lap as he tickled me.

"I'm not sure you should be the judge of appropriate royal behavior," I retorted, choosing to ignore the heated look and returning to my own reading. Brigid had suggested I go through her journal and study the quoted passages she had found for me from my father's writings, but so far nothing new or exciting had drawn my attention. "I recall you defiling me on a dining room table once."

"Hmmm," Carnon hummed, attention wholly focused on me now. "And a very enjoyable defiling it was. Didn't I promise to do the same in an armchair?" His fingers found my foot again, trailing teasingly up my calf.

"The one in *your* room," I pointed out, trying to

ignore the tickling sensation. "And you never followed through on the threat."

"Promise," he corrected. "And an oversight I intend to remedy as soon as possible." He lifted my foot to his mouth and planted a kiss on the delicate arch. "Have I told you how much I like your feet, Red?"

"Carnon," I warned, looking up from the diary to find him staring at me hungrily. "We are supposed to be working."

"We *are* working," he argued, trailing kisses down my ankle to my calf.

"*I* am working," I corrected, pulling my foot from his grasp and tucking it under me.

"And you've been working so hard," Carnon teased, giving me soulful eyes.

"Weren't you the one pushing my training not two days ago?" I asked, torn between irritation and amusement. "The whole world is going to hell outside and we need to focus."

"And we will definitely focus in just a few moments," he agreed, leaning forward as if to kiss me.

I stopped him with two fingers against his lips. "Flattered as I am that you would dedicate a *few* moments to my pleasure, I'm busy," I said haughtily. "And you should be busy, too. Plus, Akela is right there," I added, gesturing to the sleeping wolf.

"You're no fun," Carnon sighed dramatically, his bottom lip pushed out in a pout. I laughed before leaning forward to kiss him soundly. "I merely thought we could benefit from letting off some steam, but if you insist on working, then I'll leave you to it. I can't focus with you like this," he said, standing and stretching out his stiff muscles.

"I'm literally fully covered," I exclaimed, gesturing to my modest blouse and trousers. Carnon gazed wistfully at my breasts, and I playfully crossed my arms over them with a laugh.

"But I know what's under all of those confounded clothes," he bemoaned, leaning down for one more kiss. "I'll be back in an hour."

"Where are you going?" I called after him as he strode from the room.

"To convince Herne to let me stab something," he called back, raising a hand in an idle wave. "Don't move from that couch, Red."

I chuckled, lost momentarily in the delight of my mate and his undeniable hunger for me. He had told me it would lessen a bit with time, but truthfully, I hoped it never did.

Elara.

The voice entered my mind so unexpectedly that I looked around in surprise.

"Was that you, Akela?" I whispered, peering down at the still sleeping wolf. Akela had a way of expressing his thoughts and opinions directly into my mind, and I was sure that must be what this was. But the wolf was sound asleep, and the voice permeated my mind once more.

Elara.

"Who's there?" I asked, looking around in sudden panic. I knew I could defend myself if I had to, but if someone had been able to get into our rooms so easily, we were likely in danger. A sudden wave of dizziness hit me again, and my gut sank.

"*Elara,*" came the voice, female now that I could

make it out more clearly. *"Her name is Elara."*

The room disappeared, and I was suddenly looking into a mirror, its edges inscribed with witch symbols, a small wriggling bundle in one arm while my other was held out to touch the mirror. I smiled down at the bundle, then back up at the man in the reflection.

"It's a good name," the man said, smiling sadly back at me. It was the same man from my earlier vision, with golden brown hair and blue eyes, looking somehow younger than he had in the hallway. He also had a hand against the glass, as if he wanted to push his way through.

"You should take her," I said suddenly, the words coming from me unbidden like they weren't my own. I felt a terrible, inexplicable sadness, like my heart was breaking in my chest. "It's not safe for her here."

Mama. That was Mama's voice. It wasn't me in the mirror at all, but Mama. And she was speaking to Alaunus. To my father.

"It's not safe for either of you," Alaunus responded, his voice cracking with desperation as he looked down at the sleeping baby in my arms. He was looking at *me*. "Please, Circe. Please just let me bring you here. *Both* of you." His eyes were sad, full of longing and pain as he looked at Mama.

"I can't," my mother said, eyes lined with silver. "Not yet. Not until *she* is gone. She's watching me too closely right now."

"I can protect you from her," Alaunus pleaded. He reached out his other hand, placing it flat against the glass, where it rippled faintly. Mirrors were rarely used this way in the Witchlands. It was far easier just to step through and converse in person. But clearly something—maybe the magic that warded the Darklands and prevented the witches from entering now—was keeping them apart. "Please, Circe."

"I can't," Mama whispered, pressing her forehead to the glass. A tear trickled down her cheek, and I felt it grow cold against her face. "I'm sorry."

My father looked like he wanted to reach out and pull us through the mirror. I wondered why Mama didn't go to him.

"I'll come when I can," Alaunus said softly. He looked heartbroken and disappointed and scared, and I ached to see it. The necklace against Mama's throat hummed softly, and she let out a sob. Alaunus' voice cracked as he added, "I promise, we will be together soon, my love."

The image dissolved, my vision clouding until I was once again sitting on a sofa in the King's chambers of the golden palace, Akela whining at me from the foot of the couch.

Another wave of dizziness had me reaching for his neck to steady myself, and I held him tightly as I waited for the room to stop spinning.

"Gods above," I croaked, feeling like my heart was cracking as tears welled behind my eyes. Akela whined soothingly, and I felt the sense of, *you're safe, I'm here,* coming from him. I laughed wetly. "You're as bad as Carnon."

I held the wolf, the tears falling into his furry neck as I grappled with the image of my mother and father saying goodbye.

Chapter 5

"And you're sure you're alright?" Carnon asked for what must have been the hundredth time.

We were working on the fire magic again the next morning, and he had been looking at me like I might break since I told him about yesterday's vision.

I didn't understand why my mother had refused to go with my father. I had assumed that Mama *couldn't* come to the Darklands for some reason. That Alaunus couldn't or wouldn't drop the wards, and they were forced to be apart. But the vision had made it seem like a *choice.* Clearly, she loved him, and it killed her to be apart from him. I knew if it were Carnon and me, I wouldn't have been able to stay away. The whole thing had me on edge and anxious. I wished I could ask Mama why. I wished I could rage at her for the choices she made that prevented me from knowing my father.

All of this compounded to make it even harder than usual to smother my flames. I could roast the world alive if I wanted to, but putting out a tiny match was beyond me. Carnon's fussing wasn't helping, and my irritation made it increasingly difficult for me to control my anger, and therefore, the fire magic.

"I'm fine," I snapped, shooting a ball of flame in irritation at my mate.

He side-stepped it easily, grinning like a cat. "Really? You seem rather tense, my love." He returned his own ball of flame, and I ducked rather than trying to douse it. It hit the golden palace wall behind me, leaving a small indentation in the gold.

"You would be tense if I asked you how you were eight thousand times," I argued, gulping down some water before he decided to throw more fire at me.

"No, I would be touched by your tender concern," Carnon rebutted, folding his arms and giving me an appraising look. "We can stop if you're tired."

"Gods above!" I cried, shooting another ball of flame at him. This time he was less prepared, barely catching and extinguishing the ball before it set his tunic alight. "Stop coddling me! The Crone is attacking our borders, and I need to be pushed!"

Brigid was busy this morning dealing with preparations for Lughnasadh, but Cerridwen and Herne were watching us from a safe distance with Akela, who growled his concern at his master, and Artemis, who hooted in what sounded like disdain. Cerridwen raised a brow at me, a mixture of concern and amusement lighting her brown face. Herne coughed, something between a growl and a laugh.

"I know there is a lot at stake, Elara, but pushing you when your anger isn't under control is reckless," Carnon retorted, flicking his fingers so that a tiny wall of flame rose to my knees. "If you think you're ready, try to master that anger now and put out the flames."

I rolled my eyes at Carnon's obvious attempt to make me even more irritated and tried to focus on my breathing. I closed my eyes, picturing the flames. I could do this. I could put out a flame. This was my father's power, and I could harness it.

"Don't hurt yourself, Red," Carnon quipped as I huffed out a breath and opened my eyes. The flames still burned around me, and I deflated. He chuckled, stepping over the short wall to put his arms around me.

"What are you doing?" I asked warily, stiffening as his hands slid around my waist, his hard chest pressing against my back.

"Helping you. Relax, Red," Carnon purred in my ear, sending a shiver down my spine. The wall of fire flared brightly, and he chuckled again. "Maybe this was a bad idea."

"You think?" I asked sarcastically, glancing at Cerridwen and Herne. Neither was paying attention to us now, both having taken up swords for their own sparring practice.

Carnon placed a large hand over my heart between my breasts. "Your anger and fear is holding you back from full control. Do you feel your magic in your gut, Red?"

"Yes," I said, breathing rather quickly. "Your hand is *not* on my gut. You know that, right?"

Carnon hummed appreciatively. "I'm aware. But this is where you calm the magic. Imagine it like a cooling rain, dousing the flames within you. Forget about the Crone and all the things that are going wrong, and focus on your power."

I tried to take another deep breath, but Carnon's scent and proximity and heat was making it very difficult to focus.

"I promise, we will have plenty of time later for whatever it is you're thinking about right now, Red," Carnon murmured as the necklace thrummed against me, signaling heightened emotions in our bond. "But work before pleasure. Try."

I sighed dramatically, earning another rumbling laugh behind me as I closed my eyes and tried to focus. I often thought of the demon magic inside me as twisting snakes, one bright and one shadowy, writhing in my stomach. A new snake, one of flickering flames, had joined the others since my showdown with the Crone, and there was a glimmering golden thread of a fourth starting to form next to it. I ignored the golden thread for now, focusing on the flaming serpent.

Sleep, I told it, taking Carnon's advice and imagining a cooling rain drizzling onto those writhing internal flames. I was so *angry* and so tired of feeling that rage. I tried to do as Carnon said and let it go, focus on the magic instead of everything that I had lost. Could still lose. I felt a tear run down my cheek as I quelled the raging magic and wiped it away, trying to picture that tear falling on the fire and dousing it. *Sleep*, I repeated, picturing more tears dousing the fiery snake until it began simmering to nothing more than embers. *Sleep*, I said a final time.

A few moments passed in silence, my mind focused on calming the storm of magic inside me as I leaned my weight against Carnon.

I felt Carnon's thumb swipe away the tears that had fallen as I had focused. "Open your eyes, Red," he whispered, his breath hot on my neck.

The fire wasn't completely gone, but in its place was a smoldering ring, spitting and hissing like the magic inside me as I quelled it.

"I did it!" I shouted, turning to beam at him and then squeaking in surprise as the flames exploded high around us again.

Carnon threw back his head and laughed, the sound so rich I couldn't help but join him. His eyes found mine again and he leaned down to kiss me soundly, before sending his own cooling shadows to smother the flames.

"Well done," he praised, tucking a wayward hair behind my ear. "Even if it was short-lived."

"Well, you made it very hard to focus at the end there," I teased, beaming back at him. "But the visualization worked. Those snakes are tricky creatures to quell."

"I'm flattered that you picture snakes inside you, whether I'm involved or not," he teased, stroking a firm thumb over my cheekbone. He kissed me, and I felt his shadow stone ring thrum where he held it against my face, a twin feeling vibrating in my necklace. The emotions coursing through me turned the kiss into something a bit more desperate and needy.

Herne cleared his throat from a few feet away, breaking us out of our reverie.

"Gods above, Herne," Carnon growled, running a hand down his face as he took in his friend. "We were having a moment."

"Apologies, most magnanimous of majesties," Herne deadpanned, injecting as much derision into the title as possible. Both he and Cerridwen were dressed in their usual leathers, and both had their usual expressions: Herne grumpy and foreboding, Cerridwen bright and alive and endlessly amused by Carnon's antics.

Akela took the opportunity to wedge himself between me and Carnon, earning a scowl from my mate as Artemis flapped to his shoulder.

Herne rolled his eyes. "If you recall, there is a lot to do before we depart."

"Are you done for the day?" Cerridwen asked me, far more chipper than her mate. "Because we have a lot of books to get through."

"Ugh," I groaned.

Carnon laughed, giving my backside a surreptitious squeeze. "Ruling is painful work, my love," he said, dropping a kiss on my head. Akela whined in sympathy, and for a moment I was envious of the wolf's inability to read.

We grabbed a quick lunch and spent an interminable afternoon in the library. Most of the books the scholars pulled seemed to be about the time after the Darklands and Witchlands were separated, and any mention of witches was vague or inconsequential, or as a nebulous, undefined threat. Only a few books spoke of the Witch Wars, painting the Crone at the time as wicked and power hungry, and responsible for the Bloodwood.

Several more books of prophecy had been added to our stacks, but none were written by Alaunus. The head scholar, a spindly ancient male I was afraid might topple over in a firm wind, apologized profusely that they hadn't located Alaunus' texts yet.

"Why would they have been moved?" I asked the others once we had settled in the reading room. Akela had settled at my feet, and he nudged my leg every so often for pets. Artemis had flapped off haughtily when Carnon had offered to bring her, and I gathered that she disliked being cooped up for research more than I did. "Who could have moved texts of such importance?"

"Probably only Alaunus himself," Carnon mused, lugging yet another heavy historical tome toward him. He paused, giving me a thoughtful look. "Why don't you go for a wander, Red? Maybe some kind of vision or notion will strike?"

My eyes narrowed as I stared at him. "You think he'll show me their location in a vision?" I asked skeptically. Herne grunted in uncertainty, but Cerridwen looked excited.

"Maybe he knew you would be here. Maybe he's showing you the past because he had a vision of you in the future," Cerridwen exclaimed, an excited and slightly awed gleam in her eye.

"Want me to join you?" Carnon asked, closing the book and rising. Akela huffed as if to say, *I've got this,* and I scratched the wolf's head. Who needed a big, scary snake mate with a wolf constantly at one's beck and call?

"Oh no you don't," Cerridwen said, dragging him back down by the arm. She and Herne were the only people other than me who could get away with treating Carnon as a normal person rather than a king, and I covered my laugh with a cough. Carnon shot me a glare. "You don't get out of research duty that easily."

"I would never," Carnon protested, placing a hand over his breast in mock sincerity. I rolled my eyes at his obvious playacting. "I'm simply offering assistance to my beloved, fragile mate."

"Elara could burn down this whole cursed place if she wanted to," Herne grunted, not looking up. "And that wolf will tear out the throat of anyone who goes near her."

"Thank you, Herne," I said, smugly pleased with the compliment. Herne and I had not really started off on the best foot, but my mating his friend and his realization that I *wasn't* trying to destroy the kingdom had softened him toward me. I smiled, and he turned a little pink. "I'll be fine," I added, turning back to Carnon and patting Akela's head. "The last vision came to me when I was alone. Maybe that makes it easier to feel them."

Carnon raised an uncertain brow, checking the position of the sun outside the huge glass window.

"I'm coming after you if you're gone more than an hour," he warned, pulling the dusty old book back toward him.

I skipped a little as I left, happy to have an escape from the unproductive research as Akela padded along next to me. I didn't think I would have any kind of vision or feeling, but I supposed a walk through the rows and rows of books couldn't hurt.

It also didn't help. Nothing struck me or called to me, and no vision made me dizzy as I wandered aimlessly through the golden library. At least forty-five minutes passed with nothing of interest happening, and I whiled away the time reading the titles of the books on the shelves.

One of them finally *did* catch my attention, a volume on snakes and other reptiles. I pulled it from the shelf, a small smile tugging on my lips as a notion struck me. I didn't know much about Carnon's snake beast, and he hadn't been particularly forthcoming about his anatomy when I had asked. Perhaps this book would have answers to my questions.

"Hemipene," I mouthed, my eyes going wide in shock at the illustration in the section about serpents. I tilted my head, trying to work out the logistics. If Carnon could do that...

Akela's growl of warning came too late.

"Interesting book?" Carnon asked, appearing out of seemingly nowhere and leaning against one of the shelves. I slammed the book shut, blushing furiously.

He looked at me with wicked delight. "Are you reading trash, Red?" He leaned over me, plucking the book from my hands and turning it to read the title. His face went from wicked delight to confused concern in less than a second. His wide eyes flicked to me. "The Complete Anatomy of Snakes and Reptiles?"

"I was bored," I hedged, shifting uncomfortably from foot to foot.

He narrowed his eyes suspiciously, seeming to decide it was not worth pursuing his questions about my choice of reading. He slid the book back onto the shelf while I blew out a silent breath of relief.

"Find anything useful?" he asked, taking my hand in his and kissing the knuckles. "Any visions?"

"Nothing," I said, letting him lead me and Akela back to the library entrance, where Herne and Cerridwen were waiting.

"Do I want to know about the snake book?" he asked, lowering his voice so the others wouldn't hear. I scowled, shaking my head, and he chuckled darkly.

"Keep your secrets then, you little minx."

We ate dinner with Brigid in a golden dining room, everything shining and gilded in an almost ostentatious show of wealth. She was clearly exhausted from a day of feast preparations for Lughnasadh, her eyelids heavy and face drawn as we ate, and she kept stifling yawns behind an elegant hand. But she refused my suggestion that she retire early, claiming she was eager to hear about our research.

"There's really not much to report," Cerridwen said dourly, poking at her food. "We didn't learn anything useful, and Elara hasn't had any revelations from Alaunus today."

All of them knew about yesterday's vision, and I felt myself grow uncomfortably warm as their attention turned to me. I had never loved being the center of attention, being raised away from crowds and people, but I supposed I would have to get used to the feeling as Carnon's Queen.

"I don't know how to control it," I hedged, frowning down at my fish. It tasted different from the fried clams we had eaten in Oneiros, but in a wonderful new way. Brigid said that the Siren trading vessels brought in a fresh catch each day to her ports, a benefit of its position on the coast.

"I'll help you when we head back to Oneiros," Brigid said warmly, patting my hand comfortingly. "The festival took all of my attention today, but after tomorrow I am all yours. We can work through the tarot deck while we travel."

I nodded at her gratefully, and dinner broke up shortly after so we could all get a full night's rest.

I must have been exhausted from training, because I

fell into a deep sleep as soon as my head hit the pillow. My dreams were muddled and strange; I saw flashes of my father's face, and my mother, and images of objects and people and places I mostly didn't recognize or understand.

Except for one.

"Are we being attacked, my love?" he asked groggily, groaning as I jolted awake. The moon was full and bright, and the ocean sparkled in the distance out the bedroom windows. Carnon threw an arm around my waist, dragging me back down to the mattress and tucking me into his chest.

"Sorry," I whispered. "I had a dream."

"Was this a pleasant, mildly sexy dream?" Carnon asked, nibbling the tip of my only recently pointed ear. I batted him away irritably.

"No, you fiend," I hissed. "I think it was a message though. About where to find the books of prophecy."

"Really?" Carnon asked, this time sounding wide awake. "Where?"

"I think they're hidden in a wall in our bedroom, back in Oneiros," I said, speaking quietly. It was hard to tell where exactly, but I was certain that's what I had seen. Excitement rose in me about what I might find there.

"Impossible," Carnon said gruffly, sounding tired again and squashing my enthusiasm. "I'd know if there was a hidden compartment in my own walls."

"So, you suddenly doubt this power you think I have?" I asked pulling away from him. Carnon groaned, squeezing me tighter.

"I don't doubt your power, my love," he murmured, pressing his face into my neck and kissing me. I knew he was trying to distract me from escaping him, and curse him, it was working. "I simply doubt your ability to be certain what is a dream and what is a vision when it's the middle of the night and you're exhausted."

"Get off," I seethed, pushing him away half-heartedly. "You don't get to doubt me and try to seduce me at the same time. Why must everything end in seduction with you?"

"Why must everything end in anger for you?" he replied, his tone light.

I paused my wriggling, considering. "Do I really do that?"

"Yes, my love," he replied, pressing a decidedly chaste kiss to my neck. "Don't get me wrong, your anger is borne of passion. I enjoy it. Most of the time."

"I suppose anger is easy," I replied with a defeated sort of sigh. "For me at least. Easier than talking about my other feelings."

"And seduction is the same for me," Carnon confessed. He lifted himself above me, his skin glowing silver in the moonlight. "I'm sorry. We don't have to do anything." He looked down at me, face more somber and sincere than I expected. "I do believe you have some kind of sight. My disbelief is because in my many years in that room, I have never found a false section of the wall."

"Have you *looked* for a false section of wall?" I asked, running my hands through his soft hair. I skated a finger up his horn, and he shivered.

"No," he confessed, still gazing at me contemplatively. "I have not. You make a fair point."

"I know," I said, grinning smugly at him.

"Very well, Red," he said, still studying me in the

moonlight. "We will check the walls when we return."

"Thank you. And I'll try to be more open," I agreed. "Less angry."

Carnon kissed my nose. "I don't need you to change for me, my love."

"But I want to," I replied, raising myself up so I could kiss him properly. "You are always so patient with me. So rarely angry."

Carnon smiled, kissing me gently. "I, on the other hand, make no such promises about my penchant for seduction." His lips curved into a smirk as a wicked gleam transformed his face from serious to sensual. "Now allow me to apologize properly for my doubt. With your consent, of course."

"I thought I was too exhausted for that?" I taunted, only pretending to be annoyed now. His fingers had been slowly trailing down my sides, and I was extremely interested in where they were going.

He smirked as if he knew about my interest, and my necklace thrummed. "You seem quite awake now. Let me convince you of my faith in you."

I had to admit, he was very convincing.

Chapter 6

The festival for Lughnasadh in the Witchlands was a somewhat pious affair. It was the celebration of the beginning of the harvest season, and the witches usually led a ceremony with a blessing and sacrifice to the Goddess of the first ripened crops. Sometimes, in bountiful years, the mortals would have feasts or small celebrations, but I had only ever experienced the religious version myself.

Clearly, the Darklands had a different view of the festivities. Everything in the city and the palace was decorated for the festival, with garlands of berries and corn and dried fruits woven together. The whole court seemed to have been invited into the palace grounds, and by mid-afternoon the halls were filled with mortals and demons alike, all drinking and laughing and celebrating as if nothing beyond their walls concerned them in the slightest. Children made and played with corn dolls under the supervision of some of the older women as several games and athletic competitions were scheduled to take place throughout the day with everything culminating in a grand feast at sunset.

"How is this festival celebrated in Oneiros?" I asked Carnon as we prepared to head down and join the festivities.

We had already conducted our obligatory training, keeping to our balcony so as not to alarm the revelers, and I was eager for an afternoon off from research. Brigid had asked the scholars to pack the books we thought we might still need, and they were on their way to Oneiros ahead of us. We would be leaving in the morning, after celebrating the holiday with the people of this court.

"It's similar," Carnon said, his back to me as he buttoned his shirt. He was dressed in characteristic black, but with gold accents that were festive enough. "But, as Demon King, I'm expected to visit the different courts for the different high holidays, so I'm usually in Sun for Lughnasadh."

"Really?" I asked. "What about the other holidays?"

"Samhain is Shadows," Carnon explained, listing the high holidays. "Fitting, as a festival for the dead. Imbolc celebrating the rise of spring is usually Blood, and Beltane is Beasts."

"Not this past Beltane," I pointed out, remembering our kiss in front of the small village outside the Bloodwood on Beltane.

Carnon flashed me a grin. "Not this year, " he agreed. "The lesser holidays I usually spend in Oneiros. Mabon and Yule and so forth. I've been remiss in my duties of late, searching for something rather important to me." He gave me a pointed look, and I blushed. "But now that I have my queen, I'm hoping we can do the holidays properly again."

"I'm still not your queen, technically," I reminded him, pinning a final curl of my hair in place. Akela, who had been watching my preparations with interest, gave me an approving snuff of his nose as I scratched his fuzzy head.

"You are in all the ways that matter," Carnon crooned, coming up behind me and kissing my neck. His arms snaked around my waist. "Crown or no crown, remember?"

"Hmm," I said, looking at us in the reflection of the mirror where I had been attempting to make my hair look somewhat elegant. "Again, the Lords seem to care deeply about the 'no crown' part." My hands dropped to my sides as I lifted my gaze to his. "How do I look?"

"Stunning as always," Carnon answered, pressing another kiss to my neck.

I smiled. I did look stunning. I had chosen a dress of bronze, that was modest in comparison with the scrap of black Carnon had dressed me in when I first met the Daemon Lords. This dress had a wide neckline that flared to show off my collarbones and sleeves that clung to my arms all the way down. But it was positively skin tight through the waist and hips, with very little left to the imagination.

"I like that gown," Carnon murmured, his lips trailing over my ear as he spoke. "You are definitely a queen tonight. If not for our discussion late last night, I would most certainly attempt to seduce you right now."

I laughed. "Thank you," I said, turning in his arms and pressing a quick kiss to his lips. "You are incorrigible."

"Is there a reason you *don't* think you look like a queen?" he asked, turning me to face him. "Because you do. You are. I have told you a hundred times, you *are* my Queen. Do you not want the title?"

"No, I do," I assured him, sighing uncomfortably. "I suppose I feel like a fraud. Like I did when I thought this was all pretend. I have no idea what I'm doing, and I'm worried I'll make a mess of it."

"You won't," Carnon said, putting a hand to my cheek and speaking with such confidence that I ached to believe him. "You are already magnificent." He brushed a kiss over my lips, then my nose and forehead. "I could ask for no one better to protect my lands with me. To rule by my side."

"But I can't control my temper," I pointed out, remembering the number of times my fire raged out of control.

"Because you are passionate," Carnon said. "We discussed this last night."

"And I don't know enough about demon history," I added.

"You'll learn," he replied with a shrug.

"And I'm a witch."

"You are perfect," Carnon said, silencing my protests with a kiss. "My perfect match. And I know that you are smart, strong, and kind. That's what matters most."

Gods, this male. What had I done to deserve his love? I wrapped my arms around him, uncertain how to express my sudden emotion to him.

"Thank you," I breathed. "I'll try to stop arguing

about it."

Carnon laughed. "That would be greatly appreciated. That's my mate you are doubting," he added, giving me a teasing peck on the cheek. "Let's go get this over with, shall we?"

"Do you not like festivals?" I asked, remembering Carnon's reticence at Beltane. "Do you not want to go?"

"I just feel like I should be working, not celebrating," Carnon sighed, placing my hand in the crook of his elbow and guiding me down to join the revelry.

"Is being with your people not working?" I asked, nudging him with my hip.

He smiled down at me, looking more than a little proud. "For someone who says they are not a queen, you certainly think like one."

"Hmm," I hummed, raising my brows at him. "I also seem to recall suggesting we work the other day, and you were very much in favor of a distraction. What is this newfound work ethic?"

"You successfully chastised me into doing my job," he joked, pinching my waist lightly in a teasing gesture. "But truly, Red," he added, stopping to turn toward me. He lifted his free hand to cup my cheek, looking down at me with such adoration that my breath caught for a moment. "My people will be lucky to call you their Queen. I will be lucky." He tilted my face so that I was looking up at him. "You were born for it. Born for me."

A gentle brush of the lips and we were walking again, our steps slow and regal as we prepared to greet the crowd. I didn't know anything about being a queen, and I prayed to the Goddess that she would guide me when the time came.

The people of Sun were as bright as their Lady.

Either Brigid's disposition rubbed off on them, or the Court of Sun was an exceptionally bright and happy place. Demons and mortals alike mingled, laughing and celebrating and bowing or nodding politely to us. Many greeted Carnon by name, with the same 'my lord' he had been subject to before I had known who he truly was.

I was also surprised at the deference they showed me, especially since I was not their queen yet. Word of our mating must have spread, because we were met with congratulations as children and their mothers handed me flowers.

"Is this normal?" I asked, trying to hold the growing bouquet in a way that wouldn't result in flowers falling behind me as I moved.

"Do you not remember how excited the people of Mithloria were when you arrived?" Carnon asked, responding to my questions in his typically roundabout way—with another question.

I rolled my eyes and whacked his arm playfully with the flowers, which left a smear of pollen on the black sleeve of his tunic.

Carnon laughed, brushing off the sticky dust and dropping a kiss onto my nose. "I love it when you're irritated with me," he purred, giving me a suggestive smirk. "And yes, the people in Sun are especially deferential. It's been a long time since there was a queen in the Darklands. Your presence brings them hope."

"Why?" I asked, feeling suddenly nervous that I would disappoint these happy people.

Carnon shrugged. "A queen means the King is happily mated," he said, still guiding me through the grounds. "Like the gods, a consort brings balance and stability."

"Am I a stabilizing presence then?" I teased, nudging him with a hip.

He chucked, smiling down at me. "More than you know, Red."

"How do so many of them know you?" I asked, gesturing with the bouquet to the crowd. "I mean, I know you're the King, but they seem so..." I trailed off, hunting for the right word.

"Familiar?" Carnon asked, squeezing my arm as he stifled a laugh. "I've been visiting all the courts since I was a boy. It was part of my duties with Alaunus."

We stopped in front of the lawns, where several sporting events were being held. I had no idea what demon sports would be like but, looking out over the fields, they seemed similar to human sports from back in the Witchlands. Most involved balls and brawling.

"Can you tell me about him?" I asked, looking up at my mate. Carnon had told me a lot about my father in the month after Mama's murder, but I wasn't sure I would ever really know enough. "Something new, I mean."

He met my gaze, his eyes soft and understanding. "The last time he brought me to Sun was for another Lughnasadh festival," Carnon began, pulling me to sit on a bench beside him, one arm wrapped around my shoulders while the other played with the petals of the bouquet. "He forced me to compete in one of the games, to show my solidarity with the people here."

"Which game?" I asked, looking out across the fields. There were so many ongoing competitions that I had never heard of, I was sure I wouldn't recognize whatever Carnon had competed in.

He gave a long-suffering sigh. "Archery," he said,

looking wistfully across the lawn, his eyes lost in a memory. "And I was atrocious."

"Really?" I asked, surprised that Carnon was not a master of every weapon. "But you fight so well with a sword."

"Hacking at things with a sharp blade at close distances is very different to the precision and patience archery requires," Carnon intoned, as if I were a student of the finer points of the sport. "Turns out I'm a 'stab first, ask questions later' sort of male."

I laughed. "But you had a bow when I met you in the Bloodwood."

Carnon smiled at me, stealing a quick kiss. "Let me tell the story, Red. Alaunus knew I would be terrible, and I railed at him for several hours for forcing me to embarrass myself in front of the whole court. I was maybe fifteen, and my ego was somewhat fragile."

"Only somewhat?" I teased.

Carnon gave me a rueful look. "I'll never forget what Alaunus told me, why he'd made me do it. He said, 'Being a king requires you to humble yourself to your subjects. Nothing is more humbling than failure.'"

"So he was wise, then," I said, tucking these words into my heart. I wished my father were around to teach me to be a queen, but these stories would have to do in his absence.

"Very," Carnon agreed. "It also forced me to learn. I worked every day after my failure to master the damned bow," he added. "But he was right. Humbling myself made the people more free to come to me. To ask for help or to offer suggestions. It made me approachable, in their eyes at least. More so here, where I never have to rip out any throats."

I patted his hand, knowing how much he hated to play the villain in Oneiros and the other courts. "People still respect you," I pointed out. "You're fair. That's more than could be said for a lot of the kings I've read about in the library."

Carnon smiled. "I—"

An explosion cut him off, the crowd shrieking in panic around us as stone and dirt rained down on us from the vicinity of the palace gates. Shadows exploded, obliterating the structure. Carnon threw himself over me, putting up a wall of magic from every court, fire and shadows and thorns writhing around us, to shield us from the blast.

"What the fuck was that?" Carnon growled, dropping the wall as the shrieks became wails and groans and orders were being shouted loudly between guards. I heard his name being called over the din and recognized the voice as Herne's.

"The gate," I said, pushing him off me so I could stand. I ran toward the palace walls, the bouquet of flowers discarded in the ashes and debris.

If people were hurt, we could heal them. Save them. I paused several times to heal minor injuries on my way, Carnon catching up to me as I magically stitched together gashes and small wounds from the demons and mortals around us. Most of the demons had fared well, their rapid healing protecting them from the worst of the injuries. But the mortals were far worse off.

"Go to the gate. I'll catch up," I said, waving him on as I set to work on a little mortal girl with a clearly broken leg. She was wailing in agony and terror, her mother holding her so tightly I had to physically pry them apart to fix the leg. The mother was crooning comforting words to the little girl, and it made me ache for my own Mama.

I finished with the little girl, giving her and her mother a tight smile as I stood to tend to other injuries. I managed to heal two more near-fatal wounds and several less critical ones on my way to the gate. Carnon was there with Herne, Cerridwen, and Brigid, and all were staring at the ground at what must have been the epicenter of the blast.

"What was it?" I asked breathlessly as I ran up to them. I gasped when I saw the small, smoking crater where the golden palace gates had been. There was gore and blood strewn about and something sitting in the center that no one had touched yet. "Is everyone alright?"

"Bloody, but fine," Cerridwen said darkly, gesturing to splatters of something red and gooey on her leather armor. Herne was similarly covered, but fine. Brigid was paler than the moonstone palace in Oneiros, but seemed unhurt.

"The guards are gathering up the injured and checking all the guests' identities," Brigid said, almost mechanically. "What is it?" Her gaze was fixed on the object sitting in the blackened crater as Carnon slid down into it, ignoring Herne's growl of protest. He nudged the object with a booted foot.

Nothing happened.

"Looks like something inside a sack," he called back, crouching to open the bag. Herne slid down the crater after him, grumbling about safety, and the rest of us followed.

Brigid's golden gown was smeared with dirt and blood, and I gripped her hand. "How many?"

"At least five," she said, her voice still reedy and face pale with anxiety and shock. "Possibly more. It will be hard to know until the injured and living have been counted."

Carnon made a sound of disgust, and Herne swore loudly as they tipped out the contents of the bag. Brigid turned away, hiding her face against my shoulder, but Cerridwen and I looked on, aghast.

It was a head. Human or demon, it was impossible to tell, but it was male and had been roughly severed from his body. His eyes had been gouged out and lips sewn shut. Flies had already begun to investigate the remains, and Carnon swatted them away, face still contorted in repugnance.

"I think there's something in his mouth," Herne rumbled, taking out a dagger and carefully cutting through the stitches that sealed the lips. I gagged as spiders erupted from the open cavity, dislodging a scrap of paper as they scurried over our shoes and out of the crater.

"Scathanna," Herne growled, as Carnon plucked up the piece of paper. He read it, swore loudly, and handed it not to Herne as I had expected, but to me.

"Elara," he said, shaking the paper to force me to take it. I grimaced, accepting the note and reading the four words that had been scrawled on the parchment in what looked like blood.

I decline your summons.

Chapter 7

Cerridwen flew back to Oneiros almost immediately at Carnon's behest to alert his commanders to prepare for a possible attack.

"Fuck!" He shouted the expletive loudly and repeatedly, as I plied Brigid with tea to calm her nerves. Herne was brooding over a glass of some amber liquid while Carnon swore up and down the balcony, so it was left to me to comfort my friend.

"The head belonged to my messenger," she said, her voice shaky with shock and sorrow. "He had a family. A child. Many of the guards who died did."

"It's not your fault," I soothed, stroking her back and encouraging her to sip the tea. "You couldn't have known."

"I'm responsible for my people," she whispered. "I'll

have to speak to the families."

My gut twisted in a mixture of guilt and remorse. "I'll go," I offered. "And Carnon. We can go on our way out of the city."

She nodded, still pale and shaking, and I made her drain the teacup. Out of curiosity, I glanced at the remains.

"What does the broken sword or knife mean?" I asked, studying the pointed shape in the bottom of the cup.

Brigid swallowed, standing to prepare for our departure. "Disaster."

"We leave tonight," Carnon said from the door to the balcony, his face stern and unfeeling as he addressed the two Daemon Lords in the room. "Brigid, command your forces to fortify your borders. We can't risk a larger attack from Scathanna. Herne, send a message to yours and put them on alert as well."

"Do you want them joining us in Oneiros?" Herne asked, standing to carry out his orders. Brigid stood too, looking expectantly between the males.

"No," Carnon said after a moment of hesitation. "Your casters are already at the border, and we can't leave the territories defenseless if Scathanna tries something else. Not with both of you in Oneiros."

Both nodded, taking their leave silently as Carnon glowered at nothing.

"It wasn't your fault either," I said quietly, still sitting on the couch across the room.

"Wasn't it?" Carnon snapped, locking his serpentine gaze on mine. "I made the call. I made the summons. And now I have a war on my hands."

"If you recall," I began, feeling my temper flare

alongside his. I took a breath, reminding myself to try gentleness with him. To reject my usual anger in favor of tenderness. I tried again, more calmly this time. "Herne and I both agreed with you. The plan seemed like a smart one. This isn't your fault."

"I'm the King," Carnon growled, flashing his pointed canines. Again, the anger threatened to strike, the beast inside me aching to set fire to the room. I cooled it, imagining Carnon's shadows dousing my fire.

"And I'm your Queen," I argued quietly, going to him and cupping his cheek. "Or so you keep saying. This is *our* responsibility. We face it *together*."

Carnon deflated like I had physically knocked the wind from him. "You're right," he said, placing his large hands heavily on my shoulders and squeezing gently. "I'm sorry."

"You have nothing to apologize for," I said, stroking his face once more before dropping my hands to take his. "Let's pack and go. We can visit the families of the fallen on our way."

"We will have to ride through the night," Carnon said tiredly, scrubbing a hand over his face. "I'd suggest you stay here tonight and join me tomorrow instead, but if Scathanna was willing to attack another Court, she won't have qualms about attacking you."

"We go together," I agreed, stepping in closer to wrap my arms around his waist. He responded with his own embrace, holding me tightly. "And we make the spider-bitch pay."

❊ ❊ ❊

It took us three days of hard travel to reach Oneiros. None of us said much, preferring to ride hard and sleep when we finally stopped for a rest. Traveling by mirror would have been so much faster, but the witch mirror I had enchanted in Oneiros was still shattered, and the Crone was likely watching anyway.

We were a ragged bunch when we made it to the moonstone palace, all of us dirty and travel-worn, and more than a little irritable. Brigid was, as usual, the most pleasant of all of us, although still mired in grief over the losses in Sun.

Cerridwen was waiting for us, having been alerted to our arrival by Artemis' appearance, and she and her mate embraced.

Lucifer joined us, sullen and surly as usual. The short-horned male was one of the largest demons I had met in the Darklands, and I wondered if the scales traveling up his neck meant he could shift into a snake, like Carnon. I was about to ask, but he spoke before I had a chance.

"Your forces have been alerted, and the generals are ready to meet with you tomorrow, Your Majesty," he said, speaking as we walked through the palace. "Word from the border is that the wards stand, but the sighting of witches inspecting our defenses has been steadily increasing."

"Fine," Carnon said, tone devoid of warmth or patience after our exhausting journey. He rubbed his neck, looking more haggard than I had ever seen him, and I decided it was time for me to take charge and force my mate to rest. Carnon would push himself to his breaking point for his people. He would feel guilty if he didn't.

"We will meet first thing in the morning," I said to Cerridwen and Herne. "Lucifer, please escort Lady Brigid to a guest suite, and have meals sent to all of our rooms."

"I'm afraid, my lady—"

"Whatever it is, Lucifer," I interrupted, putting a hand up to silence his protest, "I am confident you can fix it. We are all tired, and I don't want to set you on fire unless I absolutely have to."

I pushed Carnon through the doors of our room, trying to ignore Lucifer's squawk of protest and Cerridwen's laugh behind us. He needed food and a bath and a shave and sleep, probably in that order.

"Elara," he growled, turning and crushing me to him in a kiss that stole my breath. He tasted of the outdoors, and three days of stubble scratched my lips horribly, but I didn't care as he kissed me into oblivion.

He pulled away just far enough that he could look down at me, leaving me breathless.

"What was that for?" I asked, attempting to catch my breath as he continued to squeeze me hard.

"It's very sexy when you take control," he murmured, dropping a more gentle kiss onto my lips. "And it's been an age since I've demonstrated exactly what you do to me."

"It's been three days," I corrected, heat flooding me as I felt the hard press of him against me. "And I need a bath first."

"Mmm," he objected, nuzzling against my neck and scratching his spiky face across my sensitive skin. "You don't."

"*You* need a bath," I argued, pushing him away a little more forcefully. He didn't retreat far, but he loosened his grip to give me a reluctant pout. "Very badly. You smell like horse."

"Cruel thing," he whined as I pushed out of his arms and went to run the bath. The tub was big enough to stand in and still be mostly submerged, with benches embedded in the sides. I looked forward to swimming in some hot, soapy water.

Carnon called after me, "I did warn you I wouldn't stop trying to seduce you."

"Now doesn't really feel like the right time for it, my love," I called back. I heard the sounds of clothes being shucked off and tossed about the room, and I took a moment to inspect my own appearance. I winced. I looked pale and exhausted, and I clearly had dirt on my nose for days. I rubbed it off irritably as Carnon came up behind me, completely nude.

"It's always the right time," he said, wrapping his arms around me and bending in to kiss my neck. "You smell like heaven."

"I do not, you lunatic," I sighed, turning to face him. "Why didn't you tell me I had a smudge on my nose?"

"Because it was adorable," he said, dropping his forehead to mine. I felt his nose wrinkle against mine. "Maybe you *do* need a bath."

"Get off," I scoffed, pushing him off me so I could remove my soiled clothes. "Luckily, the bath is big enough for two."

"A very happy coincidence of design," Carnon agreed, his gaze wandering down my body as I pulled off my trousers and blouse and underthings.

Something about his heated stare at my body made me flush with pride and confidence. I grinned as I began to untangle my hair from its messy braid, but Carnon took over, weaving strong fingers into my hair as he teased my braid apart. I groaned as he massaged my scalp, and he bent to press kisses under my ear as he worked. Warmth flooded me again and by the time the huge, onyx bathtub was full, I was aching for him.

"Still want me to bathe?" he asked, murmuring into my shoulder. His stubble scraped deliciously, and I had to swallow a groan.

"Yes," I breathed. "But we can be quick."

He chuckled, scooping me into his arms and stepping into the tub, lowering himself into the hot water with me still clasped to his chest. I yelped at the sudden heat, the sound captured with another kiss.

It occurred to me that this small slice of happiness was at odds with the rest of the world. The Crone threatened our borders, Scathanna was up to the gods knew what, and people had just lost their lives in Sun.

The thought marred my enjoyment of my mate's mouth and hands exploring me, and Carnon sensed my hesitation. "What's wrong, Red?"

"It feels wrong," I replied, "for us to be happy while others suffer." Carnon paused, putting me down so we were standing chest to chest. He pulled back to look at me, and I swallowed. "For me to live and love you after my mother was killed. After my parents lost each other. For us to enjoy each other after people have died."

"Red," Carnon said, rubbing the smudge of dirt from my nose with his wet thumb and gazing at me softly. "Your happiness is not an affront to the pain of others. You don't dishonor the memory of your mother or the legacy of your father or the losses of Sun by experiencing joy in the here and now."

"But war is coming," I said, pressing a hand to his

scratchy cheek. He sighed, eyes closing as he pressed his face into my hand.

"It is," he said, turning to kiss my palm. He looked at me again, pulling me to him and grabbing a bar of soap from the edge of the tub. "And I intend to love each moment with you as if it might be our last. Because it could be, Red. And I don't plan to leave this world with regrets when it comes to you."

His hand brushed down my back, and he tapped my rear insistently. "Now turn." He gently guided me away from him until I was facing the onyx wall, sliding the bar of soap over my arms and back as he massaged the stiffness of three days of hard riding out of my shoulders. I made an indecent noise and he chuckled, pressing a kiss to the back of my neck.

"You should stop that," he said, his voice filled with promise, "or this bath will end with both of us needing a second one."

I stepped back into him. Feeling that he was indeed hard and aching behind me, I ran my hand gently over his length.

"Elara," Carnon hissed, catching my hand in his. "I was determined to finally use the armchair. You're going to make a liar out of me."

"Hmm," I said, biting my lip to hold in my grin. "I believe you are an accomplished liar without my help."

"Gods, woman," he groaned as I slid my hand down his length. He stepped closer to me, his breath hot against my neck. "You will be the death of me."

"Then I suppose we had better treat this moment as if it is our last," I said, turning over my shoulder to look at him.

He caught my lips in his and pulled me back into his

lap, all restraint gone as he ran soapy hands over my body. One went to my breast as the other trailed up my thigh to my hip. I gasped as he stroked a thumb gently over my nipple, which peaked at his attention, and he deepened the kiss. His tongue explored every inch of my mouth and the hand on my hip drifted over my backside and squeezed.

"Elara," he rasped as he broke away to catch his breath. "Gods above, how are you so fucking perfect?"

I didn't answer with words, hooking my arms around his neck and pressing myself to him. He was hard against my stomach, and I moaned a little at the anticipation of feeling him inside me. He backed toward one of the benches as I tried to position myself over him.

He chuckled at my clumsy movements, lifting me onto his lap as he perched on the ledge. He took himself in his hand below the water and stroked himself against my entrance. "Is this what you want, mate?"

He nipped at my earlobe as I whimpered an incoherent, "Yes," sliding into me with a slow, torturous stroke.

"Mmm, I don't think we've done this in this bath yet," he murmured, grabbing me more firmly and hoisting me up, like it was nothing.

"Definitely an oversight," I gasped as I slid down onto him again. He filled me perfectly, and I tensed around him at the feeling.

Carnon swore. "One I intend to immediately rectify," he growled, kissing me again as he began to move in long, deep strokes.

The hot water sloshed around us as we moved, heightening the sensations as one of his hands drifted between us and pressed firmly on that sensitive spot between my legs. The sounds I made as he kissed and touched me would have embarrassed me if they didn't drive him harder. Clearly, he appreciated them.

"I don't think I'll ever get tired of this," Carnon said, gripping the back of my head with his free hand gently but firmly as he moved beneath me. "Having you around me like this."

"Goddess," I gasped, as the other hand stroked and teased me. "Don't stop."

Carnon's smile was wicked and beautiful. "Never, my love," he purred, kissing me again as he increased his pace.

I moaned as I came, the sound swallowed by his mouth as heat and pleasure spiraled through me. He groaned into me as he followed.

"Always the gentleman," I breathed, holding him fast as we remained joined in the water. "Letting me come first."

Carnon chuckled somewhat breathlessly. He still spasmed within me, and I smiled against his lips. "I aim to please," he teased, kissing my jaw and my neck before burying his face in my shoulder. "I didn't think it would be like this," he confessed, the words spoken quietly and reverently against my skin. "The wanting and pleasure a mate could bring me."

"Me neither," I said, laughing as I stroked his hair, weaving my fingers into the damp strands. "I'm very glad you seem to know what you're doing, as I had even less of an idea about it than you did."

"Hmm," Carnon hummed, kissing my neck before pulling at and looking at me hungrily, his gaze wholly serpentine. "Allow me to shatter all of your ideas about lovemaking, mate."

He kissed me again, and I let him do exactly as he had said, as if it might be the last time.

Chapter 8

Something about our joining in the bath felt like an ending. Not of our relationship, but of the relative peace of the last month. Lughnasadh had shattered that peace irrevocably, and the next two days proved me correct.

Carnon barely had time to kiss me after magic training before he had to rush off to meet with soldiers and generals. He had asked me if I wanted to join him, but I knew nothing of battle strategy, and I felt like my time would be better served researching and mastering my magic. He accepted this, insisting that he would keep me apprised anyway. After the first day of meetings, he told me that they were planning both the defense of Oneiros and an attack on Shadow, and he spent the next day in meeting after endless meeting about it.

My mate looked exhausted, his face drawn and eyes shadowed, and I tried to get him to drink and eat something before he rushed off again.

"Should we be worried?" I asked as he quickly downed a glass of his preferred amber drink.

"I don't know," he answered, looking concerned and handing me back the glass. "With you and me defending the city, no. It honestly depends on what Scathanna decides to do."

Carnon had sent a summons to Tyr, requesting his presence in Oneiros immediately. The Daemon Lord of Blood was either too smart or too loyal to decline the summons. But that was also something that needed coordinating, and Lucifer was rushing all over the castle to prepare for the arrival and reception of a third Daemon Lord.

Brigid worked with me a little on tarot and tasseography. I spent our time mostly focused on memorizing the meaning of the symbols and seeing what I could glean from some very simple practice.

Cerridwen had also declared that it was time for me to learn how to wield a dagger, laughing when I had told her that my magic would protect me.

"What about the Crone's iron cuffs?" she pointed out. "There are a number of ways your magic could be contained or stilted, and if you're drained, there is literally nothing you could do."

I hadn't told her that, aside from my exhaustion after intense training sessions, I hadn't felt myself near the end of my magic since the Crone's manor. The exhaustion was also improving, and I hadn't drifted off at odd intervals for weeks now. But she had a point about the merits of having multiple ways to defend myself, so I agreed.

Brigid asked to learn too, so the three of us spent increasingly long afternoons working on simple, and then more complex, techniques for both defending against and disarming an opponent.

"I can't move another muscle," I groaned, after Brigid had successfully flipped me on my back while practicing disarming me. My pride in her victory was only slightly tempered by the bruises forming across my back from the hard landing. "You win. I'm dead."

Akela huffed as if saying, *stop being dramatic*, and I shot him a scowl.

"No giving up," Cerridwen chastised, offering me a hand. I took it with another groan, letting her pull me to my feet. Brigid fussed over me, apologizing profusely.

I waved her off. "I'm fine," I said, wincing as I limped a little. "Just a little battered."

"Oh gods, will Carnon be angry?" she asked, wringing her hands delicately. As often as I told her that Carnon wouldn't hurt her, she had an almost obsessive respect for his position. I made it my mission to get her to sass him at least once before she returned to Sun.

"No," I grumbled. "More likely he'll chastise me for failing to stop you." I rubbed a sore spot on my elbow, grimacing a little, and Akela nudged my hip to make sure I was fine. I scratched his head. "Well done though, really."

"Thank you," she beamed, blushing a little at the praise. "Normally, I would just incinerate my enemies, but this is a useful skill."

"*You've* incinerated someone?" I asked, surprise making my brows leap up.

"Well...no," she confessed, turning redder. "The

most I've ever done is sentence someone to community service. But I *could*, if I needed to."

I laughed and hugged her with one free arm. "I bet you could," I agreed. Akela whined, clearly irritated he wasn't part of the hug. I scratched him again with my free hand. "Maybe you should take over my magic practice, since Carnon is so busy."

"It's not forever," Cerridwen said reassuringly, throwing her arm around Brigid as well. "Believe me, it's been days since Herne and I have—"

"I'm not sure you should tell me what you and your mates do in private," Brigid said, blushing a shade of crimson so dark, I was worried she might faint from the loss of blood to her organs.

"Have you never—"

"Oh, no, I have," she said, interrupting me before I could ask what was, admittedly, a very personal question. She was still bright red, and I felt a little bad for embarrassing her. But she *had* knocked me on my back, so my pity didn't last long. "But it's different with your mate. At least, I assume it is."

Cerridwen and I glanced at each other, then burst out into a fit of giggles. Brigid rolled her eyes in uncharacteristic disdain.

"We can be adults about this," she said, her usually sweet tone laced with the slightest hint of ire.

"Sorry," Cerridwen said, still giggling. "It's your face. I cannot *wait* for you to find your mate. Then we can share all sorts of stories!"

"You do remember that my mate is your brother?" I asked, giving Cerridwen a raised brow. She grimaced, and this time it was Brigid and I who burst out laughing.

"Do you have any idea who your mate might be?" I

asked Brigid as we headed back into the palace.

"No," she said with a small sigh. "But it's fine. Despite the blush, I promise I have had *plenty* of other experiences."

She looked so austere that I dissolved into another fit of giggles, both of the other females joining me as we fell apart on the stairs.

"My lady," came an unpleasantly familiar gruff voice. I sighed, standing up to see Lucifer, arms crossed over his broad chest and a scornful eyebrow raised in disdain. "If you can spare the time, my lady, I need your approval on the menu and accommodations for our guests."

"I trust your expert eye, Lucifer," I said, stifling my mirth and trying to make myself look somewhat respectable to Carnon's head of staff. We probably shouldn't be giggling like idiots when war was imminent, but I wouldn't apologize for enjoying my friends.

"Your confidence is touching, my lady," Lucifer drawled, looking anything but touched. "But the chef requests your approval, not mine."

"Ah," I said, smiling at the idea of visiting Pierre in the kitchens. "Then lead on."

I waved back to Cerridwen and Brigid, indicating they should go on without me, and Akela and I followed Lucifer to the kitchens. The head of staff looked more and more ominous as we approached, and I grinned a little at his animosity for the jovial demon chef who made me macarons.

"Why don't you like Pierre?" I asked, jogging a little to catch up with his long stride. Lucifer growled, but I knew that he was all bark and no real bite. "Did he offend you with burnt pie?"

"He smiles too much," Lucifer growled.

I rolled my eyes. "I think he likes you," I said genially, ignoring his ire.

Lucifer let out a barked laugh. "If you say so, my lady."

We emerged into semi-chaos as Pierre and his hordes of cooks ran around the kitchen, stirring and mixing and shouting at each other.

"Finally, the oaf has brought you, my lady," Pierre exclaimed upon seeing me. He kissed the air next to each of my cheeks, threw Akela a reluctant nod, then glowered at Lucifer. Lucifer glowered right back at him.

"Now, now boys," I said, trying to sound motherly. "Play nicely. What did you want my approval for, Pierre?"

Pierre went into a long winded explanation of the menu planned to welcome the Daemon Lords, while Lucifer stood like a stone sentry at my back.

"You may leave," Pierre said dismissively to the head of staff, peering around me to shoot the hulking demon another glower.

Lucifer crossed his arms, clearly marking a line in the proverbial sand. "I think I'll stay."

Pierre narrowed his eyes and gave me an eloquent look I couldn't decipher. "Being micromanaged is taxing on an artist," he sighed dourly. "Anyway, Lady Elara, this is what I need your opinion on."

Pierre waved for me to sit at the counter, placing two dainty porcelain plates in front of me. On one was a wispy swirl of caramelized sugar spun around a golden pastry. On the other was an elegant tart, topped with berries and browned sugar.

"Which do you think for the dessert?" Pierre asked, looking at me seriously as if my answer could mean life or death. The rest of the staff continued to work around us, and I noticed Lucifer rolling his eyes out of the corner of my own.

"Both look lovely," I said. "I think either will be perfect."

"But which to impress the Lords?" Pierre pushed, waving his hands at the desserts. "I know they are so different, but you must help Pierre by choosing." He handed me a golden fork, and gestured to each of the desserts.

"Oh my gods," I said with a mouthful of pastry and sugar. "It's divine." I tried the tarte and made similarly indecent noises. It took me two more bites to decide which I preferred. "This one. The pastry."

"Ah, the profiterole, yes," Pierre said, nodding gravely. "An excellent choice."

"Profituh-what?" Lucifer asked irritably behind me.

Pierre gasped, his shock only partially feigned. "Uncultured male," he cried. "You have never had a profiterole? My gods above, I must instruct you. Here."

He came around the counter and pushed Lucifer onto the stool next to mine. "Sit. Eat."

Pierre placed the pastry in front of Lucifer, thrusting a golden fork into his hands. I took another bite of each of the desserts, working hard to stifle my moan of pleasure.

"Eat," commanded Pierre, somehow scowling down at Lucifer, who was at eye level with him in the stool.

"I don't like sweets," grumbled Lucifer, poking at the pastry.

"I'll eat it!" I volunteered, moving my fork to Lucifer's

plate.

Pierre stopped me with a jab of his own fork and speared his gaze on Lucifer again. "Everyone likes sweets. Try it."

"I don't," said Lucifer, crossing his arms and making no move to taste the dessert.

"You are wrong," Pierre growled. "Try it. Or are you too cowardly to admit that you fear pleasure?"

I looked between the two males, realizing this argument had less to do with the dessert in front of us and more to do with some unspoken history between them. My head bobbed back and forth between them as they lobbed sullen insults at each other, Lucifer finally slamming his fist on the counter with a growl and practically bending the fork as he stabbed the pastry.

"Well?" I asked, curious if his attitude would soften with sugar.

"It's fine," Lucifer said with a shrug, clearly restraining himself from taking a second bite.

"Fine?" shrieked the chef indignantly. "*Fine?!*"

I backed away as they argued, Pierre insisting that Lucifer was unfairly biased against his dessert, and Lucifer arguing that maybe he just didn't like dessert.

"Out, peasant!" Pierre exclaimed.

Lucifer's lips twitched up into an unmistakable smirk.

I took my leave, not wanting to see the war that was about to ensue.

"There will be wedding bells any day, I'm sure," I told Akela conspiratorially as I walked to our rooms to bathe and change. Akela huffed his agreement with me, and I laughed.

I pushed open the doors of our room and felt a

wave of dizziness crash over me. "Not again," I groaned, clutching the door and struggling to stay upright. Akela whined in concern, but the flash of memory was over as quickly as it had started, and I was able to right myself after a few moments.

The flash had been the same one I had dreamt before we left the Court of Sun, and my eyes went to the wall above our bed.

When Carnon walked in a few minutes later, he found me perched on my toes, balanced precariously on the headboard and holding one of the wooden bed posts for support.

"Do I want to know what you're doing?" he asked wearily, dropping his sword with a clatter and coming to stand next to the bed to observe me.

"Probably not," I gritted out, trying to dig my nails under one of the stones where I was certain I had seen Alaunus hiding something. "Ow!"

"Gods above, Red," Carnon sighed. "Let me do it. I'm taller than you."

"You don't know what *it* is," I pointed out, shaking my fingers out. I had broken one of my nails, but the healing magic swept up almost unbidden to heal the small hurt.

"Then tell me so I can help you," he said, laughing as he gripped me by the waist and pulled me down from the headboard. He lifted my fully healed fingers to his mouth and kissed them tenderly.

"That's the stone," I said, pointing to the spot on the wall I had been trying to pry open. "The one Alaunus hid something behind."

Carnon lifted a brow, looking up at the wall. "Are you sure?" he asked, looking down at me skeptically.

"Of course I'm sure," I snapped. Carnon's brows climbed even higher. "Sorry," I sighed, giving him a rueful smile. "Sore fingers."

"Hmm," Carnon said, looking unconvinced. "Well, if Alaunus hid something there, I'm certain he intended to retrieve it himself."

"What do you mean?" I asked, as Carnon set me aside and kicked off his boots.

"I mean," he replied, climbing up onto the bed and frowning at the wall. "That he probably intended to retrieve whatever it is with his magic."

Carnon released his shadows, snaking them up the walls to investigate the cracks in the stone. When the shadows sunk into one, he pulled.

With a groan, the stone came free.

Chapter 9

"I told you so," I said smugly, after Carnon had felt around in the space behind the stone and pulled out several folios and parchments.

"The sentiments of a happily mated female," Carnon quipped, straining as he felt in the space. "I think that's everything."

He leapt down from the bed as I gathered up the papers he had tossed down. There were several notebooks and leather-bound manuscripts, as well as loose papers and parchments. If there had been an order to them, it was lost when Carnon removed the stack haphazardly from the wall. I set them out on the coffee table to examine each document.

"Well?" Carnon asked, coming to crouch next to me. He touched a loose parchment and made a noise in his throat that I couldn't interpret. "This is his handwriting."

"You recognize it?" I asked, separating the papers with shaking fingers. The room tilted sharply, and Akela growled in warning. "Oh no," I sighed, gripping the table as I toppled.

"Easy, Red," Carnon said, worry lacing his voice as he caught me, settling me in his lap on the ground. "Just breathe through it. I've got you."

My reply was lost as the room blurred, and a hazy vision of Alaunus, sitting at what was now Carnon's desk in his office, filled my mind. The old King appeared to be writing a letter, hastily scribbling the words on parchment.

He looked up, seemingly at nothing, and smiled.

"I wondered when you'd start having visions," he said. He was looking directly at me, which was... impossible? He smiled warmly, lines crinkling at his eyes. "I know you don't understand yet, but you will. I love you, even though we will never get to meet."

He looked down and dripped hot, red wax on the parchment to seal it. He pressed a gold stamp to the wax and blew on it, then held the letter up.

"Read this one first," he said, again speaking to no one in the room.

"Father?" I asked. He didn't reply, just shook his head as if trying to clear it. The room went fuzzy again, and the vision slipped away. Everything around me slowly came back into focus as I blinked up at Carnon, who was almost nose to nose with me, his face a mask of concern.

"Is this going to happen every time?" I asked, my voice weaker than I intended.

Carnon let out a relieved breath. "Gods, I hope not," he said, helping me sit up and holding my back, just in case I collapsed. "It's very inconvenient."

"Ass," I muttered, shooting him a glare.

He grinned. "You know you love it." He kissed my cheek and the grin faded. "What did you see?"

"Alaunus," I said, feeling like he was still too unknown for me to refer to him as my father. "I swear that..."

I trailed off, and Carnon pushed, "What?"

I shook my head, trying to picture exactly what I had seen. "It was like he knew I could see him. Like he was having a vision of me having a vision of him. Does that make sense?"

I looked to my mate, whose face had transformed to one of puzzled interest. "Not really," he said slowly, "but I believe you. Did he say anything?"

"He held up a letter," I said, trying to remember. The red wax seal floated across my memory and I leaned forward, rifling through the papers to see if it was there.

"This one," I said, finding the red wax and picking it up with a slightly shaking hand. "Gods above."

"What?" Carnon asked curiously, leaning over me.

I had flipped the letter over and there, in an elegant scrawling script, was my name.

"He left it for you," Carnon said, tracing the swooping letters gingerly. "Will you open it?"

"I think I have to," I said, voice a little unsteady as I broke the seal. I bit my lip and looked at him.

"I'm here," Carnon said, putting his hand over mine. "We're in this together."

I nodded and unfolded the papers. The note was far shorter than I had imagined it might be, especially as this was the only message my father had left for me, as far as I knew. I read it aloud, my voice hoarse.

> *Elara,*
>
> *I already know that I will be dead when you read this letter.*

I swallowed, clearing my throat to continue.

> *I'm not sure how yet. These things reveal themselves in their own time, but I know that we shall never get to meet.*
>
> *I want you to know—*

My voice broke, a tear falling on the paper and smearing some of the precious words.

"Can you—" I rasped, passing the paper to Carnon. "Can you read it? Please?"

He nodded, tucking a wayward strand of hair behind my ear he took the letter from me and read aloud.

> *I want you to know that I loved your mother, fiercely. I still love her. I know she won't tell you how we met, or came to fall in love, but I believe the Goddess led me to her. The moment I saw her I knew, and I knew that together we would create you.*
>
> *I have a feeling that this is the last letter I will write, and while I don't have the words to express my sorrow at never holding you in my arms, or calling you my daughter in front of my kingdom, know that I love you with everything I am.*
>
> *Something is happening. The reason I found your mother and the reason you were born. I swore to her I*

would find a way to keep you safe. To bring you here.

Should I not return, I think the Hag will have the answers you need. Trust Carnon. He will be an exceptional mate.

All my love,

Your Father

I sobbed as Carnon read the final lines, and he folded me into his chest. I cried, long and hard, for the mother I had lost and the father I would never know, finally letting myself feel the pain of their loss instead of smothering it with anger. It hurt, and I wondered if it would ever really stop hurting, that hole inside me that could never really be filled.

Akela padded over, dropping his head in my lap with a little whine of sympathy. Carnon held me, careful not to damage the letter–my only connection between me and my father. "My love," he murmured, over and over, as if he wasn't sure what to say other than to reassure me that I was not alone.

"He knew," I said at last, voice thick and mouth dry. Carnon's shirt was soaked, but I clung to him as if he were my only anchor to the world. "He knew he was going to die before meeting me. He knew we were mates."

Carnon kissed my hair. "I know," he said somberly, his arms still holding me fast. "He never told me he was going to die."

"Why not?" I asked, pulling away, a little surprised at the anger I felt flare up in me. I tried to breathe, to be calm. To remember my vow to try to control my temper. But something about the letter niggled at the back of my mind. At the truth Carnon had claimed to tell me about how he found me. "You were his protegé. His heir. Why would he not have told you?"

"I don't know, Elara," Carnon said calmly, running strong hands down my arms to soothe me. "There were clearly a lot of things he didn't tell me."

But Carnon had been looking for me. Specifically for me. And there was no reason for him to be looking in the Bloodwood for his mate, which he must have thought would be a demon, when none of them could cross into it. The thought dislodged something as realization dawned.

"He told you," I said, working hard to maintain my composure and not snap. "He told you that I would be your mate. How else could you be *so* sure you would find me in the Bloodwood?"

The color had drained from Carnon's face, and he shook his head at me slowly. "Red—"

"Don't condescend to me right now," I hissed, anger growing as he attempted to circumvent my questions. "And don't lie. Tell me the truth. How did you *know*?"

Carnon swallowed. "I didn't know it would be you or that it would be his daughter," he said, voice low and urgent as if he could make me understand. "And I *did* tell you the truth. It was Akela who was sure he had found you."

Akela, who had backed away when I had begun yelling, let out a short growl as if to say, *"Don't blame this on me."*

Carnon ran a hand down his face, looking torn. He glanced at Akela, who huffed. *Go on.* Finally, he turned back to me.

"Alaunus told me I would find my mate in the

Bloodwood," he confessed. "He didn't tell me when or where," he continued in a rush, sensing my building fury at another lie he had failed to disclose, "and I honestly didn't believe it was you when we first met. I told you the truth about that."

"And when were you planning to tell me that *he* knew?" I spat, standing and stomping to the other side of the room.

"I swear, I was going to tell you," he said, rising and taking a step toward me. I looked daggers at him, tempted to light the carpet on fire to keep him at bay. He stopped a step later. "I was waiting until the right time."

"You suspected for *weeks* that he was my father. *Months*. My mother *confirmed* it," I snapped. "What else were you waiting for?"

"You didn't know Alaunus might be your father when you found out about the mate bond," he said, spreading his hands out placatingly. "I didn't want to lay that on you when you were barely accepting our connection. And then your mother died and I thought—"

"Thought what, exactly?" I interrupted. "Thought that you knew best? That I should be protected and lied to? I already told you that lying to me is *not* protecting me!"

"Elara," Carnon begged, his face so anguished and miserable that it fueled my anger. I wanted him to be angry too. Anger I could manage. Remorse and sadness? Those were trickier emotions to navigate. "I swear, I didn't intend to lie. I honestly forgot that he told me until your mother confirmed, and then I didn't really want to bring it up when you were already grieving one parent."

"He was my father," I cried, struggling against the grief that threatened to overwhelm me. "It matters that he knew about us."

"I know, Elara," he said again. "My love, I am more sorry than you can possibly know."

As quickly as it had started, my anger fizzled. It was as if Carnon had sent his cooling shadows into me to quell the raging beast that tried to burn me alive from the inside. I sank to my knees and sobbed, letting the grief and loss consume me.

Carnon approached gingerly, as if uncertain that I wouldn't lash out again. He crouched tilting my chin up to look in my face. "Can I hold you?"

I nodded, and he wrapped his strong arms around me, reminding me that I wasn't completely alone, even if he *was* a liar.

Not really a liar, the rational part of my brain reminded me. I knew he had probably genuinely thought it wasn't the right time to tell me. That he had forgotten, like he said, and that he didn't want me to drown in even more grief than I was already. A small part of me didn't care. It wanted anger and revenge and suffering. But the stronger, larger part of me won out.

"No more lies," I gritted out between sobs. "No omissions. You tell me *everything* about him, as soon as you remember it. Even if you don't think it matters."

"Done," he agreed, speaking into my hair as he gently rocked me, like I was a child who needed soothing. It was working. "I am so sorry. I should have told you."

We stayed like that until the sky had grown dark and Akela, who had returned to my side and dropped his head back on my knee, whined that he was hungry.

"You're like fireworks, you know," Carnon

murmured.

"What are fireworks?" I asked, frowning against his chest.

"You've never seen fireworks, Red?" When I shook my head, he sighed. "Your childhood sounds truly dismal. They're like colorful explosions in the night sky. You light a special powder and they explode in different shapes and colors, then fizzle out quickly. Oneiros has them for Beltane every year. I'll have to show you."

"Why am I like them?" I asked, not seeing how explosions in the sky had anything to do with me. I was reasonably sure I wouldn't dissolve into another flood of tears at that point, so I looked up, trying to summon quizzical interest. The look he gave me told me that I had only managed watery curiosity.

Carnon hummed thoughtfully. "You burn so hot and bright it's blinding, but then it's gone a moment later," he said. "Your rage is incandescent, but fleeting,"

I thought about this, trying to picture lights flashing in the sky, quick and hot, and then gone. I thought about Carnon's cooling shadows, his ability to soothe my fire and my soul with tender words and touches. The walls of fire I summoned, uncontrollable until he subdued them with darkness.

"I suppose that's true," I agreed, looking up at him. His eyes were bright, even in the fading light of evening. "And I suppose that makes you the night. The cooling shadow to my flame."

He looked down at me, eyes tender. "You are the most beautiful female—woman—I have ever known," he said, stroking my tear-stained cheek. "Even when you are raging at me. Especially when you are raging at me." He kissed my forehead, smiling softly. "I am honored—no, privileged to be in your line of fire."

I gave a miserable, wet chuckle. "You like me exploding all over you?"

Carnon choked out a laugh. "I'm not sure that sounded the way you meant it to, Red," he said, dropping another kiss on my head. "But yes. Explode on me all you want."

I grimaced, realizing that it really *didn't* sound the way I had intended. "You know what I meant."

"I do," he agreed, tilting my face up to look at him. "Do you forgive me?"

I nodded, and he had the audacity to look a little crestfallen. "Shouldn't you be happy about that?" I asked.

Carnon shrugged, pulling me closer to him. "If you had said no," he murmured, "I was prepared to do some *very* elaborate groveling."

I chuckled, still feeling puffy and miserable. "You can still grovel," I said.

"Very generous of you," Carnon said, stroking a gentle hand down my neck. "I'll make sure it's truly lavish groveling. Top tier groveling. Only the best."

I laughed again, and Carnon held me for a long time until I accepted that, despite his propensity to try to protect me, my father had been right.

I had found an exceptional mate.

Chapter 10

Once we had removed ourselves from the floor of our room, bathed, changed, and fed Akela, we were finally able to discuss the other parts of my father's letter with our inner court.

"He said the Hag would have the answers?" Cerridwen asked, scanning the letter skeptically.

Carnon and I sat side-by-side, fingers intertwined on a sofa in one of the more casual sitting rooms of the palace. The walls were made of the same elegant moonstone that formed the rest of the palace, but plush navy rugs and furniture made the room feel cozier than the formal halls or dining rooms elsewhere.

I had left the other notes and books in our room, not wanting to share them until I had the chance to study them first, but I had brought the letter down with me so our friends could see it.

Cerridwen sat across from us, Brigid perched next to her on the couch, with Herne pacing behind his mate and scowling at the ground.

"What are you proposing?" Herne asked, pausing to give Carnon a piercing look. "You want to run off to the Bloodwood while a war is brewing?"

"I have no desire to run off anywhere," Carnon replied irritably. "But we need answers we aren't finding, and Alaunus hasn't been wrong."

"You just returned," Herne pointed out. "You can't leave Oneiros again so soon."

This was a problem Carnon and I had already discussed, and we had also already come up with a potential solution. One that Herne definitely wouldn't like.

As expected, he balked when we told him. "Absolutely not," he growled.

"My love," Cerridwen started with a sigh.

"It was a disaster last time," Herne shouted, waving his hands in our general direction. "I'm not letting you jump through more mirrors."

"We won't be going to the Crone this time," I argued, giving Carnon's hand a squeeze in a request to let me handle this. He nodded slightly, and I continued. "We'd be going to the Hag. Not only can the Crone *not* enter the Bloodwood, but the Hag's cottage is fiercely warded."

"It will take hours instead of days," Carnon added, apparently unable to remain silent any longer. I frowned at him, and he shrugged apologetically. "No one will even know that we are gone this way."

"And what if she's watching?" Herne asked, still ignoring his mate's attempts to get a word in. "We don't need a repeat of the hand incident."

I sighed, rueing the day I had accidentally opened a witch mirror and ended up with the Crone's severed hand on Carnon's desk. I would never live it down.

"I think it's the wisest course of action," Brigid said, biting her lower lip as she disagreed with Herne. Brigid, I was realizing, was perhaps the most brilliant and strategic of the Daemon Lords. The problem was she was delicate and soft-spoken, and easily overruled as a result.

Herne spluttered his disagreement, but Cerridwen finally managed to interject. "I agree with Brigid," she said, giving the Lady of Sun an approving nod. "And you're right, my love. They can't be gone from the city for days and days. This is the safest option."

"We can go to the Bloodwood and be back within the hour," I said confidently. I had seen a mirror in the Hag's cottage, and I thought it was reasonably large enough to travel through, as long as she didn't have the mirror warded with blood magic. I had a strong suspicion that maybe she expected us, so I hoped it wasn't.

"What do you think she will know that you need to hear?" Herne asked gruffly, stopping behind Cerridwen and dropping a hand on her shoulder. She patted it absently, and I smiled, remembering our giggling fit the other day.

"Alaunus seemed to think she would have knowledge we need," Carnon said, gesturing to the letter on the table between us all.

"Perhaps the reason the Crone wants to bring down the Bloodwood," I suggested. "She seemed like a prescient old bat when I met her."

Carnon snorted appreciatively at this description,

and I shot him a grin. He squeezed my hand affectionately, and Herne rolled his eyes at us.

"I see that I am outvoted," he rumbled, shooting a dark look at his mate. Cerridwen gave him a bright smile, pretending not to notice. "What next, then? We need a plan for the Spider. Do we attack? Do we wait?"

"I want to hear what Tyr has to say," Carnon said. "Either way, we are in a precarious position. We can't pull our forces from the border, so an attack would be difficult if not impossible. But if Scathanna retains her seat of power, she could build enough support amongst the more old-fashioned demons and actually oppose me."

"So we're fucked either way?" Herne asked, clearly not expecting a real answer.

"If you're not going to be helpful, you can leave," Cerridwen snapped, turning to glare at her mate. Herne growled at her, but Cerridwen seemed to be immune to his fury. "Growling and stomping isn't going to help anyone. If you can't be helpful, then you can go."

I glanced at Carnon, who regarded his sister and his friend with raised brows. He looked down at me and gave an almost imperceptible shake of his head. *Let them work this out.*

Herne deflated. "Fine," he grumbled, folding his arms. He winced at Cerridwen's narrowed gaze and added, "Sorry."

Cerridwen turned, beaming at us. "If that's settled then we need to figure out what to tell Tyr. How much he should know."

"You mean about my powers?" I asked, frowning at my friend.

She nodded her curly head. "That, and the visions,

the prophecies, your father…" She trailed off, giving me a sympathetic smile. "Whatever you are not comfortable telling him will stay between us."

Brigid nodded her agreement, and I turned to the Lady of Sun. "What do you think?" I asked. I had disregarded her ideas when it came to Scathanna, and I was determined not to do it again. "Do you think he can be trusted?"

"I know he can't," Herne said darkly, earning a smack on the arm from Cerridwen.

"I'm not sure," Brigid said thoughtfully. "I haven't known him long, or well. He came to power before me and he's always seemed rather…" She hesitated, searching for the right words.

"Treacherous? Selfish? Far too interested in blood and sex?" Herne offered.

Cerridwen shushed him again, and Brigid blushed. "Yes, all of those things."

"Tyr will come to heel if he knows what's good for him," Carnon said, voice edged with a growl of anger or frustration. "He's agreed to the summons, so the chances are good."

"Then I think we tell him everything," Brigid suggested, earning somewhat skeptical looks from Herne and Cerridwen. "We can bind him in a blood bargain not to reveal anything or betray us."

"And if he refuses the blood bargain?" Cerridwen asked, looking at her brother.

"Then he dies," Carnon replied unfeelingly. "For defying a direct order from his king."

"You can't afford to be down two Daemon Lords," Herne said, his lips pursed in disapproval.

"I can't afford to have two Lords betraying me

either," Carnon replied, standing in a stretch. The muscles of his back rippled beneath his shirt, and I had to remind myself to focus on the words, not the muscles. "So we had better convince him to agree."

※ ※ ※

Tyr arrived in Oneiros the next morning, entering the castle with the same smirking swagger he'd displayed when I first met him.

I really didn't have a solid impression of Tyr's character in my mind yet. He had vaguely suggested a threesome and he had waxed almost poetic about the magic in blood, but I couldn't really pinpoint his alliances or thoughts on his king. Carnon had suggested that he was not to be trusted, and I chastised myself for never asking him why. I would have to ask now, if I had any hope of deciding how to bind him and keep him on our side.

"My King," he proclaimed, bowing in his finery before Carnon and me in the ornate throne room with the stained glass windows. "And my lady, you look ravishing as always."

Carnon and I had also dressed up, as was expected when receiving a Daemon Lord. At least, one we weren't friends with.

My glittering black gown felt like a silken dream, the plunging neckline and long sleeves emphasizing the creamy white of my skin. Carnon was in his typical black, a crown of twisted gold and silver upon his brow as he gazed coolly at the Lord of Blood.

Tyr looked no less magnificent. His long, dark red

hair swept his shoulders, and he had chosen a jacket of the same dark hue, emblazoned with gold. His athletic form was on display in the form-fitting coat and trousers. He gave Brigid a rakish smile as he rose from the bow, his golden tan skin practically glowing.

"Well met, Lord Tyr," Carnon intoned, inclining his head in the barest sign of respect. Herne, who had refused finery in favor of his usual leathers, humphed gruffly behind us. Brigid, dressed as usual in a gown of flowing gold, curtsied politely.

"Where is the Lady of Shadows?" Tyr asked, his eyes darting between us. They were the same shade as Carnon's, but less intimidating without the snake-like slits. His lips curved upward into a wicked smile. "Or is this meeting purely for my benefit?"

"Scathanna has refused my summons and attacked Sun," Carnon proclaimed matter of factly. Tyr raised a brow in surprise, but it was impossible to know if his reaction was genuine or an act. "Which means she has also signed her own execution orders. I summoned you to find out if you wish to join her."

"I am rather fond of my own head," Tyr said, crossing his arms in a defensive posture. He didn't drop the lazy smile, but there was something edged about it, as if he feared Carnon might try to rip his throat out any moment. "Is your lovely betrothed the cause of this division?"

"Scathanna has never wanted to serve me," Carnon replied, gaze still icy on the Lord of Blood. "It's no secret that she doesn't respect me, and it's no surprise that after centuries of subservience, she would attempt to gain more power than she is owed."

"Then what is to be done, Your Majesty?" Tyr

asked, arms still crossed. His eyes flicked to Brigid and widened momentarily, before sliding back to my mate. "With Lady Scathanna."

"We need to determine the best course of action together," Carnon said, beginning our rehearsed ending to the formal portion of the meeting. "You should alert your forces to guard your borders. Scathanna has no qualms about attacking innocents, and your people should be on alert."

Tyr paled visibly, and I was inclined to believe his sincerity.

"Of course," he agreed with a reverent nod. Casting a look at me, his mouth split into a catlike grin. "How else may I serve?"

Carnon growled and took my arm as we walked out of the throne room, the other Lords and Cerridwen falling into step behind him. He clearly didn't like Tyr's flirtation any more than he did when I had first met the Lord of Blood.

"For now, recover from your journey," Carnon said with an idle wave. "We will discuss our plans over dinner."

Lucifer was waiting outside the throne room to escort Tyr to his guest suite.

"I want every move he makes watched, noted, and reported," Carnon had told his head of staff before we entered the throne room. "I want to know when he sends a message, who he sends it to, and what it contains. I need all of this information to come directly to me only, and for Lord Tyr to be unaware of it. Do you understand?"

"Of course, Your Majesty," Lucifer had drawled, as if Carnon were greatly underestimating him by laying this all out.

Lucifer nodded to Carnon as he escorted Tyr away, giving us a few hours to decide how to proceed, now that we had judged his initial reaction.

"What now?" I whispered, as the rest of us proceeded to Carnon's and my private room.

"Now," Carnon said, removing the crown and running a hand through his hair, "we decide whether he's telling the truth.

"And how to kill him if he's not," Herne added in a far too gleeful growl.

"And how do you suggest we decide that?" Cerridwen asked, ignoring her mate's somewhat uncharacteristic bloodthirstiness. "I suppose Brigid could do a reading? Or we could bind him to the truth before we ask him anything?"

"He'd be a fool to agree to an undefined blood bargain," Carnon sighed. "And I'd be a fool to try to force one on him."

He sat down heavily, rubbing his temples as if the crown had given him a headache. I sat next to him, replacing his hands with my own and circling gently with the pads of my fingers. I imbued just a tiny bit of my healing magic into the movement, and he sighed in relief.

"So, we need a way to be sure he's telling the truth without him knowing it, and without the margin of error that my readings have," Brigid said thoughtfully, perching on the arm of the sofa.

A thought struck me, something that I couldn't believe occurred to me before the others, and I allowed myself a tiny, wicked grin.

"I have an idea."

Chapter 11

It was difficult to act normally as we took our seats at the dinner table.

Lucifer confirmed that Tyr had sent word to his commanders and no one else. We had told him the plan, giving him very strict instructions, but his dislike for me was strong enough that I worried he might claim amnesia and defy them. Carnon told me that I was being silly, because Lucifer knew he would have his internal organs liquefied if he tried such a stunt.

It was a conversation not very conducive to hunger, and I sat at the table between Carnon and Tyr, more anxious than I thought I would be.

Brigid, Cerridwen, and Herne took their places across the table from us, and Lucifer appeared with drinks, placing a glass at each of our settings.

"To the Darklands," Carnon said, holding his glass high.

"The Darklands," the table echoed, each of us taking a long drink from our goblets. It was Bloodberry wine, the sparkling red liquid fizzing pleasantly on my tongue.

Tyr made a face. "Your wine has turned," he said, grimacing as he lowered the goblet.

Carnon snapped his fingers and Lucifer appeared as if he were summoned out of thin air. "Replace Lord Tyr's wine. It is not to his liking."

Lucifer bowed and filled a new glass from the bottle, placing it before Tyr, who took an experimental sip. He made another face of disgust.

"Are the berries from Sun so poor this year?" he asked, frowning at Brigid.

Her face was impassive as she sipped her wine. Clearly, Brigid didn't have the capacity to lie to anyone outright, so she had chosen blankness instead. I smiled internally at the guilelessness of my friend.

"The wine tastes fine to me, my lord," I said as innocently as I could. "May I?" I held out a hand for his glass and made a show of taking a sip. He was too busy watching my lips to notice the spell I had been mentally crafting settle over the wine. I prepared my own truth in payment.

"I can't drink much bloodberry wine," I said, smiling and returning the glass. "It affects me as it affects mortals. But this does taste a bit off."

Tyr took another sip, grimacing again, and I mentally shut the trap. *The spell is cast.*

"Probably because we dosed both of your glasses

with concentrated bloodberry," I said, sipping my undosed wine unconcernedly as I felt the truth spell take hold. "And I've spelled your wine with truth, just in case the bloodberry wasn't enough."

Tyr's face became a mask of horror and fury. "You bitch."

"Lord Tyr!" exclaimed Brigid, at the same time Cerridwen muttered, "I'd say it's working."

Tyr shot Brigid a furious look, and she blinked her eyes at him as if seeing something clearly for the first time. His scowl faltered as Carnon, playing the unfeeling king, spooled out his shadows to wrap around the Lord of Blood and bind him to his chair.

"Where should we start, my love?" I asked conversationally, taking another sip of untainted wine. I was pleased that Lucifer had been smart enough not to dose mine as well. Finding a new head of staff would have been a nuisance.

"You have no idea how much this wicked plan is turning me on," Carnon drawled quietly, clenching his hand and tightening the shadows as he gave me a heated smirk. Tyr turned a bit red as Carnon threatened to choke off his air. Carnon turned on him, his eyes flashing wholly green. "If you call my mate a bitch again, Lord of Blood, there will not be a truth in this world that can save you."

"You mated her without our blessing," Tyr gritted out, struggling against the shadows.

"True," Carnon said, looking at Tyr with a flat smile. "But you only forbade me from crowning her Queen, not from mating her. And truly, you can't really *forbid* me from doing anything as long as I have the blessing of the majority." He waved a hand at Brigid and Herne.

Herne was looking at Tyr like he'd quite like to squish him under his boot.

"Anyway, to business," Carnon said, taking a sip of his wine. "My lovely mate's truth spell, alongside the bloodberry, should be enough to convince me of your honesty. If you pose a risk to my rule, you will not live long enough to see the dessert, and I assure you it will be excellent."

"I've given you no reason to distrust me," Tyr gritted put, eyes flashing angrily.

Truth, at least in his mind.

Carnon laughed mirthlessly. "You murdered your sire to take his position of power," he said, tipping his glass toward the Lord of Blood. "That's reason enough."

I raised my eyebrows, looking at Carnon in surprise. It made sense now that Carnon wouldn't trust the male who had killed his own father for gain, especially after his own was taken from him.

"I didn't do it for power," Tyr replied, clearly struggling against the bloodberry and the truth spell. He was fighting a losing battle against his lips, which were twitching to open and reveal all of his secrets.

Brigid shifted uncomfortably in her seat as if she regretted our strategy. I reached across the table and patted her hand.

"Really?" Carnon said, raising a brow at the helpless Lord. "Why did you kill him, then?"

Tyr struggled, clenching his teeth against the magical demand for truth. "Let me go and I will tell you this willingly," he pleaded.

Despite the fact that this was almost certainly the truth, Carnon didn't waver. "If you are really loyal to me, then it shouldn't matter that you are bound."

I winced internally, remembering having a very similar conversation with Carnon when I first learned his identity. Still, it had to be done, and I wasn't about to undermine my mate in front of his court.

Tyr struggled for another moment, glancing once again at Brigid. I looked at her questioningly, but she shook her head. *Later.*

Tyr deflated, slumping against the shadows as he let the truth pour out of him. "My father was a cruel Lord. He followed the old laws, bleeding mortals against their will. He wanted to kill you," he confessed, looking at Carnon. "He hoped that it would mean I would take the crown. He had been sure I would be the next heir, and he resented that the Horned God chose a worthless boy over a Lord's son."

Carnon narrowed his eyes at this description, but he didn't move to punish Tyr or tighten the restraints. This was the truth he had asked for. I took Carnon's hand beneath the table and squeezed it in solidarity.

"He tried to murder you as a babe," Tyr confessed, looking pleadingly at Carnon. "I didn't know until the day I killed him. He confessed it all to me that same day."

"He tried…" Carnon broke off, fury radiating from him as Cerridwen, making some realization at the same time, covered her mouth and gasped. "He killed my parents."

Tyr nodded, his head slumping once more. Carnon's hand gripped me tightly, and for a moment I was afraid he might kill Tyr then and there.

"You can't be down two Lords," I said, placing a soothing hand on his knee.

"I can if they're the bastard who MURDERED MY FAMILY!" The end of this sentence was shouted so loudly that Brigid cowered, Herne growled, and the very room seemed to vibrate with his rage.

If anyone could understand Carnon's rage at Tyr, it was me. Even now, that pit of anger threatened to swallow me, and it was clear that Carnon's still lived deep inside him. But the stakes were high, and I knew Carnon would regret acting out of anger.

"His father, not him," I said, stroking a gentle caress down his arm. He met my eyes and I tried to convey my sorrow and understanding in my gaze before I turned back to the Lord of Blood. "Why did you kill him, Lord Tyr? Why not help him and try to take the crown?"

"He..." Tyr swallowed, and I couldn't tell if he was resisting the truth magic, or just the truth itself. "He killed *her*."

They way he said *her* required no further explanation.

"Someone you loved," Brigid said quietly. Tyr's eyes went to her as he nodded, and he looked to be in complete agony. "A mortal?"

He nodded again, closing his eyes and sagging somehow farther into his chair. "He said she was *just* a mortal. That I could dally with another. That they were all the same."

He took a deep breath, opening his eyes again. Brigid looked like she might cry, but something resembling resolve seemed to strengthen the Lord of Blood. "I vowed that I would be a different Lord," he said, now speaking directly to Brigid and ignoring the rest of us. "But my people, the nobility...they are cruel and power hungry. They want a return to free bloodletting and blood magic. They view mortals as less than slaves." He swallowed, turning to Carnon. "I realized if he would murder a child, he was irredeemable. I killed him, and the power passed to me, and I have since worked to keep the nobles in line while tempering their darker impulses."

"How have you tempered them?" I asked, partially out of curiosity and partially to make sure he was truly the male I was beginning to suspect he was.

"Through lies and fear, mostly," he said, turning his gaze to me. "I blame the king when they don't get their way, while secretly working to undermine them. I kill the ones who can't be controlled, in secret if possible. And the mortals who are most at risk, I get out of the mountains and into Oneiros, if I can."

Carnon took a sip of his wine, face impassive.

"I don't know what is going on," Tyr continued, speaking in a rush as if trying to convince my mate not to execute him. "Scathanna is a fair-weather ally at best, and she has never trusted me with any information of importance. She liked my father, and had always suspected me of being weaker than he was." He licked his lips, his eyes pleading as he held Carnon's gaze. "I have never betrayed you. I have worked, albeit in secret, to follow your laws and keep my people in line. I will continue to do so for as long as you are my King." He turned to me. "And my Queen."

The room was silent as Tyr slumped again, shaking his head as if it pained him. I looked at my mate, who regarded the male thoughtfully.

"I believe you," he said at last, flicking his fingers so the shadows released the Lord of Blood. Tyr slumped, catching himself on the edge of the table with a groan as he worked to right himself.

"Good," Herne said with a growl. "Because I'm

starving. Can we eat yet?"

Dinner was stilted and silent, all of us contemplating Tyr's truth. Tyr seemed visibly uncertain whether or not Carnon would change his mind. He kept shooting furtive glances at my mate, and Carnon seemed content to let him suffer. I had very little appetite after the whole display, and it seemed that only Herne was really able to eat.

Once dessert had been served—it *was* excellent—Carnon broke the awkward silence. "So, Elara," he said, turning to me. "What shall we tell Lord Tyr first?"

I sighed, blowing out a candle from the middle of the table. "I suppose we had better show him," I replied, pressing my finger to the wick and relighting it.

"Witch magic?" Tyr asked, a brow raised as he regarded us warily.

"Not exactly," I said, holding out my hand and letting a ball of fire form there. I twisted it into several shapes before smothering it, forcing that fiery snake back into submission. I plucked one of the oranges from the centerpiece, there for decoration rather than consumption, and withered it. Tyr stared wide-eyed as I revived the fruit, peeled it, and handed him a slice.

"How...what...how...?" Tyr stammered as he took the piece of fruit.

"It took us a while to figure it out," I said, watching the lord intently. "My father was Alaunus. Somehow—we are still not sure how—I inherited not only his gifts from Sun, but also the King's power of life and death."

"And you all knew she could do this?" Tyr asked, holding the slice of orange like it might explode.

Everyone nodded.

"I found out last," Brigid said, trying to sound

conciliatory, "but I've known since the ball."

"Are you surprised we hid such gifts?" Carnon asked. He was studying the Lord as if trying to read his thoughts.

"No," Tyr said with a derisive laugh. "There's no way Scathanna and I would have agreed to your match."

I frowned, wondering if it was our combined power that frightened Tyr, or the fact that it was power he didn't have.

"As previously stated, you wouldn't have had a choice," Carnon drawled, something icy coating his tone. "But if it makes you feel better, Herne also opposed it."

"Not because of the magic," Herne cut in gruffly. "Because of her bloody grandmother."

"But you are a witch," Tyr said, turning back to me. "How can Alaunus be your father?"

"That's another long story that I don't have all the answers to yet," I replied, glancing at Carnon to see if he wanted to weigh in. He made no move to comment, so I continued, "Suffice it to say, we failed to destroy the Crone and now she is sending witches to attack the wards. We don't know exactly what she wants, except to tear down the Bloodwood. And she believes she needs me to do it."

"Ultimately, our immediate problem is Scathanna," Carnon cut in, taking my hand and squeezing comfortingly. "Elara and I will worry about the Crone."

"And what is your plan for Scathanna?" Tyr asked, gaze traveling over our clasped hands.

"We were waiting to decide that until we knew if you would stand with us," Carnon said, nodding toward Brigid and Herne. "We may have to go to Shadow and remove her from power. I need to know, Lord Tyr of Blood, if you stand with the Demon King."

Tyr looked at Brigid again. Did she have some kind of sway over him I didn't know about? I looked between them, but I couldn't glean any specific understanding or secret conversation.

"I do," Tyr said, breaking the silence.

"And will you make a blood bargain and swear it?" Carnon pressed. "Will you swear not to sell my mate to the Crone? Not to reveal her gifts to our enemies?"

Again, Tyr looked at Brigid. She nodded once, holding his gaze.

"What is—"

"I will," Tyr cut in, interrupting me and preventing me from asking what in the name of all the gods was going on with them.

"Good," Carnon said, pushing back from his chair. He took a steak knife from the table and sliced his palm, handing the blade to Tyr as he held out his hand. "Swear it now."

Tyr stood, drawing the blade over his own palm and clasping hand with Carnon. A silvery light glowed for a moment, then faded as each pulled their hands away.

My mate smirked, his eyes gleaming in the light of the candles as he regarded our new ally. "And now, we get to work."

Chapter 12

It was incredibly frustrating to feel that, despite the fact that we were doing all that we could, we were still doing nothing.

We moved from the dining room to the war room to discuss a plan of attack. The map of the Darklands in the middle gave me a better idea of the difficulties we would face getting to the Court of Shadow in the mountains.

Tyr argued that there was very little we could do until we had intelligence, suggesting that Carnon send spies to Shadow to report on Scathanna's movements, if he hadn't already.

It was very hard to read the Lord of Blood. After the episode with the wine, I expected him to be angry or wary, but he reverted back to the flirtatious, graceful lord as soon as the meal was over.

"I already have spies in Shadow," Carnon replied, looking at Tyr thoughtfully. "But it's difficult for them to get word to me. I'm also afraid they might have been compromised, based on the lack of communication we have received from them."

"Why don't you have Artemis go?" I suggested. The large strix usually stayed outside or in an aviary in one of the towers of the palace, but I hadn't seen her a great deal lately. "Unless you already have?"

"Artemis is still watching the Crone for me," Carnon confessed, pointing to the Bloodwood. "Her spies meet her here," he added, pointing to a spot outside the Bloodwood, "and sending her to Shadow as well would tax even her strength."

"We could use blood magic," Tyr suggested, raising his palms in submission and wincing at the hard look Carnon gave him. "Not against any mortals. I can send spies to infiltrate the court. Change their appearance to look like prominent members."

Carnon chewed his lip, thinking the plan over. "They need to imprison their targets, not kill them," Carnon said finally. "I want to question her court, and I don't want to risk killing anyone who is loyal to me."

"Agreed," Tyr said, smirking at his victory. He was standing at attention rather like a soldier, his hands clasped behind his back. Brigid kept shooting him furtive looks as we discussed.

"What is going *on* with you two?" I whispered as Tyr and Carnon worked out the particulars of the scheme, with Herne dropping in suggestions every so often.

"I'm honestly not sure," Brigid whispered back, looking at me in panic. "I think maybe—"

"Lady Brigid," Tyr said, snapping us out of our whispered conversation. We looked up to see everyone staring at us, Carnon and Herne with varying degrees of annoyance on their faces, and Cerridwen and Tyr with looks of amusement.

"Sorry, What?" Brigid asked, using her sweetest voice.

"Do you agree to the plan, my lady?" Tyr said, still looking at her with that strange intensity he had been regarding her with all night. The way he said 'my lady' was like a caress, and I felt Brigid shiver slightly next to me.

"Yes," Brigid said, sounding confident even though I was fairly certain she hadn't heard the plan. "Just tell me how I can help."

"Can you ask your best seers from Sun to focus their attention between the Crone and Scathanna?" Carnon asked her, looking between her and Lord Tyr with the same confusion I felt. "We need to know when either makes a move, and the more eyes on them the better."

"Of course," Brigid said, straightening and adopting her 'Lady of Sun' voice. "I'll send a missive tonight."

"Until we know more, we should work on a plan for attacking Shadow," Carnon finished, standing and cracking his neck. "Scathanna is unpredictable, but she's smart. The safest choice for her is to stay right where she is."

"Tomorrow," I agreed. "It's late. We should retire before none of us are able to think straight."

Carnon nodded, taking my arm to leave. I ached to speak more to Brigid, but Tyr was already walking to her with a purposeful glint in his eye. I glanced at Cerridwen who shrugged warily, indicating she would stay.

"What is going on with them?" Carnon asked me when we were far enough down the hall that we wouldn't be overheard.

"I'm not sure," I replied snappishly. "And you whisked me away before I could find out."

"Anxious to be left with Lord Tyr?" he asked, giving me an arch look.

I rolled my eyes, and Carnon chuckled. "Apologies, my love. But I have one more rather important task for us to complete tonight."

"I hope she will be alright," I said ruefully, but quickly remembering that my friend *could* summon fire. She'd probably be fine. "What task?"

"One that I don't need the Lords knowing about until I am ready to tell them," Carnon said, propelling me down a different hallway than I had expected and bypassing the stairs to our room. "And one that I need you to keep secret until the time is right."

"Okay..." I said, hesitantly. "When will the time be right?" I didn't recognize this part of the castle, but Carnon moved with a clear purpose in mind.

"I promise you, Red," he said, stopping to pull me into a quick but fierce kiss. "You'll know."

He continued to pull me down the hallway, veering off again when I finally recognized our location as being near the throne room. Instead of turning to the great double doors that led into the hall, Carnon took me to a smaller chamber, whose door was barred with a series of very sturdy looking locks.

"This door is locked and warded at all times," Carnon said, taking my hand in his and pressing it to the door and smirking down at me. A series of clicks and whirs sounded from within the door itself, and the door popped open with a tiny creak. "Only the Demon King may enter. Or the Queen."

"I'm not the Queen yet," I protested, pulling my hand back and staring at it, as if there might be some visible marking of the magic that allowed me entry.

"I already told you, Elara," Carnon reminded me, taking my hand again in his. "You are my Queen, with or without a crown."

My heart was thundering as he pulled me into the room, and I was uncertain what I should expect. What I saw when Carnon brushed a hand against the moonstone wall next to the door was far from what I could have imagined.

His touch somehow lit the room, the moonstone glowing from within as tiny lights illuminated small alcoves in the walls. Something glittered from each space, and it wasn't until the room was fully lit that I could understand what I was seeing.

"Oh," I gasped, turning in wonder as I took in the gold and silver and sparkling jewels that filled each of the little alcoves.

"Oh," Carnon chuckled, catching me around the waist. "These are all yours."

"Mine?" I asked, a note of panic in my voice.

He laughed again. "Well, ours technically." He took the band of gold and silver from his head and placed it into one of the alcoves that had no other baubles. "These are the royal jewels. The crowns and bedazzlements of the Demon King and Queen."

"They're lovely," I said, looking at each alcove and running a finger over the delicate metal and gem work. There were crowns and necklaces and bracelets and diadems, and it was honestly a little overwhelming. "But I could never wear all of these."

"You don't have to," Carnon said with a chuckle, pulling a box from one of the alcoves. "Most Kings and Queens find a few pieces they like and never bother with the rest. The room is warded against dust and theft, so you are the only other living person to see the trove."

He held the box between us, looking down at me with his usual wicked amusement. "While I am happy to let you choose which of these sparkly trinkets you like best, Red, I am rather hoping you'll agree to wear this one."

He opened the box, and I gasped as I took in its contents. Nestled on a little velvet pillow was a crown, silver and shining, wrought with individual strands of metal that were woven together with diamonds and pearls. I lifted it gingerly, finding it lighter than I had expected, and admired the intricate metalwork.

"Do you like it?" Carnon asked, sounding almost anxious that I might say no. "I commissioned it for you the day we first arrived in Oneiros together."

"You what?" I asked, looking up at him in shock. He grinned, which almost hid the blush blooming across his cheeks.

"I had some of the more archaic and ostentatious pieces reworked to make it," he said, gently stroking a finger over the silver points of the crown. "In demon culture, pearls represent the purity of love." He lifted his finger from the crown to stroke my cheek. "And diamonds represent strength and inner light." I tore my eyes from the crown to look at my mate who was smiling down at me with adoration. "I knew long before we entered the city that I loved you, Red."

"It's beautiful," I said, beaming up at him.

"You're beautiful," he countered, brushing a whisper soft kiss against my lips. "Will you wear it?"

"Of course," I replied, sneaking another look at the beautiful thing. "But can I wear a crown if I'm not technically your queen? I don't want to offend anyone, or break tradition, no matter what your magic door thinks."

Carnon smiled, a beautiful, wicked, soul-melting smile, and my heart gave a little leap in my chest. "That brings me to the other little task you and I have for this evening," he purred.

※ ※ ※

The mirror was ready the following afternoon, all the runes in place to facilitate our travel as we gathered in Carnon's office. It was faster to enchant this time, since I had done it before, and I looked at Carnon warily as we prepared to step through the glass.

I had spent the morning sorting through my father's papers, which still lay scattered on the coffee table in our room. The oddest find was a notebook, clearly aged with use, its pages dog-eared and yellowed, but completely and utterly blank. I had studied the little book for over an hour, trying to figure out its secret, then decided to bring it with us to show to the Hag. My father had said she might have the answers we needed, but I was beginning to think that his messages contained multiple meanings. Perhaps it wasn't the answers I assumed she would have that he had foreseen.

"Ready, Red?" Carnon said, squeezing my hand at my side. "She won't like us stepping into her cottage without warning."

"I know," I said, biting my lip. "Although, I have a feeling that she might be expecting us."

"I still think this is a bad idea," growled Herne from the sofa where he was sitting like a rather grumpy statue.

The office was cramped with all of us present, including Tyr, who was very interested in the travel magic. He and Brigid had barely looked at each other, and I wondered what was said between them the previous night. I still hadn't had the time to ask, and I was glad Cerridwen was nearby to keep her company.

I believed I could trust Tyr with the kingdom, but it was another thing entirely to trust him with my friend.

"This will just take you directly into the Bloodwood?" Tyr asked, walking around the back of the mirror to inspect the frame.

"If I'm right about the Hag, then yes," I said, looking nervously at Carnon, who smiled reassuringly.

"And if you're wrong?" Herne asked, still looking thunderous.

"Then the mirror won't do anything," I replied, shrugging in what I hoped was a confident way. "At least, it shouldn't. A path should only open if there is indeed a mirror to travel to when you make the request."

"And if the mirror is too small?" Cerridwen asked, looking nervously between us and her mate. I remembered the story Vera had told me about the witch trapped in the hand mirror and decided not to repeat it. It couldn't be true, anyway. Probably.

"Then we return and go the old-fashioned way," I said, turning back to face the glass.

I intoned the incantation for travel, trying to picture first the Hag's cottage in the Bloodwood, and then the floor-length mirror I had seen in her bedroom after she had magicked her house to increase in size. The glass wavered, a ripple flowing across its surface as the magic took hold.

Akela growled faintly, clearly not a fan of mirror travel after our misadventure with the Crone.

"Ready?" Carnon asked, squeezing my hand and scratching Akela's head with the other.

"Only one way to be sure," I replied.

Carnon nodded, turning to the others. "If we get into any trouble, I'll send Elara back through," he said. "Artemis is at the border, and she'll sense it if I need help."

"I will not be returning without you," I said determinedly. "We'll send Akela."

"The wolf won't leave your side," Carnon pointed out as Akela huffed in agreement. "But we will figure out something to alert you all."

"Don't get into trouble," Brigid said, wringing her hands. Tyr made a move as if to go to her, then paused, clearly thinking better of it. He clenched his fist as Cerridwen patted Brigid on the shoulder.

"You'll be fine," she said. "But try not to die."

"Thank you for the vote of confidence, sister dear," Carnon drawled. He gave an irreverent little wave and then stepped confidently into the glass.

There was the cold, terrifying sense of nothing and everything swooping past, and then we stepped out onto wooden floorboards, a fire crackling in the little bedroom hearth. Carnon looked at me, partially surprised that this had worked.

A voice floated into the room through the open door, ancient and terrifying and alluring all at once. "About time you got here. The tea is getting cold."

Chapter 13

The Hag was waiting at the rickety wooden table, a steaming pot of tea and two empty, wooden bowls before her. A sinking swoop in my stomach told me what those bowls were for.

"You're late," the Hag croaked, motioning to the empty chairs before her. She looked just as ancient and decrepit as the first time I met her, the skin of her hands and face sagging and wrinkled, hair gray and brittle. "I expected you a full fortnight ago."

"Forgive us for not receiving your summons," Carnon drawled, giving the Hag an unamused look.

She waved him off, knowing very well no summons had been sent. "It took you far longer than it should have to put things together. I thought you were bright, boy?" Akela growled at this slight to his master and the

Hag rolled her eyes. "You can be quiet, or I can muzzle you. Your choice, wolf."

Akela quieted, narrowing his eyes at the Hag in dislike.

"Much better," the Hag crooned approvingly. "Who is first then?"

"Elara will not be giving you her blood," Carnon said sharply, rolling up his own sleeve and taking the spot across from the old woman.

"She will if she wants answers," the Hag cackled, slicing into the soft skin of Carnon's forearm and catching the blood as it dripped into the first bowl. "Why don't you let the witchling speak for herself?"

I raised my brows, trying not to laugh at the antics of the ancient woman. She was such a batty old thing, and her treatment of Carnon both amused and puzzled me.

"It's fine," I said, putting a hand on Carnon's shoulder as he growled. "I'll pay."

"Smart girl," said the Hag, running a finger across Carnon's forearm to seal the wound. I wondered if she knew that Carnon could do that himself, but he didn't protest as he rolled down his sleeve. "Your turn, then."

I sat, Carnon scowling as I offered my forearm to the Hag. She made a swift, neat slice, and I winced as blood trickled into the bowl under my elbow. I had to wrestle with the healing magic to stop it from flaring to the surface, only allowing it to heal me once my bowl was nearly at the same level as Carnon's.

The Hag's eyes widened in interest as my wound flared silver and knit itself back together. "Well now, I suspected you were an *interesting* witch. Turns out you're not a witch after all."

"I am," I countered. "Half."

"I know," the Hag said, her smile a little gruesome with her rotting, browned teeth. "Now then, you've both paid. How can I help you?"

"I thought you were expecting us?" Carnon said, watching warily as the Hag poured tea.

She waved her hand again irritably. "Yes, but it helps to know what you *think* you should ask before I go telling you things."

Carnon and I looked at each other, his nod indicating that I should start. I cleared my throat. "Well, you may or may not know that my grandmother is the Crone of the Witchlands," I began. The Hag continued to pour us tea, making no comment on this, so I went on. "She says she needs me to bring down the Bloodwood, and we don't understand why."

"And?" questioned the Hag, setting her piercing gaze on me. She settled into her chair, hands around her mug like she was no more than a helpless old woman.

"And my father left me a letter saying you would have the answers," I continued, getting irritated with the old bat.

"Ahh," the Hag replied, sipping her tea genially. The flowery teacups were at odds with the ramshackle nature of her cottage, and I felt a prickling sensation at my neck as if I were being watched. I didn't like it.

"It has been ten years since I last saw Alaunus," the Hag said, draining her teacup and studying it thoughtfully. I tried to see what was so fascinating, but she covered the cup with a withered hand. "He died for you, you know."

"He what?" I asked, feeling the color drain from my face. My heart began to pound at the implication, and Carnon took my hand.

"Explain, old woman," he growled, his eyes turning wholly green with his temper.

The Hag cackled as if this was ridiculous. "You can't hurt me, boy. Not only is this place warded against your magic, but I'm centuries older than you. I could kill you in five hundred different ways."

"Why don't you then?" he asked, squeezing my hand tightly. If we had to run, there was every chance we wouldn't make it back to the mirror.

"Because you amuse me," the Hag said, chuckling lightly as if Carnon were a rather silly grandson. "Now do you want the story, or not?"

"What story?" I asked.

"They're all *one* story, child," the Hag said, seeming to look a little more softly at me. "Everything that was and is and will be is connected. The same players from a millennia ago have returned to the game to see it reach its end."

The Hag cleared her throat, leaning back in her tiny, rickety chair. "I suppose the story you know is that nine hundred years ago, the witches declared war on their daemon brethren, believing themselves to be the true representation of the Goddess. This was before the days of their separation, you see, and although witches were borne of unions between mortals and daemons, they began to see themselves as both separate and superior to daemon kind, believing daemon magic to be unnatural and uncontrolled."

I nodded, having read as much from the many, *many* history books Carnon had thrown at me.

"What is *not* common knowledge," the Hag continued, "is that a thousand years ago, and for many hundreds of years before that, the Witchlands and the

Darklands were one. A single realm united under a Witch Queen and a Daemon King, who ruled in the name of the Triple Goddess and the Horned God and kept order and peace."

"A Witch Queen?" I asked, interest piqued.

"Hush, child, and let me tell the story," the Hag snapped, giving me a sharp look. Akela growled, and she hissed at him. "Anyway, nine hundred years ago, the Witch Queen Lilith mated with the Daemon King as had happened hundreds of times before." The Hag poured another cup of tea and took a sip as Carnon and I remained riveted in silence.

"But one particular witch, Morgana, wished to rule over all the lands herself. She was the younger sister of Queen Lilith, and she began to dabble in blood magic. Though it was forbidden by the Coven, she learned in secret from the Court of Blood how to wield unnatural power. In this way, she began taking territory and gaining followers, until eventually, a full coven of witches rose up behind her, waging war on daemonkind and declaring themselves a separate people."

The Hag paused, looking sadly into nothing for a moment before clearing her throat to continue. "Morgana couldn't stand the idea of her sister, a witch, consorting with a 'demon,' as she called them, and she murdered the Daemon King, destroying the tradition uniting the lands for thousands of years."

"Unable to stop Morgana and grieving her mate, Lilith fled deep into the forest that connected the lands. She learned enough blood magic to raise the Bloodwood between the two realms, separating the witches and daemons—now referred to as demons by the witches and mortals alike—and enraging Morgana, who began calling herself the Crone." The Hag looked up at me, raising a brow. "I'm certain she chose that to seem fearsome. The aspect of the Triple Goddess representing wisdom and death."

She scoffed. "Anyway, in order to keep the Crone out of the Bloodwood," the Hag continued, her story like a spell holding me in place, "Lilith had to tie her very blood and magic to the spell that raised it, leaving her unable to leave this place as long as the Crone still lived. Should she fall, the Bloodwood would fall with her."

"How many Crones back was Morgana?" I asked in a hushed tone, trying to figure out how many generations had passed in nine hundred years.

The Hag gave me a pitying smile. "She is the very same Crone who rules the Witchlands now, child. Your grandmother. The pompous old biddy."

I startled. "No," I argued. "My grandmother was Crone for a hundred years. She is only three centuries old."

"No," Carnon said, frowning at me. "She is the same. It was she who terrorized the demons a millennia ago. As far as all of our intelligence and histories say, she's been in control for a thousand years."

"How?" I asked. "Everyone in the Witchlands believes she ascended only a hundred years ago."

"Blood magic can do terrible and wonderful things, Elara," said the Hag, looking at me thoughtfully. "It can kill and silence and bind and maim. It can give life and take it. It can warp memories and change one's appearance. The Crone is over a thousand years old, child, and well-versed in using blood magic to reverse the effects of time. What do you think she did with the blood of all those witches who 'consorted with demons'?"

The Hag put this last part in quotations, and my blood ran cold. Carnon had said he had never come across any witches in the Bloodwood, except for the Hag and me.

"She lied," I said, eyes wide in understanding and shock. "She made them confess to treason when they had done nothing."

"And stole their youth," the Hag agreed. "Used the blood magic to make elder witches forget. A few clever pieces of magic would be all she needed to stay in power for so long, with no witch questioning her rule."

"It's barbaric," I argued, feeling a little sick to my stomach.

"No arguments there, girl," the Hag said, grinning wickedly. "You will note that I have not used my donations in the same way." She gestured to herself, the withered skin and frail bones and rotting teeth, and an idea struck me.

"How long have you lived in the Bloodwood?" I asked.

The Hag wheezed out a laugh. "Clever girl," she praised, reaching across the table to pat my hand with her bony, withered one. "To finish the story, then. For nine hundred years, the Crone plunged herself deeper and deeper into the darkest of blood magics in an attempt to bring down the wood and rule over the Darklands. The two realms were never meant to be separated, you see. Without the magic of demons and the mortal dreams that fuel them, the Witchlands has begun to die."

"It has?" I asked, wracking my brain for any evidence of this from my childhood.

The Hag waved her hand impatiently. "Yes, child. Witches are less powerful. Crops sicken and the land fails. Fewer witchlings are born each generation." I thought of Vera's struggle to control her magic. Of how rare and precious witchlings were. Of the growing and healing spells that Vera's mother and mine would provide the mortals.

"Anyway," the Hag continued, drawing my attention back to her. "For the last thousand years, Morgana's sister has stood as the sole warden and protector of the Bloodwood. Magic is a funny thing, you know," she mused, looking wistfully out the window. "When I tied my own life to this forest, I meant only to keep my sister out. Magic is very literal, it seems, as the Demon Kings have no problem passing through."

I stared at the Hag, at Lilith, who I supposed was technically my aunt. The sheer age and power she possessed baffled me.

"But ten years ago," she continued, "My magic began to fail."

"Why?" asked Carnon, who was equally absorbed the the story.

The Hag gave him a wry look. "If you haven't noticed, boy, I'm very, very old. These things happen. Anyway, your father," the Hag continued, turning to pin me with her sharp gaze, "had a vision of the Bloodwood falling and ruin befalling his people. But I believe what drove him to finally seek me out was the vision of your death in the bloody war that would take place when the woods fell."

"Alaunus had no idea who I really was, other than a powerful witch with an interest in keeping the Bloodwood alive. I had met him a handful of times.

Met your mother, too, as a matter of fact," she added, nodding to me. "And I told them the same story I am telling you now."

"You what?" I asked, shock filling me. "My mother was here?"

The Hag nodded. "I thought maybe they were the ones who would end this all. But alas," she added, looking at me sadly. "Your father came to me with his vision and begged me to stop it."

"And you did," I said slowly, having a dark sense of where this tale was going.

"For a price, my dear," the Hag said quietly. "All magic—witch magic, demon magic, gods-blessed magic, even blood magic believe it or not—has a price. Since my blood and magic would no longer hold the wood, a sacrifice was required. Another had to tie their life and blood to the wood to keep it standing."

The Hag patted my hand again, almost tenderly. "King Alaunus tied his life's blood to the wood, so that only his child or one of his blood could bring it down."

"How much of his blood?" I asked quietly, already knowing the answer in my bones. Carnon's hand had turned to ice, the answer becoming clear to him as well.

"All of it," said the Hag sadly. "Blood is powerful magic. In giving his life, he saved the life of the daughter he had never spoken to. It is an ancient, complicated spell, and only one person now has the power to undo it."

"Me," I said, feeling the blood drain from my face.

The Hag nodded, looking truly sorry for the burden she was laying upon me.

"Alaunus and his mate failed to reunite the realms. His death destroyed their chances of ending the thousand-year-old war. But," the Hag added, patting my hand in a motherly way, "his sacrifice ensured that the fated consort of the next Demon King, herself an aspect of the Goddess, would come of age to oppose her grandmother. To live and take her rightful place as Witch Queen alongside the Demon King. To fulfill the destiny set in motion when Morgana killed my mate, and unite two peoples under one crown, as it was in the old days."

"You think Elara is an aspect of the Goddess?" Carnon asked, still crushing my hand in his. "A fated Witch Queen?"

The Hag cackled, the tension in the room palpable. "I don't think it, boy, I know it. Just as you—and every Demon King before you—are an aspect of the Horned God, your *mate* is an aspect of His consort. I knew it the moment she first stepped foot in my cottage."

"And you didn't think maybe to tell us?" I asked, voice rising in indignation, then softening again as understanding struck. "That you were a Queen? That you are…what? My aunt?"

The Hag—Lilith, now that I knew who she was—dismissed me with another wave. "You weren't ready, child," she said, looking at me seriously. "You're barely ready now. But the hands of fate are forcing mine, and time is running out."

"Why didn't Alaunus tell me then?" Carnon demanded. "He must have known all of this."

Lilith shrugged, an infuriating gesture. "How am I to know that, boy? He didn't ask for my advice. My guess is he kept you in the dark to protect his mate. And Elara." She pinned Carnon with a pointed stare. "If you had known your mate was on the other side of this wood, would you not have gone after her?"

Carnon shifted uncomfortably, and Lilith made a triumphant sound. "Thought so." She stood, shuffling over to one of the many worn-looking cabinets, and withdrew what appeared to be a heavy book.

"When I die, which will be very soon," Lilith said, looking between me and Carnon, "you, Queen Elara, will be the last force standing between our two worlds." She blew the cover of the book, launching a cloud of dust into the air that made me cough. "When the time is right, you must bring down the wood and unite the realms. But you need to be prepared."

There was a loud bang in the distance, and Carnon and I both looked to the window in alarm. Akela growled again, and Lilith made an irritable noise.

"You will need allies on both sides of the wood," she said, speaking more quickly and lowering her voice. "And you must learn what you can to oppose the Crone. I stole this from her nine hundred years ago, and now I am leaving it in your hands."

She pushed the heavy book toward me, and I craned my neck to read the title. *The Blood Grimoire.*

"I can't learn blood magic," I said, balking at the book, which she pushed toward me with greater urgency.

"Elara," Carnon warned, the noise outside the cottage growing louder as moments passed. He rose and went to the window, swearing at whatever he saw.

"You must," Lilith hissed, pushing the book toward me again. She knocked over her teacup in her haste and I saw the signs in the bottom she had been trying to hide, a cross and a broken sword. Loss, and disaster.

"We need to run," Carnon said, turning back and

grabbing my arm. "Now."

"What is it?" I asked, pushing the book away from me and rising to follow my mate.

"Witches," Carnon growled, striding toward Lilith's bedroom. "Lots of witches. How did they get in here?"

"The Bloodwood keeps the Crone out," I answered, peering out the window in horror. Sure enough, there was a small army of witches surrounding the cottage. "But others can enter just fine."

"The book, girl," Lilith screeched, floating the tome toward me on a phantom wind. It hit me in the chest, knocking the breath from me as I instinctively caught it.

"You too, Lilith," Carnon said, holding out his hand to the old woman, who gave him a look of amused fondness at his use of her true name. "You can't defeat so many witches."

"I cannot," Lilith agreed, rolling up her sleeves and putting the first bowl of blood she had drawn to her lips. I gagged as she drank, the whites of her eyes turning red as the blood began to fuel her unnatural magic. She drank the second bowl, an eerie red glow emanating from her skin. "But I can hold them off. Make sure you smash the mirror on the other side."

Carnon nodded, pulling me with him to the mirror. The pounding and banging grew louder as Akela jumped through after us, and I heard Lilith open her front door.

"You really shouldn't bother an old woman while she is getting her beauty rest," she said, her voice somehow more ethereal as it wrapped around her cottage and the witches outside.

Carnon pulled me through the mirror just as the screaming began.

Chapter 14

We landed on the floor of the office, me on top of Carnon and Akela on top of me. The book fell from my arms with a thunk as Carnon rolled out from under us and shattered the mirror with his fist.

"We have to go back for her!" I cried as Carnon swore over his bloodied knuckles.

"Gods above," cried Cerridwen, rushing over to us as Tyr caught the broken mirror before it crushed us. "What happened?"

"Witches," Carnon said, breathing heavily and healing his knuckles where the broken glass from the mirror had embedded in them. "Lots of witches."

"The Hag?" Herne asked, offering Carnon a hand. He took it gratefully as Cerridwen and Brigid helped me to my feet.

"Gone," Carnon said, lips pressed tightly together. "Or she will be. There was nothing we could do, Elara. I think she knew she was going to die."

"How did they know we would be there?" I asked, my mind still reeling at the history that had finally been revealed.

"I'm guessing the Crone has her monitored," Carnon replied, pulling me into his arms and dropping a quick kiss on my head. "Or she was watching the mirrors."

I realized in horror that I had forgotten about my father's journal tucked into my pocket, and that I'd probably never figure out what was concealed inside it. The tear that ran down my cheek was more about the loss of this last piece of my father than Lilith's sacrifice, but I said a little prayer to the Goddess to guide her spirit. Even though I had never known her as my aunt, she was family. Yet another piece of my life's puzzle I had lost.

"Are you alright?" Carnon asked, looking down at me and brushing the tear away.

"Fine," I lied, clearing my throat.

"I told you this was foolhardy," Herne grumbled, leaning against Carnon's desk with his arms crossed. "Did you at least learn something?"

"Lots of somethings," Carnon said, glowering at his friend. "But we should go somewhere more private to discuss them."

"Our room," I said, not really thinking straight and wanting to be near my father's papers.

"Our room," Carnon agreed, giving my arms a reassuring squeeze.

I walked almost mechanically, letting Carnon drag me along with Akela nudging me from behind as my mind worked. Lilith had answered some of my questions, but not the ones that would actually help us with a plan. The idea that I was some prophesied aspect of the Goddess didn't really do much to help me defeat the Crone, especially if she had an army of witches willing to follow her blindly.

I said another little mental prayer for my estranged aunt as we settled around the coffee table. I hadn't realized I was still clutching *The Blood Grimoire* until Carnon was prying it from my arms. He dropped it heavily on the table, and Tyr studied the cover with interest.

"Well?" Herne asked irritably once we were all settled.

I let Carnon relay the story that Lilith had spun, telling the tale of the two sisters, the creation of the Bloodwood, and my own father's sacrifice to keep it standing. As he spoke, I pulled out the little blank journal I had failed to ask Lilith about, flipping through its worn pages.

Blood is powerful magic, she had said, the words coming back to me as I flipped through the empty journal. The pad of my index finger caught on one of the edges, slicing my skin. A bead of blood dropped onto the empty page before the healing magic rose in me to heal the small cut.

"Ow," I muttered, sucking my finger as the magic repaired the wound.

"Red?" Carnon asked, turning to me in concern.

"Just a papercut," I said, closing the book.

"So now what?" asked Cerridwen, looking between me and my mate. "Elara is the fated aspect of the Goddess who somehow must unite our realms to make up for her grandmother's murderous ways? How exactly does she do that?"

"I have no idea," I sighed, turning to Brigid. "Did the prophecy say anything specific? I haven't had time to go through all of my father's writings."

I remembered one of the phrases she had recorded: *A sacrifice of blood will keep her safe until the Demon King can claim her.* I supposed I understood what the sacrifice was now. The Hanged Man from my tarot reading. Not Carnon, as I had feared when we had faced the Crone, but my father.

Brigid picked up the journal she had left with me, which I had abandoned on the coffee table with my father's other writings. She flipped through until she found the prophecy about the Goddess and the Horned God, reading the passage aloud:

> *A thousand years shall see them wed, the Goddess and her consort, made flesh once more and united by fortune. As they are mated, so shall their lands be, until at last what was torn asunder by the Crone shall be made whole.*

"That's ominous," Tyr quipped, brows raised as Brigid finished. "Also not extremely detailed."

"No," Brigid agreed, frowning at the words. "Although it sounds like you'll be successful perhaps?"

"This was supposed to be my mother and father," I argued, frowning at Carnon. He nodded in agreement, lips pursed. "If they failed, how can you know that we won't?"

"Because you have us," Brigid said, with so much innocent confidence that I wanted to hug her.

"Failure isn't an option, Red," Carnon said seriously,

his eyes boring into mine. "I *won't* live without you, and I don't plan on dying anytime soon." I nodded, feeling a lump of emotion rise in my throat.

"What's with the book?" Tyr asked, nodding toward the grimoire.

I grimaced, trying to clear my throat. "Lilith used it to raise the Bloodwood. To fight the witches. She wants me to learn blood magic too."

"Blood magic?" Brigid asked in surprise. "But you can't."

"I don't want to," I agreed. "I think it's a perversion of the Goddess' gifts."

Tyr scoffed loudly at this, and I turned to him expectantly. He sighed. "Blood magic is no different than any other magic," he argued. "It can be wielded for good or evil."

"I've never seen it used for good," I pointed out, remembering the demon that Carnon had sentenced to death for taking blood from an unwilling victim.

"Raising the Bloodwood wasn't a good cause?" Tyr asked, crossing his arms as he regarded me. He was leaning against the hearth, and his eyes kept flicking to Brigid, as they had done the previous night.

"That was a necessary evil," I argued.

"Enough," Carnon said, sighing heavily. "I don't like the idea either, Elara. And aside from that, you need to have an affinity for blood magic. Not everyone can do it."

"The Crone can do it," Tyr pointed out, "as could your father. All Demon Kings inherit the gift. Maybe you did too. The Hag seems to think you have. Why would you not use every tool in your arsenal?" Tyr asked, his cool tone belying the anger I could sense rising in him. "You are allowing your prejudice to blind you to powerful magic."

"And who will help me?" I asked, giving him a sardonic look. "Who's going to volunteer to let me practice on them? To give me their blood? You?"

"Yes," Tyr said, giving me a steady look.

I balked, uncertain what to say to that.

"Why?" I asked finally, feeling a curious mix of suspicion and warmth toward the Lord of Blood. "Why put yourself in danger? Why give your blood?"

"I have my reasons," Tyr replied, eyes flicking to Brigid. She blushed, looking away.

"We'll discuss this another day," Carnon said, standing as a clear sign that the meeting was over. "We need to hold court and explain the situation with Shadow. Put the people on their guard, and ask anyone with information to come forward. Ensure their loyalty and make sure there are no spies or traitors among them."

"When?" Herne asked, offering Cerridwen a hand and pulling her up.

"Tonight," Carnon replied, receiving wide-eyed looks in return. "I sent the summons yesterday. It's time for the people to meet their Queen."

"Elara isn't Queen yet," Tyr said, frowning between us. "There's been no coronation, no ceremony."

"Ah," said Carnon, his face splitting into a wide, wicked grin. "About that."

He shot me a tender smile and told the Daemon Lords and Cerridwen what we had done. How he had crowned me himself after the dinner when we had drugged Tyr, witnessing my vows and carrying out the whole ceremony without pomp.

I blushed, a little embarrassed that we had defied protocol so brazenly, especially as Tyr and Herne shot me accusing looks. Brigid was impossible to read, but Cerridwen beamed widely.

"I was done waiting for your permission," Carnon argued, cutting off Herne and Tyr's protests. "Either you accept Elara as your Queen tonight, or you abdicate your posts. Tell me your decision at court."

* * *

Carnon and I stopped before the doors to the throne room, the moment so oddly like our first time at court that I had a strange, fluttering feeling in my gut.

"You ready?" Carnon asked, smiling down at me.

"As I'll ever be, I suppose," I said, biting my lip nervously. Akela was at my side, as always, and I took a moment to study the image carved into the door, the one of the Triple Goddess and the wolf.

"Carnon," I asked, trailing a finger over the stone wolf. "Why does Akela have a connection to me?"

Carnon frowned, looking at where my finger traced the door. "I'm not sure, Red," he said, placing his own hand over mine as I traced. "Why?"

"Maybe it's related to this," I said, indicating the door. "Here is the Goddess, a wolf at her side. Did Lilith not call me an *aspect* of the Goddess?"

"She did," Carnon said slowly, looking down at Akela. The wolf huffed as if disappointed it was taking so long for us to figure it out. "I bonded with Akela when I came of age. When magic emerges in the Court of Beasts, it's traditional for males to be sent into the woods to test themselves." I gave Carnon a sidelong look, and he chuckled. "Very sexist, I know. Anyway, Cerridwen's gift was flight, of course, but my magic took days to figure out. Herne actually sent me out into the Bloodwood after nothing happened in his court to draw it out of me."

"And that's when Akela attacked you, and you tamed him?" I asked.

Carnon nodded. "And I shifted for the first time. Fighting off a pack of leshy brings out the beast."

"I wonder what else brings out the beast," I teased suggestively, remembering the book on serpents and a surprisingly pleasant interlude that involved his tail back in the Sacred City. I felt heat course through me as my necklace thrummed.

Carnon ignored this completely, still studying the wall with an intensity that was immune to my filthy thoughts. "I wonder..." he said, trailing a finger over the stone wolf. "That other stone panel in the hall, the one with Cernunnos. You remember it?" I nodded, the heat fading a bit, and Carnon continued. "The strix has always been the companion of the Horned God. Just as it is in that portrait. But the wolf..."

Akela huffed, looking at me impatiently. "Did you bond with Carnon to claim me, my friend?" I asked him. Akela cocked his head in a wolfy way, revealing nothing. "Fine," I sighed. "Keep your secrets."

"The Horned God and the Triple Goddess, united once again in flesh," Carnon murmured. He raised my hand to his lips, looking at me thoughtfully. "No pressure, Red, but it's possible we have a destiny to fulfill."

"A little late for that concern I think," I said

ruefully, sighing under the enormous pressure of a thousand years of expectations and fate. "Maybe I did inherit other kingly powers from my father, like Tyr suggested."

Carnon took my hand, gripping it tightly, and bent to kiss me. "We'll figure it out together, Red," he murmured. "Whatever it is. You are my Queen, and only death will take me from you."

"You'd better not let it," I growled, pulling him down for another, hurried kiss. "We should go. I think I hear Lucifer coughing pointedly beyond this door."

Carnon grinned, pushing the heavy stone doors. "As you say, my Queen."

Court was assembled just as Carnon had declared, the noble and wealthy houses as well as the less well to do all gathering in the throne room as the sun set. Carnon was resplendent in his sharp crown of gold metal horns and black finery, and I was attending as his mirror opposite.

The crown of silver and pearl and diamond sat upon my head. I had left my hair loose, and it curled over my shoulders in soft waves. I wore a dress of pure white, tiny diamonds sparkling all over like I was living, walking moonstone. We were light and dark, healing and death, Triple Goddess and Horned God incarnate, whether the people knew it or not.

The crowd hushed as we walked toward the thrones, a second identical one having been commissioned weeks ago by Carnon for this very occasion. He held my hand as we sat, daring the crowd to protest my elevation to Queen.

"My friends," Carnon boomed, his voice amplified by some magic of acoustics so that the whole room could hear. "I have summoned you here for two reasons. The first is to warn you about a threat to our safety from within the Darklands itself."

Hushed, panicked whispers rose from the crown, and Carnon raised a hand to silence them. "Lady Scathanna of the Court of Shadows has declared war against us." More muttering and outraged cries erupted at this, and Carnon waited again for the crowd to quiet. "I have vowed as king to protect you and protect these lands. Tonight I would ask for your fealty and support in those endeavors, as my council discusses the best path forward to eliminating the threat.

"I ask that you report anything you might have heard about Shadow to me, to offer your service and your magic to the protection of our lands, and to reaffirm your loyalty tonight in face of this treason." Carnon paused, seemingly for dramatic effect. I tried not to roll my eyes at his showmanship. "Anyone who does not wish to swear their fealty to me tonight has until dawn to flee this city."

More murmurings and rumblings went up from the crowd, and again Carnon waited for their silence. "The second reason I have summoned you is to give you an opportunity to swear fealty to your Queen." Carnon raised our joined hands to his lips, pressing a kiss to them. "Anyone who does not wish to swear their fealty to *her* tonight also has until dawn to flee this city."

A line formed as soon as Carnon was done speaking, with nobles and merchants and soldiers and common demons all lining up to pledge their loyalty and strength to our cause. All pressed their fists to their chests, kneeling before us and pledging their loyalty, until at last only the Daemon Lords and Cerridwen were left.

Cerridwen came forward first, dropping to one knee in her flying leathers and placing her hand over her heart. "My King, I pledge my fealty to you in the name of the Horned God, master of death and resurrection. My Queen," she added, turning a beaming smile upon me, "I pledge my fealty to you in the name of the Triple Goddess, mistress of life and death and mother of all." She bowed her head at the end, but not before she had given me an irreverent wink.

I smiled, and Carnon nudged my arm. Realizing I was supposed to say something, I had a moment of panic before the words Carnon had practiced with me returned to my mind. He had said the words to everyone else, but he felt strongly that it should be I who accepted the fealty of his family and lords.

"We accept your fealty in the name of the Goddess and her Consort," I intoned. "May we serve and protect with their fairness and honor."

Cerridwen stood, stepping to the side of the thrones as Herne approached next. In his sonorous tones, he repeated Cerridwen's pledge, and I responded in kind. He smiled, giving me the slightest of nods. Approval from Herne was hard won, and I had trouble stifling my grin.

Brigid was next, all somber elegance and poise until the end, when she gave a little squeal and hugged me tightly.

"I am proud to call you my Queen," she whispered, squeezing me again before she took her place next to Herne.

Tyr was the last to approach, and the room seemed to still as he knelt before us. Clearly, his reputation for cruelty was far-reaching, and I wondered how much of it was because of his father, and the act he perpetrated to keep his people in line. Here was another male, like Carnon, with a reputation he didn't deserve.

At least, I hoped he didn't.

"My King, I pledge my fealty to you in the name of the Horned God, master of death and resurrection." he said, his words crisp and elegant as they echoed through the throne room. "My Queen, I pledge my fealty to you in the name of the Triple Goddess, mistress of life and death and mother of all." He looked up at the end, something hesitant in his gaze, as if worried I wouldn't accept.

"We accept your fealty in the name of the Goddess and her Consort," I intoned, giving him a reassuring smile. He had offered to teach me blood magic, and if his reasons were what I expected, then perhaps I should take him up on the offer. "May we serve and protect with their fairness and honor."

"Bow," Carnon commanded, the room obeying before he had even finished the command, "before the Witch Queen."

Chapter 15

"Witch Queen?" I asked after Court had finally disbanded and Carnon and I found ourselves alone in our room.

The informal coronation had gone exactly as Carnon had planned, and he was clearly feeling very smug about it. He was grinning widely, his eyes dancing with mischief. Not a single member of court had failed to swear fealty and the relief in his expression was palpable.

"I'm leaning into our destiny," Carnon quipped, giving me a feral grin. "Plus, it seemed more exciting in the moment than 'Demon Queen'. But name your title, my love, and I will call you anything you desire."

"Only if I get to call you the Snake King," I replied,

lifting the crown from my head and shaking out my hair. It was light, but I wasn't used to wearing anything on my head for any length of time, and it felt wonderful to rub my scalp. "Should we have told them?"

"The Daemon Lords?" Carnon asked as he came up behind me, his hands taking over the massage as I sighed against his warm chest. "I like to keep them guessing a little." He kissed my ear, and I shivered. "You will be a spectacular queen."

"You think?" I asked, stifling a groan as his hands worked miraculous circles into my scalp. "I have no idea what I'm doing."

"You'll learn," he said, brushing his nose against my cheek. "I'll learn with you. I have no idea how to do this with a queen."

"You'll tell me," I said, turning in his arms and putting my arms around his neck, "if I overstep?"

"My love, you have nothing to be worried about," he replied, face turning serious. "You have a loving heart and a strong, kind spirit. That is what's most important in a queen."

"I hope you're right," I said, rising on my toes to kiss him. "I think…" I paused, considering. I had been thinking about my role as Queen for some time, and the idea had come to me after Lughnasadh. "I think I want to do what Mama did. To use my gifts to heal and help others. Mortals and demons, and even witches if we can actually unite the realms. She always said that our gifts were a blessing from the Goddess, and that it was our duty to bless others. What do you think?"

Carnon's smile was warm, almost awed, as he kissed my head. "I think that you are incredible."

"Maybe we can even set up a clinic in the palace," I

suggested, getting excited about the idea. "Or the city, if you'd rather I use my own space."

"Set up a clinic wherever you want, Red," Carnon said, grinning down at me. "Set it up in our damn bedroom for all I care. I think it's brilliant."

"Will you be able to spare me from my Queenly duties?" I asked, only half joking as I had no real idea what those duties would be.

"Your duties are what you want them to be, Red," he said seriously. "If you want to use your power to heal injuries and sickness, then I can think of no better way for you to serve as Queen."

A little squeal of excitement left me as I leaped at my mate, catching him by surprise as I kissed him fiercely.

Carnon groaned feelingly. "Gods above, Red, I've missed you."

I laughed, lowering myself to the floor. "I've been with you almost every moment for the last two days."

"Mmm," Carnon hummed, practically breathing me in as he bent to kiss my neck. "And yet I'm still desperate for you. What does that say about me?"

"That you love and desire your mate?" I suggested, pressing a kiss to his nose.

"A mild way of putting it," he countered, brushing a kiss over my lips. "My Queen."

I shuddered at the purr and promise in his voice, and he kissed me again. This kiss turned feral, his hands roaming lower until he was cupping my backside and lifting me.

"Lest I be accused of attempting to seduce you prematurely," Carnon purred, "I should check that I have your willing and enthusiastic consent."

"You do," I breathed. He peppered my collarbone

with kisses and I moaned, wrapping my fingers around his horns and making him shudder in response. "You definitely do."

"Then how shall it be tonight, Red?" he murmured as he carried me toward the bed. "Whatever My Queen desires. Slow and sensual? Fast and rough?"

I swallowed, the memory of our mating chase and his tail wrapping gently around my throat making warmth flood me, just as it had in the hallway before court. An ache built as I hesitated to ask for what I wanted.

"What is it?" Carnon asked, pulling back and raising his brows at me. "I can literally deny you nothing."

"I think…I know…I want the snake," I said, voice hushed as if I might be overheard. Carnon raised his brows and I blushed. "I mean you as a snake, not *your* snake. I mean, of course, I want that too—"

Carnon cut off my insane babbling with a kiss, for which I was extremely grateful.

"You don't want me as a snake, Red," he said, lowering me to the bed and tugging my gown over my head. The gown was cut in a way that there was little practicality in donning undergarments, and he groaned at my bare breasts and sex, kneeling between my legs. "I'm much better at this as a male."

"I believe I should be the judge of that," I argued, gasping a little as he lowered his face to me and flicked that forked tongue up my center.

Carnon chuckled darkly, pulling back again to meet my heated gaze. "If I show you that, Red, there is no going back. You won't be able to unsee me like that. I'm not sure you're truly ready for it."

I frowned, cupping his face in my hands. "Are *you*

not ready?" I asked, realizing that his hesitation wasn't about me at all. "We don't have to. I shouldn't have pushed."

"Elara," Carnon said, turning his head to kiss my palm, then turning back to face me with a hesitant smirk. "It's true that I've never...been with anyone as a beast. You'd be the first. I don't know how it would be."

"I love you," I said, running my fingers through his dark hair and trailing them up to the tips of his horns. He shuddered a little, a sound of pleasure escaping him. "All of you. I want to know you in every way."

I must have said the right thing because Carnon's eyes became purely serpentine, his pupils black slits against a marbled green gaze.

"Are you sure?" he asked, unbuttoning his jacket and shirt to reveal an expanse of golden chest and swirling tattoos. He stood to unlace his trousers and boots, shucking them off until he was completely bare before me, aside from the golden crown. "Only for you, my mate, would I do it."

I licked my lips as I watched him harden, my core going hot and tight. "I'm sure," I whispered, looking into his eyes and trying to will him to believe me. His smirk went from hesitant to feral as, in a flash of green smoke, he changed. His legs became an expansive golden tail, the scales intricately overlapping as he undulated before me. He cracked his neck as claws emerged from his fingertips, his tongue flicking over his bottom lip as he regarded me with those snake eyes.

"As always, Red, I can deny you nothing," he said, almost a hiss as he braced his clawed hands on either side of me and lowered his mouth to my center.

"Gods," I breathed out, falling back on the bed as he

began to work me with his tongue and lips, one of his clawed hands splaying over my stomach to hold me in place. The tips of his claws scratched me in a way that was surprisingly arousing.

I felt the bed shift, and then cool scales wrapping around my waist as he replaced his hand with his tail, the length of him wrapping around me until he was holding me like a snake holds its prey, wrapped so tightly in his coils, there was no escape. The end of his tail flicked around my throat, squeezing gently.

"Carnon," I gasped, feeling pleasure building as he held me, unable to escape even as I wriggled to test his grip. I felt him smile against me as he worked me, his tongue circling and flicking and pressing in and in until I was coming undone around him, my release shattering through me and again.

"Do you want more, Red?" he asked, his tongue flicking lazily over me as I shuddered.

"Yes," I pleaded. "Please."

His tail uncoiled gently as he rose above me, and I would have protested had I not been so eager for him. He gave me a catlike grin and slid onto the bed.

"Oh," I said, trying not to seem a little crestfallen as I propped myself up. He paused, frowning at me.

"What's wrong?" he asked, sitting up to cup my face between his clawed fingers. "Did I hurt you?"

"No," I assured him. I felt my face turning red as I tried to explain. "It's…that book. The one about snakes."

Carnon raised his brow in wary anticipation. "What about it?"

"It said that they…I just thought you might have…" I trailed off, gesturing to the still extremely impressive length of him. Length, singular. I sighed, accepting my inevitable embarrassment. "I thought there would be two."

For a moment, Carnon said nothing. He looked at me in a mixture of horror and disbelief. Then he threw his head back in a resonant laugh that shook the bed.

"It's not funny," I whined, crossing my arms over my bare chest as he laughed at my embarrassment.

"You are the most fucking adorable creature I have ever met," Carnon said through his laughter. "But no, Red. There's just one. I'm utterly devastated to disappoint you."

"You know what," I started, scowling at him. My protest was cut off as Carnon kissed me deeply, the beast melting away until my mate was before me, now wholly demon again, hands and legs restored to normal.

"You are a delight, my love," he said, planting a kiss on my nose as he pulled away. "What would you even do with two of them?"

"I don't know," I snapped, flushing even hotter in my embarrassment. "I assumed you'd have ideas about that."

"Oh, I have ideas," Carnon agreed with another chuckle, one hand weaving into my hair as the other trailed down my arm in a light, teasing stroke, "but I'm afraid they'll have to remain in the realm of fantasy."

"So no snake beast then?" I asked, gesturing to his now very normal-looking hands and legs.

"Hmmm, I think for tonight, my love," he teased, "I would rather ravage you as a somewhat ordinary male than a rather disappointing snake beast." His hand dropped to my breast where he gently ran the pad of his thumb over my taut nipple.

"You told me you were no ordinary male," I said with

an intake of breath, remembering one of our earliest times together. My disappointment about Carnon's snake form quickly dissipated in the pleasure he was beginning to rekindle in me.

"I said somewhat," he reminded me, nipping my lip between his teeth as his fingers scraped my scalp and my pinched nipple in tandem. "And I will make up for the shortcoming of my snake beast, I assure you."

His tongue found mine as he kissed me, and it didn't take long for my embarrassment to melt away into feral need for him as he fell back on the bed and pulled me against him.

Truly, *this* was what I needed. What I wanted. Just him and his tongue and his hands and his body worshiping mine.

"You liked my tail around your throat though," he murmured between kisses as his hand trailed between my legs, stroking the wetness gathering there. "Admit it."

"I did," I breathed, digging my nails into his arms as he worked a finger inside of me. "Gods."

"Two of them, honestly," he teased, chuckling as he nipped my ear. He trailed kisses down my neck and slid a second finger into me.

"There will be zero of them if you don't get on with it, mate," I threatened, earning a rumbling laugh against my neck.

"As my Queen commands," he murmured, withdrawing his fingers and positioning himself at my entrance. He captured my lips as he thrust in, filling me with aching pleasure.

"Good boy," I teased, earning a pinch to my rear as Carnon silenced me with his tongue, his fingers digging almost painfully into my waist as he pulled me to him.

He thrust into me, each move patient and rhythmic like the rolling of the sea at the Court of Sun, until I was gasping from the rising pleasure gathering in my core. His legs wrapped around mine, holding me in place as I built and built and built. I cried out, and he followed me, gripping the back of my head as he bit down on my lip.

I rolled off him, panting and sending a spark of soothing, healing magic into my abused lip.

"Sorry," he breathed, turning on his side and cupping my face in his hands. His thumb ran over my lip, all traces of the small hurt already gone. "Too rough?"

"Just right," I answered, kissing him lightly and nestling into the warmth of his arms.

"Once again I forgot completely about the armchair," he said into my hair, running a hand down my back in soothing lines, his continued apology for the bite to my lip.

"Mmm, maybe it's just not meant to be," I said, smiling against his warm chest.

"I love you," Carnon murmured, his voice light and playful and loving. "You are utterly fucking perfect. And insane," he added, kissing my nose and smirking at me, "and adorable."

"Insane?" I asked, tilting my face up to look at him.

"What kind of person wants to fuck a snake beast?" Carnon asked, raising a brow as he teased, his eyes sparkling with warmth and love. "Insane little witch."

I smiled, kissing his chin, which was the only part of his face I could reach. "Someone who loves that snake beast," I replied, sighing contentedly. "And I suppose I should be glad you don't shift into a whale."

"Why?" Carnon asked, his voice both contented and

resigned to whatever silliness I would suggest next.

I smiled. "Theirs are ten feet long."

Carnon laughed loudly, squeezing me tightly as he shook his head. "I love you. Remind me to never let you back into the damn library," he said, kissing my head.

I smiled, letting his warm arms and rhythmic heartbeat lulled me to a dreamless sleep.

THE WORLD

Part 2

MADELEINE ELIOT

Chapter 16

"This definitely won't work if you're too terrified to actually take my blood," Tyr said, crossing his arms and raising a brow at me.

I scowled, examining the cup of blood in my hands. "I didn't think I'd actually have to drink it," I replied, frowning. "Is all blood magic done this way?"

"Most," Tyr said, regarding me steadily. We were in the stone courtyard of the palace, a little apart from Brigid and Cerridwen who were practicing with blades. Carnon had been cornered by Lucifer to take care of paperwork for the management of the staff, and he'd been forced away grumbling about bureaucracy.

We had decided that Scathanna would need to be removed from Shadow by force, and if he wasn't with Cerridwen, Herne was usually with the commanders discussing strategy and provisions if Carnon couldn't attend himself.

I still hadn't had the chance to talk to Brigid about Tyr, and my agreement to let him guide me through *The Blood Grimoire* was based equally on my desire to snoop into his feelings and to master blood magic. Based on their inability to look away from each other, I knew something was happening between them, and I was determined to find out what it was.

I had spent a day alone in my room examining the book. Many of the spells were similar to witchcraft, the primary difference being the requirement of blood as payment. I had quickly tested all of the spells that required only my own blood, finding them incredibly simple to perform. Things like moving objects from a distance or glamouring rooms like Lilith had done required only an incantation, intention, and a drop of my own blood.

But the section that required the blood of another was more daunting and required a volunteer—or victim—so I accepted the offer to work more closely with the Lord of Blood. I refused to flip through the section completely, afraid I would find the spell that cost my father his life. But I supposed that both Lilith and Tyr had a point about the potential value of mastering some blood magic.

"Carnon agreed to this?" he asked, slicing his palm and letting his blood drip into a goblet as if it was the most normal thing in the world.

"Carnon technically doesn't know I'm doing this right now," I hedged, "but he's not my master."

Tyr raised his eyebrows but said nothing as he handed me the goblet. "Drink."

Cerridwen and Brigid had come to train ostensibly to keep up our regimen. After catching Brigid glancing at Tyr for the tenth time, I couldn't stop myself from saying something. "What's going on between you and Brigid?" I asked, throwing caution to the wind in a bid to put off drinking Tyr's blood.

He raised a brow, reminding me so much of Carnon that I almost laughed. "Drink, and perhaps I'll tell you."

"How exactly will I get the Crone's blood in the first place?" I asked, still frowning at the cup. "Or Scathanna's for that matter. It's not like they'll offer me their arm and tell me to drink."

"That's not how this works," Tyr said, frowning at me. "You don't need the intended *victim's* blood, just blood that isn't yours. Offensive spells require sacrifice. The blood of another serves to power the magic. The spells are difficult to master, but easier for someone with a lot of magic." He nodded pointedly toward me, and the cup in my hands.

I grimaced, frowning down at Tyr's blood. His words made a lot of sense, especially with what I had seen in Lilith's hut. She had used our blood to power some devastating magic.

"Elara," Tyr said, closing the distance between us and putting a hand on my shoulder. "May I call you Elara?"

"Yes," I said warily.

"Blood magic, like any magic, is not inherently wicked," Tyr said. "Like your healing or your withering, blood magic is as wicked as the wielder. It can be used to alleviate pain, to create pleasure." I blushed and Tyr grinned, clearly pleased to have embarrassed me. "You have seen only the bad. And unfortunately, if you plan to use it against your enemies, you will probably only learn the darkest of blood magic. But there is nothing to fear from the magic itself."

"Elara," came a lilting male voice from only a few feet away. I jumped back, and Tyr dropped his hand, giving my mate an irreverent bow.

"My King," he said, grinning like he knew exactly what Carnon had suspected he was up to. "Your lovely mate asked me to help her master the finer points of blood magic. Surely you recall?"

"Elara," Carnon repeated, ignoring the Lord of Blood. His voice was cold and unyielding, and my stomach did a little flip of panic. "Can I speak with you? Now. Please?"

I bit my lip, handing the cup back to Tyr and jogging over to where Carnon leaned against the gleaming moonstone wall of the palace.

"What exactly are you doing?" he asked, looking down at me with narrowed eyes.

"Learning blood magic," I said, crossing my arms as I mirrored his posture. "Tyr offered to help, and I decided to accept."

"We agreed to proceed with caution, not dive right in," Carnon rumbled, lowering his voice. "Offensive blood magic is forbidden."

"Only if you use an unwilling victim, or attack an innocent," I pointed out, citing the loophole I had double-checked with Lucifer earlier that day. "And Tyr is willing, both as a donor and a practice target. You make blood bargains, and those aren't forbidden."

"I don't trust him," Carnon growled, shooting a thunderous look at Tyr. "And I don't like you dabbling in something so dark."

"Do you trust me?" I asked. I was genuinely curious

about his answer. This was the first time we had disagreed about some aspect of my magic and, if we were to build a life together, it would need to be based on trust. Trust that he wouldn't forbid me from learning, and trust that I could handle my magic and anger.

Carnon pursed his lips. "I trust you, Elara. But I'm worried. Blood magic can be dangerous, and I don't want to lose you to its darkness."

"So you *don't* trust me?" I asked, raising a brow.

"I don't trust *him* not to bait you," Carnon bit out. "To not corrupt you. This isn't my first time tangling with darker elements of blood magic, Elara, and it didn't go well for me last time."

Oh. *Oh.*

"My love," I said, softening my tone and cupping his cheek. "I am not Keaira." Carnon flinched at the sound of his old lover's name, but he didn't turn away from me. "No magic could steal me from you or turn us against each other."

"You can't know that for sure," Carnon said, sounding more panicked than angry now. He had been forced to kill someone he had loved to save her from an excruciating death, all because blood magic had warped her mind.

I rose on my toes to kiss him, not caring about our audience. "Stay with me," I suggested. "Be part of it. That way you can be sure he won't warp my mind. I know he won't, but I want you to know it too."

"Are you sure?" Carnon asked. He sighed as he scrubbed a hand over his face. "Now I just feel like a territorial prick."

"You *are* a territorial prick," I laughed, kissing him

again. "But you're *mine*, and I understand. If anything Tyr does feels off, you tell us to stop. So far, I haven't actually done anything with him, since I have to drink his blood first." Carnon grimaced, and I laughed. "That's how I feel about it too. Plus, maybe it won't even work. Maybe I won't have inherited the gift for anything really powerful."

"Fine," Carnon conceded. "I suppose I could even be convinced to play victim for you, with the right inducements."

"Pig," I laughed, kissing him again. "Promise you won't get all growly and bossy though."

"I will *promise* no such thing," he said haughtily, letting me lead him to where Tyr was waiting. "But I'll try."

"I suppose that will do," I conceded, releasing his hand. "Where were we, Lord Tyr?"

"I was reminding you that blood magic is not inherently evil while you dithered over drinking my blood," he said without missing a beat. "Lovers' quarrel?"

"Nothing that concerns you," I said, accepting the cup back from Tyr. I decided to damn the consequences and gulped down the blood. It was *not* pleasant and tasted exactly as I imagined blood would taste—metallic and vaguely meaty. I grimaced.

"Well, damn," Tyr said, looking mildly impressed as I swallowed. "Let's begin."

* * *

It became clear very quickly that I *had* inherited the

ability to use darker blood magic. I did not enjoy the feeling of foreign power churning through me as Tyr had me practice some basic offensive spells. It was viscous and strange, not at all like my serpents who normally coiled and writhed inside me until called upon. They didn't like the blood magic either, raising their heads and hissing at the interloper as Tyr's lifeblood flowed through me.

And yet, some dark part of me also felt that power and preened. I was strong. I could make people *hurt*. So far I had slowed Tyr's heart rate, controlled his movements, and inflicted pain throughout his body. It worried me a little, that dark part of me.

"Good," Tyr gritted out, his teeth bared as the pain spread. This was barely scratching the surface of blood magic, and it already felt wrong. The bright healing magic in me was writhing and squirming in a bid to end Tyr's pain, and I had to concentrate on keeping it at bay as I finished the spell. When I could bear it no longer, I ended the spell. He gasped as I released my healing magic into him to soothe the discomfort. "Thank you."

"Gods above," I exhaled, swaying a little as I felt the last of his blood leave me with the completion of the spell.

Carnon caught my elbow to steady me. He had been our silent observer for the past two hours, only stepping in when I struggled with something that he had an idea about. "Are you all right, Red?" he murmured.

"I'm fine, thanks for asking," Tyr said, earning a dark look from Carnon.

"Fine," I said, smiling weakly at him. "It's almost addictive, the feeling. I can see how people would come to crave the use of blood magic."

"It takes a strong mind not to bend to it," Tyr agreed, wiping sweat from his brow. He had stripped down to his shirt sleeves, removing his usual elegant jacket as the magic took its toll on him. He looked rather pale, and I let my healing take another pass at him. "I'm fine," he snapped, narrowing his eyes at me. "You can stop that."

I rolled my eyes at the stubbornness of males, feeling my body relax as I let the magic go.

"The problem with this plan, as I see it," Carnon said, guiding me to the wall to sit and thrusting a water skin into my hands, "is that it will require you to use someone's blood to power the magic. More tricky to arrange in battle."

"That's why we have fangs," Tyr said, indicating his significantly sharper than normal canines. "In the old days, we would simply drain our victim on the battlefield to power our magic."

"I don't have fangs," I pointed out, grimacing as I remembered Carnon ripping out a male's throat. It was bloody and gruesome, and I couldn't imagine myself doing that. "And I don't really want to tear open any throats if I can help it."

"Preparations can be made," Tyr said, drinking deeply from his own water skin. "We can bottle our blood in advance. We have a similar system in place for our own wielders in Blood."

I didn't relish the idea of my friends or mate bottling their blood for me, but I didn't say anything about it yet. Tyr had made a good point about not prejudicing myself against magic that might be useful.

"We can work out the details when I have more control," I said, noncommittally.

"You did well," Tyr said, nodding at me with an approving gleam in his eyes. It was strange, feeling like we were on the same side after being warned against trusting Tyr for so long, but I supposed war made strange bedfellows. "You'll have control in no time, especially with my blood powering the magic. You must have a blood demon somewhere in your family tree if both you and your grandmother can use the magic."

"How is that possible?" I asked. "She's one of the oldest witches alive."

"We found that answer in the Court of Beasts, Red," Carnon said. He scowled at Tyr, who was stripping off his sweaty shirt. "Witches were born of demon and mortal mates."

"Really?" Tyr asked, eyebrows rising in surprise. His bronze skin was on full display, and I noticed Brigid carefully *not* looking at him. "I've never heard that."

"I'm guessing a thousand years of war caused that little fact to be swept under the proverbial rug," I said, taking another sip of water.

Carnon was still glaring at Tyr, who threw him an irreverent grin. "I'm going to bathe," he said, taking a last moment to look at Brigid, who was laughing about something with Cerridwen. "And take a cold shower."

"If you're drinking anyone's blood from now on, Red," Carnon rumbled as Tyr moved out of earshot, "it will be mine."

"Feeling a little possessive, are we?" I teased, kissing Carnon's scowl. "I don't particularly want to drink *anyone's* blood. Do you see the value in learning the magic though?"

"If it gives you an edge against our enemies, then yes," Carnon relented with a sigh. "But you won't really be able to test the ability until you find yourself in battle, and I'd rather avoid that outcome if possible."

Before I could reply, we were interrupted by Herne, who appeared in his stag form running at top speed and braying angrily. Akela, who had been dozing happily in a sunny spot, rose with a growl.

"Carnon!" Herne bellowed, his voice deeper in his stag form, as he skidded to a stop in the courtyard. "The border."

"What is it?" Carnon snapped. He ran to his friend, and Cerridwen and Brigid hurried to join us. I saw Tyr look back and change his trajectory as well.

"Scouts..." Herne panted, breathing heavily. "From the border...attacked. Casters from Shadow." He took another moment to breathe as foreboding filled me.

"Casualties?" Carnon asked, voice hard as his eyes flared green.

Herne shook his head. "Uncertain. Only three scouts returned."

"We have to go to the fucking border," Carnon said, whirling around and stomping toward the palace.

"Carnon," I shouted, running to catch up and grabbing his arm. "Stop and think. If we leave, who will guard Oneiros?"

"She's right," Tyr said darkly, giving me a nod. "This could be a trap to lure you away."

"It's *your* casters she is killing," Carnon growled. "Someone *needs* to go. If scouts just returned it's been at least three days."

"Only one," Herne corrected. "All three were mine. They flew."

"Then let me," said Brigid, putting a gentle hand on Carnon's arm. "With Lord Tyr. We can send a scout back with word once we have a handle on the situation."

Tyr gave Brigid a strange look, and I forced myself to mind my own business. "The wards will hold, yes?" I asked, looking to Carnon. "Even without the casters?"

"For now," Carnon gritted out. "But it will take you three days to get there, and a full day to send word with a scout beyond that."

"Maybe not," I said, biting my lip as a thought struck me. "What if I could enchant a mirror? Something small enough that the Crone wouldn't be able to use it for travel. I could enchant them for speaking across distances."

"I thought mirrors didn't work that way?" Carnon asked.

"They can," I said, still thinking through the problem. "I had a vision of my parents speaking through them. If both parties touch the glass, it becomes like a conduit."

Carnon's eyes softened for a moment, and I remembered the desperate press of Mama's hand to the glass as my father said goodbye.

"I'll work the enchantments tonight," I said. "And show you how to use them. It's simple magic if you can master the words and intention."

"I can spare ten guards," Carnon said. "But all of my casters are already guarding Oneiros. Are you sure about this, Lady Brigid?"

Brigid nodded, snapping her fingers once. An inferno of flames, gold and yellow and orange and blue, rose around us in a fiery whirlwind, gone a second later at another snap of her fingers. "Save your guards, Carnon. They'll only slow us down. Lord Tyr?"

Tyr looked like a man struck by the beauty of

the first sunset that had ever existed. His eyes were wide, gleaming brightly as he turned to her. "Yes, Lady Brigid?"

Brigid pursed her lips, her face set with grim determination. "Are you with me, Lord Tyr?"

Tyr's eyes remained locked on Brigid's as he answered, "Always."

Chapter 17

"What the hell is going on?" I hissed, pulling Brigid into my room after she knocked hesitantly on the moonstone door.

Carnon was making preparations for Brigid and Tyr's departure with Tyr and Herne, while Cerridwen and I successfully plotted to finally get Brigid alone under the guise of teaching her how to work the mirrors. Obviously, I planned to do that too, but a serious discussion about whatever was going on between her and Tyr was necessary before she left with him on a three-day ride.

I'd made that journey with a handsome male. I knew what could happen.

"Nothing," Brigid sighed forlornly. "I swear, nothing

has happened."

"But he wants it to," Cerridwen said, pouring Brigid a glass of wine. "His eyes have been having their way with you for days now."

"Is that it?" I asked, sitting across from her. "He wants you, but you don't reciprocate?"

"No..." Brigid hedged. "It's more complicated than that."

Cerridwen and I waited, staring Brigid down until she dropped her face into her hands.

"I think it's the Pull," she said, her voice muffled by her palms.

Cerridwen and I both gasped, exchanging a glance that was part horror, part excitement. The Pull was the attraction felt by mates when they first recognized their partners, and it would only grow stronger and more difficult to resist until the pair accepted the bond. Most demons searched for years to find their mates, waiting and hoping to feel the Pull. Only mated pairs could produce children, and many spent centuries without finding their match.

But Brigid looked anything but relieved.

"But it's Tyr," she said, sounding like she might cry. She looked up at us and her face was stricken. "The wicked Lord of Blood who my family has warned me away from as long as I can remember."

"But maybe not so wicked," I suggested, resting a comforting hand on her knee. "We heard his truth."

"I know," said Brigid, still sounding agonized. "But my family..."

"Are they still alive?" I asked. I immediately cursed myself for such an insensitive question. If Brigid were the Lord of Sun, it meant someone had died for that power to pass to her. Succession of the Daemon Lords was hereditary.

"My mother," she said, pressing her lips together. "My father died only a few years ago. She still lives in the golden city. I would have introduced you at Lughnasadh if not for the attack."

"And she won't approve?" Cerridwen asked gently.

Brigid scoffed. "No," she said, voice sounding teary. "She remembers Tyr's father too well. My father used to bring back stories of the Lord of Blood's black heart and his cruel son."

"But if he's your mate..." I said, hesitating. What would I have done if Mama had hated Carnon? It would have been difficult at best, torture at worst, to have the two people I loved so dearly at odds.

"And what if he's not?" Brigid asked. "What if this is just attraction and not the Pull? Shouldn't I have felt it before this?"

"At some point you'll just know," Cerridwen said. "This is the first time you've worked in close quarters for any real length of time."

"And what if he's using blood magic to warp my mind?" Brigid countered, looking skeptical at Cerridwen's assessment.

Cerridwen looked uncertain as an idea struck me. "I think I can help with that," I said, kneeling on the floor. I pushed my father's papers off the coffee table, wanting to do this properly instead of hastily building a mental altar. I grabbed my little pouch of supplies and drew a pentagram on the table, remembering fondly how Carnon had once sat on my coffee table altar and been covered in chalk.

"I need some sage and peppermint," I said, looking at

Ceridwen, who nodded and ran to the balcony. She shot into the sky, then swooped down, hopefully toward the kitchens. "And an amethyst," I added, looking around.

"I have one," Brigid said, producing a necklace from under her gown. It was hung with a small, purple stone, and she lifted it from her neck. "I had a dream last night that I needed it for something, so I thought I should wear it today. Will it work?"

"Perfect," I said, beaming up at her from my spot on the floor. I placed the amethyst at one of the points, then rummaged in my pouch and pulled out the athamé and the quartz. Those would be fine as amplifiers. I could fudge the spell a little with my demon magic.

My, my, Elara, how far you have come, I thought to myself.

"Since this spell is about you, I'm afraid you'll have to bear the cost," I said thoughtfully, looking apologetically at my friend. "A strand of hair pulled straight from the scalp should work."

"What spell are you doing exactly?" Brigid asked, wincing as she plucked a golden hair from her head. I placed it in the center of the pentagram as Cerridwen flapped loudly back onto the balcony.

"Got them!" she called, producing far more sage and peppermint than I could possibly use. "And Pierre sent macarons," she added, dropping a little white bag in my lap.

"Perfect," I replied, plucking some sage and peppermint from the bundles and adding them to the remaining points of the star. "This is a spell for mental clarity. If your mind is not your own, this spell should lift any tampering."

"Okay…" Brigid said warily. "And what if my mind *is*

my own?"

"Then you'll have to decide how you feel about Tyr," I said, patting her shoulder. "Ready?"

Brigid nodded, and she and Cerridwen stared raptly as I held my hands over the altar to perform the magic. The incantation for this spell was in a long-dead language, and most were words that had been lost over the millennia. Only two were familiar: *ansuz* for 'insight,' and *algiz* for warding off evil. When I was done, I looked at Brigid expectantly. "The spell is cast."

"I don't feel anything," Brigid said, frowning.

"Well, how do you feel about Tyr?" Cerridwen asked.

Brigid pursed her lips, thinking. She groaned and dropped her face back into her hands. "Like he's beautiful and I want to do unspeakable things to him."

I stifled a laugh, patting Brigid on the shoulder. "Well, that's your answer. It's not blood magic."

"What am I going to do?" she asked, looking forlornly up at us. "I already told him I don't feel the same."

"You did?" Cerridwen and I squeaked in unison.

Brigid nodded. "After the dinner. He asked if I was feeling it too."

"And you told him no?" I asked, surprised at the lie. Brigid had always struck me as almost naively truthful. Clearly, I had more to learn about my friend.

"And now I can't stop thinking about him," she groaned. "It took all of my willpower to not rescue him from the blood magic today."

"Oof," Cerridwen winced. "It does sound like the Pull."

I nodded in agreement, and Brigid groaned again.

"On the plus side," I said as I reached for a macaron,

"long journeys of forced proximity are an excellent way to find out if you're truly compatible."

Brigid gave me a depressed look. "This is a rescue mission. A battle. I don't have time to get my head all twisted up over a male."

"Sounds like the perfect time, actually," I quipped, grinning at the annoyed look she leveled at me. "And the mirrors mean you'll be able to tell us all the details."

* * *

"You meddled," Carnon said, as we saw Tyr and Brigid off at dawn. They left riding fast but, eventually, they'd have to stop. And talk.

Despite Brigid's claim that they didn't need assistance, a small contingent would be following them to help secure the border once they took care of Scathanna's casters. They were under orders to capture if possible, kill if necessary.

I hurriedly wiped the grin from my face. "I have no idea what you mean."

Carnon raised a brow. "Their lives are in danger. The lives of their people. Now is not the time to play matchmaker."

"And when is the time?" I asked. "If I recall, we first expressed those feelings under similarly urgent circumstances."

"That was different," Carnon argued.

"The Crone set the Bloodwood on fire to try to get me back," I pointed out. "It feels similar."

"Should we not go with them?" Cerridwen asked nervously, watching them ride away. "What if they walk into a full-scale war?"

"Scathanna would be mad to send a large force," Herne said gruffly, putting an arm around his mate. "The scouts didn't have firm numbers, but the border wasn't overwhelmed. It's more likely that Tyr is right and she's trying to lure us away."

"I showed Brigid and Cerridwen how to work the mirrors," I said. The three of us had spent a good hour shouting at each other from opposite ends of my chambers through mirrors, and I was confident that they had mastered the spell during our practice. "It's actually given me some ideas for how demons might apply and use witch magic."

"Your mirrors for one," Carnon agreed, leading us back toward the castle. "Instant travel and communication would be a boon. The current system of couriers and mail is nowhere near as efficient."

"We could install them at the courts to start," I mused. "And maybe some other strategic points throughout the kingdom."

"Now we just have to figure out how to get out of this mess," Carnon muttered, running his hands through his hair as we approached the side door to the kitchen. "Scathanna has me well and truly fucked. She's almost certainly watching us. If we leave to attack her, she'll attack Oneiros while it's defenseless. If we stay to defend the city, she'll hide in her mountain."

A new thought struck me, one that made my blood run cold. "Do you think she's working with the Crone?"

Carnon turned sharply to look at me. "Why do you ask that, Red?"

"It just doesn't make sense for Scathanna to oppose you alone," I said. "She must know she couldn't defeat all three of the other lords and you. But if she had an ally…"

"Fuck," Herne growled, coming to the same realization.

"How would they communicate?" Carnon asked, looking between me and Herne. Neither can pass through the Bloodwood.

This time, it was Cerridwen who supplied the answer. "Spiders."

"You sent creatures into the wood," I pointed out, "to spy on the Crone. Scathanna could have done the same."

We had arrived in the kitchen by this point, our party stopping at the broad counter in the middle of the room. Pierre was cooking something and humming to himself, but I could tell he was listening.

Carnon sat down heavily on a stool and put his head in his hands. "Fuck."

"If Brigid and Tyr can get the border secured, maybe we can find a communication trail," Cerridwen suggested, sitting next to her brother. "How exactly do her spider messengers work?"

"I'm not sure," Carnon sighed. "Maybe they speak in her head like Artemis and Akela. Or maybe they just do her bidding."

I shuddered. The idea of a spider speaking in my head felt far more unpleasant than Akela's shared thoughts and feelings.

Cerridwen put a comforting hand on Carnon's shoulder. "We will figure this out."

"It would be easier if we had some allies in the Witchlands," Herne mused. "Is there no one, Elara, who opposed the Crone?"

"My mother," I said, swallowing the lump of grief

that clogged my throat. "Maybe a few others. But no one publicly, aside from her."

"Maybe if Scathanna is sending messages through the Bloodwood, we can too," Cerridwen suggested, looking at me, clearly hopeful I would confirm. "Is there anyone you trust there? Someone who could spread the word?"

Carnon's eyes snapped to mine, and the name erupted from both of us simultaneously. "Vera."

I bit my lip. Vera had been my only friend in the Witchlands, but I had realized that our friendship was shallow at best.

"Vera could spread the word," I said hesitantly. "But I don't know if she'll believe me. She swallowed every lie the Crone fed us. She's the one who told me most of the terrible stories about demons."

"We'll have to convince her then," Carnon said. "Both that she's been lied to, and that it's in her best interest to side with us."

"I could speak to her through the mirrors," I said, thinking carefully about how I'd have to go about this. "Carnon and I passed through the mirrors once, into the Crone's mansion. How *did* we do that?" I asked, turning to my mate.

"The Demon King can pass through the wards of the Darklands," Carnon replied, gesturing to himself. "It's how I went there in the first place to test my powers. How I found Lilith. I assume that your father's blood gives you the same power, since he was King before me."

"And how will we distract the Crone?" I pressed. I stifled a groan of desire as Pierre started setting out crepes and bacon on the counter before us.

"We will have to make sure she's not watching,"

Cerridwen said thoughtfully as she and Herne joined us at the counter.

"Artemis," my mate suggested as he tossed Akela a piece of bacon. "I promise, she can cause a commotion worthy of the Crone."

"Artemis was gravely injured the last time she went into the Witchlands," I reminded Carnon, frowning at his suggestion.

"That's why I'll be with her this time," Carnon replied. His expression told me that a truly insane plan had entered his mind, and I decided I didn't want to know what it was yet. "But can you do it, Red? Convince Vera of the truth? Convince her to gather others and not turn you in?"

I hated to quash his hope, but realistically this seemed impossible.

"I don't know. How do we convince witches to side with the Demon King?" I asked in exasperation, looking to my mate for answers. "They've been taught to hate your kind—our kind—for centuries. How do you even begin to unite a people who have been at war for a thousand years?"

"Simple," Herne said. We turned to the Lord of Beasts who was watching us with a raised eyebrow. "You give them a common enemy."

Chapter 18

It was clearly not going to be quite as simple as Herne had suggested.

Waiting to find evidence that the Crone and Scathanna were working together was trying. The added difficulty of having to weave that evidence into a believable tale for Vera was a task I wasn't excited about tackling.

With Tyr at the border, it could be weeks until we heard back from his spies in Shadow, so both Akela and Artemis left for the Bloodwood to search for any sign that Scathanna was sending spiders through the wood. Their goal was to intercept a message that would confirm the alliance. I was left wolf-less for the first time in what felt like forever.

I realized I had spent most of my life without Akela padding next to me, but I felt strangely forlorn as I went through training and meetings with Carnon and Cerridwen and Herne without my wolf companion.

On the first day of Akela's absence, I spent the whole day with *The Blood Grimoire* in my lap, a page of notes on the table in front of me. It was while I was reading on combining blood spells that I realized my magic would be most effective if I could blend it together: witch magic that drew on the Goddess' powers of nature, the demon and gods-blessed magic gifted by my father, and the blood magic in the book.

By the evening, I had a workable list of spells to try out the next morning, with which Carnon begrudgingly agreed to help me.

"Are you sure?" I asked as he sliced his forearm and held it out to me. "We could get a cup or a bowl."

"If you do this in battle, there may not be time to get a cup," he said wryly. His smirk was warier than usual, as if he were acting against his own better judgment. "Drink, Red, before I change my mind."

"How much?" I asked, taking his arm in my hands. His flesh was warm, and I could see him trying to hold back his own healing magic to keep the blood flowing.

"I have no idea," he said. "Start with a mouthful or two, and we will see how far it gets you."

I pressed my lips to his flesh, feeling all kinds of wrong about drinking my mate's blood. It tasted... different from Tyr's. Less like blood and more like Carnon, the scent and feel of him. It felt warm and nourishing and somehow a little arousing as I drank, and Carnon groaned as I pulled from him.

"Stop," he rasped after I had taken a few mouthfuls,

the buzz of his blood making me warm and a little desperate for him.

I sent my healing magic to close the wound and stepped back, feeling sheepish. "Sorry," I said, panting a bit. "Did I hurt you?"

"The opposite," Carnon groaned, kissing me once and licking his blood from the corner of my mouth. Clearly, he felt the same as I did about the blood drinking, and I flushed a little at the idea of trying it under more intimate circumstances. "It's possible that my own unexplored blood magic likes this. Very much." He stepped away before our passions could overwhelm us. "What's it to be, then?"

I was still a little breathless, but I managed to outline my plan to Carnon. He gave me a nod and looked at me thoughtfully.

"Why wouldn't you use your death magic for the last part?" he asked softly.

I swallowed. Of course the thought had occurred, and that was as good a backup plan as any, but it felt too simple. Too quick.

"Because I want her to feel what Mama felt before she died," I said, looking into his bright green eyes. "I want her to suffer."

Carnon nodded, gripping my shoulder in comfort. I didn't waver though, and just as I thought he would protest this very bloodthirsty decision, he surprised me. "Test it on me then," he said, walking a few feet away.

"You're not going to argue?" I asked, surprised that my desire to see someone suffer didn't make him bat an eye.

"Not kind, remember?" he said, still looking at me

seriously. "But fair. This sounds very fair."

I swallowed, my love for this male growing as he encouraged me to seek my vengeance, rather than talking me into mercy. Maybe Mama's death had broken the softness in me. Just a bit. "No weapons then," I said, "just in case I can't control it."

He tossed his daggers and swords away from him as I tried to work all three magics simultaneously. I started with the fire, the easiest magic to summon, trapping Carnon in a ring of flames as the fiery beast inside me purred with contentment. Then the binding spell, which took longer as I had to build the altar in my mind first to feed the magic, then will the spell into being. I fed the spell some of the death magic as payment, and a flash of white light told me it had worked.

"Good," Carnon shouted over the wall of flame. "Last part now."

I had to feel for Carnon's blood flowing through me to make the blood magic work, picture harnessing the blood and feeding it into the incantation drop by drop. I pictured Carnon in my mind's eye, imagining his hand rising to his throat. Across from me, Carnon's own hand mirrored the mental image. Had he been holding a blade, he would have slit his own throat.

I dropped the blood magic, feeling suddenly exhausted from holding all three spells at the same time. "The spell is cast," I gasped out, unbinding my mate from his position in the ring of fire.

Carnon doused the fire for me, beaming at my success. "I think this will work," he said, handing me a water skin and stroking soothing lines down my back as I breathed heavily. "We just have to work on speed. The crone will figure out what you're doing and try to counter-spell within seconds. Less if you're unlucky."

After performing the trio of spells six more times, I declared myself too drained to continue. Carnon had given me blood twice more to feed the magic, and I worried about the amount it would take to have any real success.

I groaned tiredly as I trudged up to our room, feeling a little lonely at Akela's absence. I needed a nap and a bath.

The mess that awaited me made me groan again. The papers I had shoved to the side to make room for Brigid's clarity spell were all over the floor. Sighing, I carefully picked up letters and notes, many of which I still hadn't read. My gaze went to where my father's empty journal had fallen on the floor.

Or rather, the previously empty journal. Because the page the book had fallen open to had writing on it.

I quickly put down the other papers and flipped through the journal, bath and nap forgotten. It was the only page with writing, and it seemed to start in the middle of a thought. I flipped back and forth a few times, looking for the rest of it and trying to figure out what I had done to reveal the text.

I couldn't remember doing anything special. Except...

Frowning, I stuck the tip of my finger with the sharp point of my dagger and smeared the drop of blood on the page next to the one with writing. Words bloomed to life where my blood had smeared, swooping elegant handwriting filling the page. My father had spelled it with blood magic, and the paper cut I'd received while first flipping through had unlocked it.

Flipping to the front of the journal, I smeared

another drop of blood on the first page, willing the healing magic to wait so I wouldn't need to prick my finger again. I managed to get through ten pages before my natural swift healing closed the wound.

Eagerly I flipped back to the first page, and began to read, my eyes welling with tears as I realized what this was.

It was an account of my father's courtship with my mother. The first few pages detailed their first meeting: how he snuck into the Witchlands to watch the mortal Beltane festivities, only to see a witch among the mortals. How my mother danced like her life depended on it, laughing and acting as mortal as any of the other villagers. How he glamoured himself so he could dance with her, spending hours with her under the full moon, until at last the sun began to rise and he had to leave her. How he asked her to meet him again near the Bloodwood the following night.

I wiped my eyes as I pricked my finger again, smearing my blood on as many pages as possible before the wound healed.

I read about the moment he realized he was feeling the Pull. How he kissed her in the woods. How she ran when he told her the truth and removed the glamour.

I read about how she returned anyway, and how they spent every night together, when he told her what he suspected. How she agreed to the mating bond, and how he showed her the mating mark that was burned into the skin by those in the Court of Sun. How he gifted her the necklace and took her to the border, only for her to refuse to go back to Oneiros with him. To have her tell him she had unfinished business with the witches.

I read about the little cottage he built for her near

the edge of the Bloodwood, and how she told him she was expecting, and that she had decided to stay in the Witchlands to oppose her mother. I read about his panic when he realized that she and his unborn child would never be safe in either the Darklands or the Witchlands.

I stifled a sob when he kissed her goodbye. When he promised to return as soon as he could, to kill the Crone and reunite the lands and bring us with him. When he spoke to her through the mirror, when he told her he loved her, and promised to visit.

I read about his secret visits during my childhood. I read about how he kissed my mother as she welcomed him with love and relief. How he kissed me while I slept. How he promised to visit more, and how he was forced to break that promise, finding it harder and harder to get away without suspicion. How he begged my mother, just before my fifteenth birthday, to come with him. To bring me and flee to the Darklands with him. How she refused.

And then there was no more. The diary stopped after that visit, and I knew what must have happened. My father had a vision, saw my death in the war that would destroy the Bloodwood, and gave his life to stop it.

I sat on the floor in front of the coffee table for what must have been hours. I clutched the journal to my chest, this gift from my father, feeling the loss of my parents so heavily on my shoulders that it was all I could do to remain sitting upright as I sobbed.

Carnon came in as the sun was setting and found me. I had cried all of my tears by then. He knelt next to me and held my face in his hands, gently tilting it up so I was looking at him. Wordlessly, I held out the journal. Carnon glanced at a single page before folding me into his arms, pulling me onto his lap as he held me.

The sun had fully set when I finally spoke. "She *chose* to stay," I croaked out, my face buried against Carnon's shirt. "He wanted her to come here, and she *chose* not to. Why would she do that?"

"I don't know, Red," Carnon said, speaking against my hair as he cradled me. "But I'm sure she had a bloody good reason. Nothing short of that would keep me from you, if we were in the same position."

"She never knew what happened to him," I said. "Not for sure at least. She must have thought he abandoned her."

"No," Carnon said, so confidently that I pulled away from where I was nestled and looked up.

"How can you possibly know that?" I asked. I finally felt like myself again, enough to inject some irritation into my tone.

"There you are," Carnon said, smiling tenderly as he stroked my cheek with his thumb. "Because, my love, she sent you to find him. To find the Demon King and beg for his protection. When it mattered most, she trusted him to keep you safe."

"I wish I could ask her why," I sighed, forcing myself out of Carnon's arms and off the floor. "She never did anything to overthrow the Crone, as far as I know at least. Other than opposing her at a few Coven meetings, what good did her sacrifice do?"

"I don't know, Red," Carnon said, standing more gracefully than I had and lowering onto the sofa. "It's never easy when you can't ask the dead why they made the choices they made. I wish I could ask my parents why they stayed in Asterra. Why they didn't take me straight to the King or Herne when Artemis came to me." He sighed heavily. He cocked his head as a thought struck him. "But maybe you *could* find out."

"How?" I asked, sliding in next to him. He tucked me in close, heedless of the fact that I still hadn't bathed or changed and was tear-stained and splotchy. Gods, I loved him.

"I'm not positive," he said, mulling over his idea. "But maybe you could find a way to direct your visions. To see what your mother did with her time spent in the Witchlands."

I frowned. "I have no idea how to do that."

"Neither do I," said Carnon, kissing my forehead. "Back to the library, I fear. Although I would beg you to stay far away from the section on reptiles and their anatomy."

I tossed a pillow at his face, and Carnon caught it neatly, tucking it behind him. "You are the worst," I laughed, as he caught me in another quick kiss. "It's not nice to take advantage of my naïveté."

"You love me," he said confidently.

"I do," I agreed, looking bemusedly up at him.

"And you'll love me even more when I draw you the best bath you've ever had in your life," he added as he rose swiftly and strode toward the bathing chamber. "If you recall, I am *excellent* at washing your hair."

Chapter 19

Cerridwen and Herne joined us in our room for an intimate family dinner around the coffee table. We had plans to contact Brigid by mirror. We didn't need any of the staff observing my witch magic in action, especially since Lucifer was still understandably wary of mirror magic.

There wasn't much I could do in regards to the witches until Akela and Artemis returned with something that would help me prove my story. I had already decided that my father's journal about his relationship with Mama would serve as a critical piece, as well as a written account of what Carnon and I had both witnessed in the Crone's manor, when she had tortured Carnon and killed Mama, and what Lilith had told us about the history of Morgana.

So we focused our energies on the border, hoping that Brigid and Tyr would have good news. It took several shouts of her name for Brigid to retrieve her mirror. The glass showed a black canvas, and male voices could be heard in the background as we waited.

"Holy Goddess, it works," she exclaimed, waving someone over to look in the small mirror with her.

Whereas Brigid looked travel-worn but relatively unscathed, Tyr looked like he had seen battle. Blood smeared his lip, and a deep gash across his temple was slowly knitting itself back together. It was too dark to see much behind them, but at least they were alive.

"What's happened?" I asked, wishing the mirror were bigger. "Why is Tyr injured?"

"Why my Queen, does this mean you care about my well-being?" Tyr quipped, earning a warning nudge from Brigid.

She cut in before he could continue. "We arrived this morning to a bit of a stalemate. The casters from Shadow are contained well away from Mithloria, but they are refusing to surrender." Brigid glanced at the Lord of Blood, standing close enough that they were pressed shoulder to shoulder. She bit her lip, and turned back to face us. "One got a good blast in at Lord Tyr."

"You scorched him quite nicely for me, my lady," Tyr responded, his voice pitched low to a sensual rumble. Brigid blushed and I hid a smile at his obvious infatuation with my friend.

"We were just trying to decide how to proceed," she continued, glancing off to the side to where the remaining casters must be. Her voice was sorrowful, and she sounded exhausted. "We lost a handful of our own, may the Goddess guide them." Brigid dipped her head for a moment before continuing, "There are only ten remaining from Shadow. What do you want us to do with them?"

"Capture and interrogate them," Carnon said, his voice hard and unflinching. "I trust, Lord Tyr, that you can convince them to speak truthfully?"

"If I can't, Lady Brigid will probably charm them into a confession," he replied fondly. Brigid scowled at this, but Tyr continued. "And after we interrogate them?"

Carnon pursed his lips, glancing at me.

"It's your call," I said.

"It's *ours*," he corrected. "Scathanna betrayed us all. What is a fair response to her treatment of Sun?"

Cerridwen and Herne watched me as I considered. I knew what Carnon would probably do. I also knew he was asking me to make the call so I could practice in front of our friends before having to make judgments in front of the whole court. I nodded, resolved.

"After you interrogate them, decide if you believe they were coerced or threatened or forced to act against us," I said. "If they were, bring them back as prisoners. If they were willing participants…" I trailed off, looking at my mate. He nodded once, and I steeled my shoulders. "Kill them. Send their heads to the Spider."

Brigid blanched, but Tyr nodded. "It shall be done," he said. "We will contact you tomorrow when we know more, Your Majesties."

I spoke the incantation to close the channel, looking up to see Cerridwen staring at me wide-eyed. Herne's face was impassive as usual, and I frowned. "What?"

"You want to send their heads to the Spider?" she asked, looking between me and Carnon.

"Only if they chose to attack our casters," I confirmed, feeling like perhaps I had chosen wrong. I looked at my mate. "Was it too much?"

He looked at me seriously, but with pride in his eyes. "Not kind, but fair," he said, giving me a nod. "Handled like a true Demon Queen."

"I don't want to be cruel," I hedged, rethinking my decision. Seeking revenge on the Crone was one thing, but seeking it on demons I didn't know made me second-guess myself. Cerridwen still looked at me disbelievingly, and I worried I had gone too far for her gentle nature.

"A firm hand is needed where Scathanna's court is concerned," Herne grunted, startling me out of my panic. "Mercy would be seen as weakness. You know this, mate." He looked down at Cerridwen, who only pursed her lips in response. He turned back to pin me with a piercing look. "Win this war, root out the disloyal, and then be whatever kind of Queen you want."

"How does that make you any better than the Crone?" Cerridwen asked, still looking somewhat pale. Her question hit me like a slap in the face, and Carnon put a heavy, comforting hand on my shoulder.

"The Crone would have killed them all," he said, speaking to his sister. She had crossed her arms as if readying for a battle, but Carnon didn't let her interrupt. "And for what it's worth, so would I. I would have had Tyr bleed them dry."

I looked back at my mate in surprise at this bloodthirstiness and he shrugged.

"You want to unite the demons and the witches," Cerridwen argued. "But at what cost? How will you convince the witches to join you if you live up to every single one of their rumors and fears?"

She stormed out of the room before either of us or Herne could reply, and I felt something crumple in my chest. That warm ball of friendship, of sisterhood, cooled and hardened uncomfortably.

"She'll come around," grunted Herne, rising and giving me an apologetic look. "She's more idealist than strategist."

Herne followed his mate out, and I turned to Carnon in dismay. "Maybe she's right, Carnon. Maybe this *isn't* the way forward for us. How can I go to Vera and say she's been lied to if we are every bit as cruel as the Crone says?"

"My love," Carnon said, frowning down at me. "Give Cerridwen a little space. I'm sure she didn't mean to upset you."

"But she's right," I said, throwing up my hands in frustration.

"This is war, Red," Carnon sighed, cupping my face in his hands. "There is a time and place for mercy, and there is a time and place for violence. Sometimes violence is the only option."

"After this war then," I said, feeling unmoored and adrift with the disagreement between Cerridwen and me hanging in the air, "we need to be different. We need strength when strength is called for, but mercy when it's not."

Carnon nodded, pressing his forehead to mine. "Despite what Cerridwen said, you *did* show mercy. You spared those who had no choice in their betrayal, and when they are brought before us we can determine a fair judgment." I nodded as he pressed a kiss to my forehead. "And for what it's worth, Red, I thank the Goddess for bringing you to me."

"You do?" I asked, looking up at him.

He smiled, tender and real. "I do. I've been doing this alone for a long time, Red. But for the first time, I feel like I have the chance to be a better king. With you by my side, we can be *more*."

* * *

I had fitful dreams, reliving the fight with Cerridwen over and over in my mind. I had never really fought with a friend before. Vera always got her way, because it was just easier to agree with her, and I didn't know enough in my former life to take a stand against her. I wondered, when all of this was over, if I could find a way to mend my friendship with Vera, too.

When I wasn't dreaming about my rift with Cerridwen, I was dreaming of my mother. Of her refusal to join my father. I wanted to shake her, to scream at her and to ask her why. But every time I came close to touching her, she faded, looking at me sorrowfully as she disappeared into nothing.

My fitful sleep was finally ended by Artemis, who returned sometime near dawn. She hooted loudly to let us know she was back, and we bolted out of bed to meet her on the balcony.

She waited for us with a dead mouse in her beak and a piece of paper clasped in one talon. She dropped the mouse with a superior sounding hoot and looked at me expectantly.

"Thank you?" I hedged, never having quite gotten

used to Artemis' brand of affection. She nodded with a satisfied hoot and turned to Carnon, giving him her attention for a full minute as some silent conversation passed between them. Another hoot, and she flapped away, probably headed for a much needed nap.

"Where's Akela?" I asked as Carnon gingerly reached for the paper, trying to avoid the mouse.

"Still on his way," Carnon said, unfolding the paper, which was a bit worse for wear. "Artemis told me she flew ahead."

"Does she speak actual words in your head?" I asked, curious how our bonds with the creatures might work differently.

"More like, she places ideas and feelings there," Carnon said, frowning at the note. "Same with Akela. I've just learned to interpret after years of learning how they communicate. You?"

"It's the same for Akela and me," I agreed impatiently, waiting for Carnon to read the note. "Well?"

"All it says is, 'Before Samhain'," Carnon grunted, handing me the paper. "This does us no good whatsoever."

"It does," I disagreed, excitement and trepidation warring within me. "This is the Crone's handwriting. I'm sure of it. Where did Artemis find this?"

Carnon raised a brow at me. "She took it from a giant spider in the Bloodwood. She blessedly did not feel we would appreciate the spider's remains as a gift."

"How giant?" I asked in horror, imagining a spider the size of Akela.

Carnon smiled faintly at my horrified expression. "Not bigger than Artemis, if that makes you feel better."

"Well, that proves it then," I said, feeling like we finally had something concrete to move forward with. "Scathanna and the Crone are communicating about something that will happen before Samhain."

"Samhain is over two months away, Red," Carnon said skeptically. "It's not a lot to go on. And what if Vera doesn't believe where Artemis found this? Or that it's the Crone's writing? Do you have anything to compare it to?"

"No," I said, irritation dampening my excitement. I paced across the balcony, trying to think. I needed Vera to believe me unconditionally and to tell others. I could ask her to cast a truth spell on me, but she was notoriously poor at spellwork, and I doubted she had improved significantly. I couldn't really afford to be turned into a toad right now. I could always cast the spell on myself, of course, but she might doubt that I cast true if she believed the Crone's lies.

"You look adorable when you pace in frustration, just so you know," Carnon drawled. He was leaning against the balcony, all gleaming gold skin and tattoos. The trousers he had pulled on hurriedly when Artemis arrived were slung low on his hips, and the sight was thoroughly distracting.

"Shhh," I snapped. "I'm thinking."

The idea came to me then, but it would be a risk. Going to one witch was dangerous. Going to a second could be disastrous. But it was the only way I could think to convince her.

"We need to tell Vera's mother," I said, finally turning to Carnon. My copper hair was a bit wild in the morning breeze, and I brushed it away irritably. "She was like Mama. Avoided the city, wanted to lead a quiet life helping mortals. If Vera's mother casts a truth spell on me, then Vera will believe me."

"Why can't Vera cast it herself?" Carnon asked.

I winced. "Because she's not a very good witch."

"Ouch," Carnon teased.

"I already feel awful saying it," I groaned. "But I'm sure this is the only way forward. She won't believe me if I cast it on myself."

Carnon pursed his lips, looking thoughtful.

"Fine," he agreed, crossing his arms as if preparing for an argument. "But if you're facing two witches, then I'm going with you."

"That is a monumentally stupid idea," I said. "Witches barely trust men as it is. The moment they see the horns, they'll write you off. Never mind when they learn you're the actual Demon King."

"Oh, my love," Carnon grinned, breaking his thoughtful pose and striding purposefully toward me. He kissed me soundly, practically lifting me off my toes with the force of the movement. "Haven't you learned that I am a master of disguise?"

"You in a cloak is not really a disguise," I argued, giving him an arch look.

"True," he agreed, stepping away from me toward the door to our room. "But how about this?"

With a snap of his fingers, Carnon disappeared into shadow.

"You *do* love to be dramatic, don't you?" I sighed, waiting for Carnon to reappear. He did so a second later, grinning like a cat.

"Tell me that won't work, Red," he said, looking smug. "I'll come and just lurk in the background. You won't even know I'm there. I'll only come out if there's danger."

"Fine," I conceded. "I suppose if I argued, you'd find a way to come along anyway."

"This is true," he agreed. "So when do we leave?"

I thought for a moment, trying to decide what preparation would be needed. With the truth spell plan, there wasn't much.

"Tonight," I said. "After I've had a chance to gather the evidence and clear the air with Cerridwen."

Carnon nodded, his grin softening. "It will be fine, Red," he said, giving my arm a squeeze. "Just be honest with her."

I threw Carnon the most incredulous look I could muster, letting my voice drip with disdain. "That is truly rich advice, coming from *you*."

Chapter 20

Unable to wait any longer, I set off in search of Cerridwen before I bothered with breakfast. I was worried about too many things to eat anyway, including Akela all alone in the wilds and the mission we would be undertaking.

As if she were of the same mind, I found Cerridwen coming in search of me, already dressed for the day in training clothes as I was, looking like a demon on a mission.

"Oh," she said, taking a step back as she nearly crashed into me. "You're here."

"I am," I said, reaching out to steady her as she stumbled. "I was looking for you."

"Me too," she said hurriedly. "Listen, I'm so sorry."

"I'm sorry too," I cut in, wanting to make sure she

knew that I had sought her out to make amends, not to fight some more. "You were absolutely right. It was cruel, and it's exactly why the witches fear us."

"No, you were right," Cerridwen said, shaking her head and taking her hands in mine. "This is war, and those casters chose to hurt ours. I shouldn't have questioned your justice. You're the Queen."

"I *want* you to question me," I exclaimed, placing a hand to my chest. "I need guidance, and I trust your counsel. I should have really listened to you instead of just defending my own ideas."

We both spoke in such a rush that when we were finished we stood, somewhat dazed, waiting for the other to speak. When neither of us did, Cerridwen threw her arms around me in a hug.

"You're my best friend, you know," she said, speaking over my shoulder. "Other than Herne, of course."

I laughed. "What about Carnon?"

"Oh no, he comes after you," she said, pulling back with a grin.

"You're my best friend too," I replied, feeling oddly uneasy. This was not how I had expected things to go, and I felt strangely awkward and relieved at the same time. "Other than Carnon, of course."

"Good," Cerridwen said, linking her arm in mine and forging a path in the direction of the kitchens. "Breakfast? I was too nervous to eat before I came looking for you."

Friendship, it occurred to me, was an odd creature. It needed to be fed and nurtured like an animal, and was as easily wounded as it was tamed.

Cerridwen and I continued to the kitchens as she told me about the time she and Herne had fought for a week straight over the color of their bedchamber. I laughed at her story, the fight between us practically forgotten as we entered the kitchens together.

Herne and Carnon were already there, watching us like twin statues, coffee cups in hand.

"See?" Carnon said smugly.

"All better," Herne agreed, clinking his mug against Carnon's.

I rolled my eyes and slid onto a stool in front of a huge pile of bacon and eggs.

After breakfast, the four of us trained with magic for a few hours. Carnon wanted me to practice using my combined magic against a larger group, rather than a single opponent. He was the first to offer his blood, slicing his arm without hesitation. After a successful demonstration proved I wouldn't accidentally kill them all, everyone else submitted to practice as well.

I spent the rest of the afternoon gathering materials to show Vera and her mother, and preparing a mending spell for the broken mirror we had used to visit Lilith.

Brigid and Tyr checked in with us via their mirror at one point, letting us know they'd be returning with three prisoners.

"Only three?" I asked, surprised it would be so few. I had thought for sure Scathanna had forced her casters to attack. "Are you positive?"

"Sadly, yes," Brigid said, her tone anxious. "The three who claim to have been coerced seem legitimate enough. Two have given us information that might be useful. But the others…"

"They were proud to have done it," Tyr spat, his face a mask of disgust. "They said they were proud to fight for the true power of the Darklands."

"Ominous," Carnon muttered.

I nodded, biting my lip. "Get back as soon as you can. We will let Lucifer know to prepare some cells so the prisoners can be questioned."

"Listen to you, acting all Queenly," Carnon said once I had ended the spell. "It does something to me, Red."

I tried to smile and enjoy my mate's amorous attention, but by late afternoon my anxiety for Akela had reached a fever pitch. Artemis had been sleeping all day, but otherwise seemed perfectly fine, but there had been no sign or mention of the wolf by any of the guards. I was beyond panic and heading into recklessness.

"It could take him another day to reach us," Carnon soothed, setting up the big gilded mirror against the wall of his office. I couldn't help but note the edge of concern in his own voice for our furry companion. "If he's not back by tomorrow morning, I'll send Artemis out to scout for him."

"Are you two sure this is a good idea?" Cerridwen asked, eyeing the mirror with apprehension. "I feel like traveling by mirror hasn't gone well any of the times you've done it."

"I do," I said firmly, trying to embrace my decision with confidence. "Carnon will be in shadow, and the two of us are more than a match for the witches if it doesn't go our way."

"I thought Artemis was supposed to cause a distraction," Cerridwen pointed out, noting the strix's absence.

"She's too tired for the trip," Carnon said, watching as I mentally prepared the mending spell. It was the same spell I had done when I'd landed on my basket in the Bloodwood all those months ago, terrified and naive and completely unprepared for what was about to happen to me. "We'll go fast."

"If the Crone shows up," Herne said. "Run. You're not prepared to take her on alone."

I nodded, accepting this advice for the wise counsel it probably was as I set up the altar in my mind and cast. The glass slid together like water until it was smooth again, but Carnon didn't take my hand as usual.

"I'll be behind you the whole time, Red," he said, cloaking himself in shadow. If I hadn't known he was there, it would have been impossible to make him out. I felt him, more than saw him behind me.

"Only come out if I'm attacked," I warned him. There was no response from the shadow, so I took that to be a yes. "And hold on tight. I've never taken a shadow through a mirror before."

I felt his weight on my back, the sensation very strange as I saw nothing behind me in the rippling glass.

"Back soon," I promised Cerridwen, shooting her a confident smile.

"You'd better be," she threatened as I stepped through the mirror into icy nothingness.

❖ ❖ ❖

When we had parted ways the day before my birthday, Vera said she would be staying with her aunt in Ostara. I had no idea where her aunt's house was, so rather than risking us getting trapped between realms for eternity, I went to the mirror I knew second best—the one in Vera's bedroom.

I briefly contemplated going to Mama's cottage, but I was certain that the Crone would have eyes on it in case I went back there, and I couldn't bear to be around all of Mama's things without her.

We stepped into Vera's room, which was dark and felt unused. I had known Vera's mother my whole life, and I knew she liked to live quietly like Mama. I hoped she wouldn't try to hex me as soon as she realized there was an intruder in her house.

"Hello?" I shouted, trying to make it obvious that I was hiding nothing—besides Carnon, of course. I heard something shatter on the floor below and winced. I supposed she knew she had company then. I went for the door to the room and opened it slowly, making sure I wasn't about to be ambushed in the hall. "It's me, Elara! I promise I'm not here to hurt you!"

"Elara?" shrieked the voice of Vera's mother as she climbed the stairs. "By the Goddess, child, you scared me half to death!"

Vera's mother, Agnes, was a shorter, slightly rounder version of Vera, brown curls bobbing and honey-gold skin practically shimmering in the candlelight. She was holding a rolling pin rather more like a weapon than a baking implement, and I held up my hands placatingly.

"I'm not here to hurt you, I promise," I said.

"What are you thinking, traveling by mirror?" Agnes hissed, glancing warily around and beckoning me downstairs. Carnon's shadow followed mine, and I too glanced around the small cottage. "You've been declared an enemy of the Coven. The Crone has been telling everyone you killed your mother."

A stab of pain shot through me, and I felt Carnon's heavy presence move closer to me. "I didn't kill her."

"What? No, silly girl, of course you didn't," she scoffed, waving her hand and indicating I should sit at the kitchen table. "I'm guessing the Crone killed her, yes?" I gave a tight nod as I sat, and Vera's mother shook her head. "It was foolish for her to come back here. She should have run with you."

"She...what?" I asked, feeling utterly confused. Nothing was going the way I had planned it to go exactly, but it was also sort of going better than expected. "What do you mean?"

Agnes gave me a kindly smile, so like my own Mama's that it hurt something in my heart. "Tea? It always helps me when I have to process heavy information," she added, pouring me a cup. "Circe told me you'd likely show up here asking for help. I just expected you to come on foot. She told me you were bright."

I was too stunned and confused to coherently respond to this. Shaking my head, I tried to take control of the conversation. "I was actually hoping to speak to Vera," I said hesitantly, "or to you both, I suppose. To ask for your help."

I had tucked the papers and evidence beneath my cloak, but I pulled them out and laid them on the table before me. Carnon's presence at my back reminded me he was with me, and I felt more secure.

"That won't be necessary," Agnes said, waving her hand again. "I already know what you're going to tell me."

"You do?" I asked, my confusion growing.

"Yes," Agnes said, setting a cup of tea before me and smiling warmly at me as she sat. "You're here to tell me that everything we've been told about demons was a lie. Or mostly a lie. And that the Crone is using blood magic to try to bring down the Bloodwood, which was created to protect the demons from her wrath in the first place."

My eyes went wide as my face drained of color.

"And," Agnes continued, taking another sip of tea as if we were discussing a rather interesting gardening technique, rather than a thousand years of lies and deceit, "you're going to tell me that you, heir to the Coven, are actually *half*-demon, the child of Circe and her demon mate, who also happened to be the Demon King."

"How—"

"I've been waiting a very long time for this conversation, my dear," she said, smiling at me warmly and patting my hand. "For twenty years in fact. From the moment your mother first started gathering a movement in secret to oppose the Crone. To unite the gods and the realms once more, and to put an end to the suffering of mortals and witches alike under her rule."

"My mother—"

"*Chose* to stay, yes," Agnes lamented. "And a very difficult choice it was for her, too. I half expected her to change her mind every other day, but she didn't. She stayed for you. For *us*. Why do you think she chose to live so far from other witches?"

"Because my father—"

"Yes, of course," she said, interrupting me yet again in a way that was becoming rather infuriating. "He built her that cottage. But she chose for it to be as far away from your grandmother as possible. So she could move unnoticed through the realm as she did her work."

"Hold on," I said, finally butting my way into the conversation long enough to ask one of the thousands of questions buzzing around in my brain. "How do *you* know any of this? How do you know about my father and my mother and the prophecy?" Agnes seemed to be on a much faster train of thought than I was, and I was at terrible risk of being left at the station.

Agnes raised an eyebrows. "I don't know much about prophecy, my dear, but I know the rest because she told me. And I took some convincing, believe me. So did the others. But once we met him—your father, I mean—and they explained, we all agreed. We've been sworn to secrecy, until you were old enough to learn the truth. Your mother said that would be the day after you came of age, but then you disappeared and she was captured, and we've all been in hiding waiting for you."

"You *met* him?" I asked, shaking my head in disbelief, then asking, "The others? What others?"

Agnes smiled rather smugly as she leaned back in her chair. "What did you think your mother was doing for twenty-five years, child? Biding her time? Circe was brave and smart. She knew she couldn't oppose your grandmother alone, and she knew you were the leverage she needed to keep the Crone at arm's length while you grew up. She was working, child. Preparing for you. Gathering allies."

"Allies?" I asked, still feeling l dumbfounded at how completely in the dark my mother had kept me. "I didn't even know you were friends. You and Vera moved here—"

"When you were five," Agnes confirmed with a nod. "When Circe recruited me. It had to be a secret, of course," she added sadly. "None of us were even able to mourn her, for fear the Crone would learn of it. We promised to hide our association for the sakes of our daughters and each other. If one of us were caught, the rest could continue on with the work."

"What work, exactly?" I asked, my brain slowly catching up to these revelations.

"Gathering an army of witches to support *you*," Agnes exclaimed, as if this were obvious. "She told us that one day, you would be ready to take your place as the new leader of the Coven. A Witch Queen of unprecedented power, born of two realms and heir to two thrones."

For a long moment, I was silent as I contemplated my mother's many, many deceptions and let my mind catch up to Agnes'.

Mama had been planning a coup for my whole life. Had introduced my father to other witches. Had pretended to have no friends or connections to keep them and me safe. Had died protecting that knowledge so that *I* could take the throne. And she had spun a tale that I would be some kind of goddess-queen to convince these witches to follow me.

"I'm no heir," I finally said, feeling very uncomfortable with the awed expression with which Agnes was regarding me. "The Darklands already have a new Demon King. My father has been dead for ten years."

The older witch's face fell at this. "I am sorry to hear that. Circe always held onto hope, but we all did wonder."

"You keep saying all," I cut in. "Allies. An army. How many of you are there, exactly?"

"Including you and Vera, once we convince her of the truth?" the witch said, mentally calculating. She grinned. "One hundred."

Chapter 21

"One hundred witches?" Cerridwen repeated in disbelief after we had returned and relayed what had happened.

I was barely able to comprehend it myself. Agnes had assured me that she would call Vera home and tell her everything, and signal the other witches to meet with me. I was to return to the cottage in two nights to meet with Agnes and the other witches who had taken over the resistance when my mother had been taken by the Crone.

"And leave your shadow behind next time," Agnes had added before we left, giving the empty space behind me a wry look. "I suspect he would put the others on edge."

"How do you think she knew I was there?" Carnon asked as soon as we had returned to the office and shattered the mirror again as a precaution. It was easy enough to fix when we needed it next.

"I have no idea," I said with a frown. "But I can't really go alone, can I?"

"Why not?" Carnon asked, looking down at me as if he was genuinely confused.

"Well...because I'm not—"

"My Queen?" Carnon suggested. "My equal and partner, perfectly capable of handling yourself without me?" I felt a flush sweep through me at his words, and it had nothing to do with his hand resting on my arm in a warm, comforting gesture. "I trust you, Red. You need to learn to trust yourself now."

"It could be a trap," Herne said gruffly, scowling at his king. "A secret meeting with a hundred witches sounds like it is definitely a trap. She could be telling the Crone as we speak and preparing to have you ambushed."

"Then she should definitely go prepared," Carnon said, sounding irritated at his naysaying. "One hundred witches will tip the balance in our favor." he added, turning back to me. "You *have* to go."

"Do you really trust this witch?" Cerridwen asked, biting her lip as she glanced between me and her brother. "Did you spell her tea or bind her word or do something to ensure she wasn't lying?"

"Well, no," I admitted, "but her story fits. It explains why Mama stayed, even though she loved Alaunus and he wanted to bring her here. Why she kept me in the dark for so long. She knew the Crone was using blood magic; that she could have forced the truth from my mind against my will, and I would have no way to defend myself until my demonic gifts emerged."

"That's true," Carnon agreed, nodding as he stood next to me like a wall of support.

"And she told me—" I swallowed, my throat becoming thick with unshed tears. "She told me, when she sent me into the Bloodwood, that she would follow me as soon as she could. She *knew* we could enter the Darklands because Alaunus was her mate. She thought he was still alive. You were right," I added, turning to Carnon, whose gaze had softened at my distress. "She was sending me to find him."

"It doesn't mean that Agnes isn't working for the Crone," Cerridwen said thoughtfully, glancing up at her mate, who was still frowning. "But it does seem like she knew your parents."

"Artemis and I will wait for you in the Bloodwood," Carnon said, as if the matter were settled. "You'll need a distraction to keep the Crone away from you, and we will be happy to provide one. That way we'll be nearby if you need backup."

I nodded, grateful for his support despite my anxiety about doing something like this on my own. "I will take Tyr and Brigid's mirror too," I suggested. "They should be back by then. That way if I get into trouble, I can call you for help. I can maybe even enlarge the mirror with witch magic if I need to escape."

"And you'll take vials of blood," Carnon agreed. "And a dagger. And Akela, if he is back in time."

I nodded, and Carnon mirrored the movement.

"I'll prepare the guard," Herne said, nodding at Cerridwen to follow him. "With two days, we can have them march on a moment's notice if anything happens to you out there."

"That won't happen," Carnon said confidently.

I wished I had his self-assurance as Herne nodded, striding out of the room with Cerridwen flapping to keep up with him. He was probably going to alert the guard anyway, which made me feel a little safer at least. Oneiros would be protected in our absence.

"I can't decide if I love your mother, or if I'm intensely annoyed with all of her secrets," Carnon sighed, sitting heavily in his chair behind the desk when we were finally alone. "It's a lot to have kept from you."

"You and me both," I agreed, perching on the edge of his desk. "You would have loved her though. She was like me, only nicer. And better at baking."

Carnon smiled warmly. "I'm sure I would have. And you're *mostly* nice." I gave him a little half-hearted kick with the toe of my boot and he chuckled.

"I feel like I didn't really know her," I sighed. Wishing I could somehow force a vision of her and make her explain. "I'm going to be a disappointment to them, Carnon," I confessed, voicing the fear that had been niggling at me since Agnes had relayed my mother's tale. "Mama told them I'm some kind of queen with 'unprecedented power,' and I'm not. I'm just—"

"An actual queen?" Carnon cut in, giving me a sardonic look. "Heir to the Coven *and* daughter of a king, and wielder of magic from *both* realms? I don't think they'll be disappointed, Red." He playfully nudged my knee. "You're exactly who they expect. You need to start believing that you can do this. That you were born for it."

I pursed my lips, frowning at my mate who looked completely serious in his praise. "What if they won't follow me?" I asked.

"They will," Carnon said with a confident shrug. He laughed as I rolled my eyes. "And," he added, "if by some unlucky circumstance they *don't*, then we will come up with a new plan. We've got this, my love. You and I are a force to be reckoned with."

I looked at my mate, feeling his warmth and confidence fill my chest and buoy my spirit. "Thank you," I said, with a little dip of my chin. "Still, it would have saved a lot of arduous research time if we had gone straight to Agnes, rather than bothering with so many libraries," I joked. "Although I suppose I might not have believed her if I hadn't learned it for myself first."

"And you would have never acquired your valuable knowledge of serpent anatomy," Carnon quipped, earning another small kick.

"When will you cease to tease me about that?" I asked, with no real vitriol behind the question. "How was I supposed to know what a snake shifter had hiding behind his scales?"

"Never," Carnon declared, pulling me into his lap. "Unless you truly despise my teasing, in which case I will attempt to limit it only to three or four times a day."

"Gods above," I sighed, feigning irritation. "What shall I do with such an inconsiderate mate?"

"I promise I will make up for it with a great deal of consideration in other areas of our mating," Carnon purred, his voice sending a shiver down my spine. "Now, if you'll consent to come to bed with me."

"Hmmm, tempting as the offer is," I said, kissing the corner of his mouth and reveling in his groan of discomfort as I ground my hips into his lap. "We have quite a lot of work to do."

"Work can wait for five minutes," Carnon protested,

capturing my lips in his and curling his tongue around mine.

"Only five minutes?" I balked with a laugh. "That doesn't sound very considerate."

"Ten then," Carnon laughed, recapturing my mouth. "But that's as high as I'm going."

"You'll need to do better," I teased, biting his lip as I pulled away from him. "And you'll have to catch me first."

"A chase, Elara?" Carnon asked, his brows shooting up. The hard length that was straining against my backside was evidence that he clearly liked the idea. "You want a chase tonight?"

"I need a thirty second head start," I murmured, kissing him again as I worked the fastest spell of my life.

"You get ten," he growled.

"Deal," I said, completing the spell and grinning as the bright light of the binding spell flashed, trapping his hands and legs against his chair.

I ran, smiling at the roar that floated out from his office as I raced up the stairs. I knew how this would end, and there wasn't much of a point in dragging it out, but at least this way I could choose where and how he would take me.

The moon was a thin crescent shining brightly in the sky outside our bedroom, the moonstone balcony bathed in silvery light. I stripped off my leathers and padded out naked in the moonlight, the summer air warm enough that only a slight chill pebbled my skin.

As I looked over the city and the mountains surrounding us and waited for my mate to find me, I took a moment to enjoy this last bubble of peace. I had a feeling that, whatever came of the meeting with the witches and Scathanna, something was going to mar the peacefulness of Oneiros sooner rather than later.

"You didn't try very hard," Carnon laughed, materializing out of the shadows behind me.

I turned, reveling in the feeling of his eyes drinking me in. "I thought I'd take it easy on you," I said coyly. "You're quite old, after all."

"Hardly," Carnon laughed, prowling toward me like a forest cat on the hunt. He began pulling off his clothes as he walked until he was standing directly in front of me, naked and hard, the moonlight gleaming off his golden skin. "Is this how you want it, Red? In full view of the city, so they can hear your cries as I take you?"

I shivered at his seductive tone, practically leaning into the heat of him and feeling my nipples peak with anticipation. He didn't touch me, not yet. It was part of the chase. Making me wait was his revenge, and it had heat flooding me already.

"You once told me to let them all hear," I replied, hopping up onto the balcony ledge so I was sitting before him, my legs slightly parted. He swore, reaching forward to grab my waist in case I overbalanced, and I grinned at my victory in making him touch me first. "You said you wanted the whole city to hear me crying out your name."

Carnon's hands slid to my back, one sliding down to cup my rear as he stepped closer to me. "So I did," he said, capturing my lips in a feral kiss. His wicked forked tongue slid over mine as he pressed against me, every hard inch of him digging into my soft stomach in a deliciously tempting way.

"Wait," I breathed, pushing him back a step as I slid off the balcony rail.

"What?" Carnon asked, concern warring with desire as he gazed at me with hungry, hooded eyes.

"What if I want to make you scream *my* name?" I asked, dropping to my knees on the cold stone before him.

"Red," he said, inhaling sharply as I pressed my lips against his length. "Gods, I certainly won't stop you."

I smiled against him, teasing his length with my tongue as I nipped and licked, then wrapping my mouth against him and sucking gently. He groaned, fisting his fingers into my hair with one hand and cupping my face with the other.

"The things you do to me, Elara," he groaned. I ran a hand down one muscled thigh, feeling goosebumps erupt where I touched. I was just getting into a rhythm when he held me away, preventing me from getting my mouth on him. "If you keep going, this will be over before it even starts," he growled, pulling me to my feet and hoisting me up into his arms.

He kissed me, not giving me time to reply as he carried me to one of the moonstone columns that connected the balcony to the floor above, pressing me hard against it. I gasped at the feel of cold moonstone against my back, and Carnon chuckled as he murmured, "Payback."

His lips trailed down my neck and across my collarbone as I rested my head against the pillar. He lifted me a little higher, raising my arms above my head and pinning them to the column above me.

"You won't be able to hold me like this the whole time," I gasped, arching as he flicked his tongue over one peaked nipple, then the other.

"Is that a challenge, Red?" he asked, looking up at

me with a wicked glint in his eye. He pressed his body closer to mine, holding me against the column with one hand and his hips while he trailed his other hand down between us. His touch was electric, and I felt that caress shudder through me as he began to work me in slow, aching circles.

"No challenge," I gasped out as I felt a finger tease my entrance. I was already wet and aching, and I longed for him to press that finger into me. "Just don't want you hurting yourself."

Carnon chuckled, his mouth pressed against my neck as he finally gave me what I needed with the press of his finger. "Mmm, already dripping for me," he purred, nipping at the spot below my ear. "I think you're a bit of an exhibitionist, my love."

"We're too far up for anyone to see us," I pointed out, a little moan escaping me as a second finger joined the first. He was stoking a fire inside me and I was going to let it burn hot and fast.

"True," he purred, kissing me again as he pumped his fingers slowly. I rocked my hips, trying to move faster and get the friction I desperately desired, and he chuckled as I moaned. "But they can hear us."

His fingers slid out of me, and I protested with a little whine. It was quickly silenced by his kiss and the feel of him pressing against my entrance. He thrust in, the movement gentle enough that I bucked against him to try to move him faster and harder. He chuckled again, enjoying his chance to tease me as he held me trapped against the column.

"Impatient," he rumbled, wrapping a hand of shadow around my wrists and using his newly-freed hand to caress the curve of my breast.

"That's cheating," I hissed as his thumb brushed my nipple, shooting a bolt of pleasure down my spine.

"No more than your binding spell," he replied, wrapping more bands of shadow around me until I was held fast to the column by his magic. One band wrapped around my eyes until I could see nothing but darkness.

"Carnon," I breathed out, the momentary panic of the dark soothed by his touch as I felt him around me and in me.

"I'm here," he said, his breathing heavy as he began to move faster, thrusting into me with greater need as his desire grew. His fingers teased both nipples, and I cried out, feeling my release shatter unexpectedly through me. In the darkness, there was only touch and sound and taste, and something about the loss of one sense seemed to heighten the others. "Good girl," he purred as I shuddered against him. "Now louder this time."

He moved a thumb down between us, working me in deep thrusts and gentle strokes, as he ground against me, his own breath ragged as he chased his release.

Part of me wished I could move my arms to sink my fingers into his soft hair, or wrap them around his horns, but there was an appeal in being bound and at his mercy that sent a thrill through me as he built me to my next orgasm

"Carnon!" I cried out, throwing my head back as release crested through me a second time, the sound of his name echoing around us and drifting off into the night.

He came, roaring as he spilled himself into me, his bands of shadow releasing as he lost control. I nearly slipped to the ground, but he caught me against him, kissing me deeply.

The night sky was bright after the darkness of his shadows, and I blinked as we slid to the ground, Carnon pulling me close as he sank back onto the moonstone balcony. I lay atop him, burying my face into his hard chest, my cheek resting on the tattoo of the symbol of the Horned God.

"Will it always be like this?" I asked when the passion had abated enough for rational thought to resume.

"Sex?" Carnon asked, his hands stroking soothing lines down my body as we lay bare in the night. He must be cold against the stone, but his body was warm and solid against mine. "Or something else?"

"Everything," I said, uncertain how to word the question. "Our mating. Our relationship. Our nights and days."

"Yes, yes, and hopefully no," Carnon replied with a light laugh. "I'm hoping there will be far less planning for war during our days and far more moments like this with you."

"But," I hesitated, uncertain how to ask. From my own experience, witches kept their dalliances short. But demon mating was for life, and I had no real model to base my understanding on since my own parents had been kept apart. "You won't grow bored?"

"Of you?" Carnon asked, tilting my head up so he could see my face. "Of this? Never. If we live for a thousand years, Red. For ten thousand years. I will never get enough of this." He kissed my forehead. "I'm hoping you feel the same."

"Hmm," I said, pretending to consider. "Ten thousand years is a *long* time."

Carnon looked completely serious as he replied, "And

it would still not be enough."

Chapter 22

The morning dawned bright and warm, and Akela had still not returned.

"I'm sure he's fine," Carnon said. He was sitting at the little iron table drinking his coffee and reading reports, but I could tell his tone of unconcern was an act. He had already roused an extremely grumpy Artemis an hour before, requesting that she search for our missing companion. I was pacing the balcony like a worried mother as we waited for her to return with news. "Akela nearly took my arm off when we first met. He can take care of himself."

"Something feels wrong," I said, unsure how to put the nagging worry that had begun to push its way to the forefront of my mind into words. "I can just feel it."

Carnon regarded me steadily, frowning a little as he

looked at me over his coffee cup.

The dizziness hit me suddenly, and I clutched the balcony rail as a vision hit me, the first I'd had in several days.

I was in the Bloodwood, the sky red and trees twisting around me, looking furiously at Akela, who's maw dripped with blood. My arm was in agony, the rapid healing of demon kind not enough to knit this kind of wound back together quickly enough. If I bled all over the forest floor, the leshy would come sniffing around.

"Are you done?" I said, hearing Carnon's voice emerge from me. This must be his memory. His past. "Because I promise I'm not a good meal."

Akela growled as Carnon stared him down, some unspoken understanding passing between them as Carnon worked his beast magic. Akela whined, licking Carnon's face.

"Good boy," Carnon murmured, groaning as he rose. "Let's find someone who can fix this now."

I came out of the vision as suddenly as I dropped into it, finding Carnon standing before me holding me up by my arms.

"Back now?" he asked, anxiously scanning my face. "What was it this time?"

"You and Akela," I murmured, shaking the fog from my mind as the vision cleared. "In the Bloodwood."

"Before or after he bit me?" Carnon asked with a wry smile, guiding me into one of the metal chairs.

"After," I said, wondering at this new magic I had yet to understand. "Why do you think I saw that?"

"I'm not sure, Red," Carnon said, kneeling before me. He touched my cheek, as if making sure I was still with him. "They seem to be directed by your thoughts and feelings, and whatever circumstances you find yourself in. Maybe control comes with time."

"I'll ask Brigid when she gets back," I said, pressing the balls of my hands into my eyes, still feeling not quite right from the vision. "I wish..."

"What, Red?" Carnon asked, still before me on one knee, one hand resting lightly on my thigh.

"I wish I could ask my father," I said with a shrug. It felt silly, and maybe a little selfish, to admit this. Carnon, after all, had lost both parents very young. But he had Herne and Cerridwen to guide him, and I had no one but him to help me with my demonic gifts. "I don't suppose you're hiding a gift for prophecy?"

"I'm afraid not, my love," Carnon said gently. "It's rare, and your gifts are inherited. I think it's safe to say that your magic is quickly outpacing mine in strength and complexity."

"Sorry," I winced.

Carnon raised his brows. "Why should you be sorry, Red?" he asked. "I'm proud to have such a powerful mate. It means you can protect our people. And me, if I get into trouble." He added this last part with a wink and a kiss, returning to his own chair and his coffee.

A screech told me that Artemis was returning, and I shot out of the chair, my heart in my throat. She swooped rapidly down to the table, knocking over the coffee in her haste and locking eyes with Carnon.

"Fuck," Carnon said, shooting to his feet and sending Artemis back into the sky. "Time to go, Red."

"What's wrong?" I asked, panic rising as he threw on a shirt and pulled on boots, not worrying about tucking anything in or looking regal. I pulled on my own clothes quickly, pushing aside the mental images of all the horrible things that could have happened.

"He's hurt," Carnon said, strapping on a blade and grabbing my waist. "Outside the city."

Without a word of warning, I was swept into shadow. Carnon had never traveled with me like this and I did not enjoy it. The world seemed to twist and bend as we hopped from shadow to shadow, materializing for less than a second at a time as he moved us through the world. We emerged in the stables moments later, and it was all I could do not to vomit.

"Sorry, Red," he said, putting a hand on my back and holding back my hair in case I lost the battle with my stomach. "It's not a fun way to travel. Can you ride?"

I nodded. I took deep breaths as Carnon left me to saddle horses, shouting orders to the stable hands. Within minutes we were racing through the city. We traveled quickly up the path in the mountains to the moonstone gate and tunnel that led out of Oneiros. Artemis screeched anxiously once we emerged, flapping ahead of us to lead the way.

Akela was about an hour outside the city, and I seemed to feel him as we neared. I pulled my horse to a skidding stop when I finally saw him, lying limply under a hedge where he must have dragged himself to hide. He had a huge gash on his side, and from his labored breathing and the angle of his legs, I could tell that several bones were broken. I sobbed as I dismounted, running to where Artemis was hooting in distress.

The last time Akela had been gravely wounded, I had hesitated to pour my healing magic into him, knowing it would reveal my secrets to Carnon before I was ready.

This time, there was no hesitation. The magic poured from me before I even touched him, wrapping around his broken body, and I was inordinately grateful that my magic worked on him.

"Oh, Akela," I cried, lifting his furry head onto my lap and stroking him soothingly as I cried. "I knew something was wrong."

Carnon dismounted and joined me, pouring his own healing magic into Akela as well. "Shame on me for doubting your instincts, my love," he murmured, running gentle hands over the bones that had appeared to reset. "How is that, old friend?"

Akela whined piteously, and I sobbed out a laugh. He would be fine, but he was a dramatic creature. Carnon gave me a wry grin.

"Come on then, you big furry baby," Carnon said, hoisting Akela into his arms like an overgrown and very hairy child. "Let's get you home."

The horse was not happy about carrying the wolf as we made the awkward journey home. It took twice as long, with Akela resting in Carnon's arms, his furry head lolling over his shoulder to look at me behind. He remembered to whine sadly every so often, and I found myself promising all sorts of treats when we got home to make him feel better.

"You get all the steak," I crooned, patting his fuzzy neck.

"You're going to spoil him," Carnon warned. He put Akela down to walk on his own when we finally reached the palace. The wolf limped pitiably.

"Can you tell us what happened?" I asked, kneeling down to meet Akela's big, yellow eyes.

Akela tilted his head to the side, whining as he

pressed his wet nose to mine. I got the sense of danger, of an attack, and a great deal of blood.

"Can you make out what he's trying to tell us?" I asked Carnon, feeling confused for the first time while trying to read the wolf. Maybe he really was still in pain, because his thoughts seemed jumbled and disjointed.

"No," Carnon said, frowning as he knelt next to me. "He's confused."

"Can you show me, my good boy?" I asked, rubbing his ears. I had no idea if I could get visions from creatures, but I tried to clear my mind and focus on Akela and his pain and fear and confusion. "Let me see?"

Akela huffed a hot breath against my face, and I gripped him more tightly as I felt a familiar wave of dizziness.

"Red?" Carnon asked, his voice going fuzzy as I saw what happened through Akela's eyes.

I was the wolf. Get home. Get to my mistress. Those were the thoughts running through my wolven mind as something hit me from the side, causing agony to ripple through me. I growled, tearing at flesh and bone as something attacked me. It tasted like demon blood, and I fought in a frenzy to get free as more pain hit me.

I saw shadows and then nothing.

"Red," Carnon said as I blinked, the vision falling away. "What did you see?"

"Ugh," I said. I tasted blood in my mouth as if I were the one who had torn into all of those shadow demons. "He was attacked. Shadow casters. He doesn't remember much though."

"Are you sure he saw shadows?" Carnon asked, looking between me and the wolf.

Akela huffed as if to say, *of course, you idiot*, and I

nodded. "Yes," I said. "What does it mean?"

"It means that Scathanna is done waiting for us," Carnon said grimly, hoisting Akela back up over his shoulder and guiding me into the palace. "She's scouting our defenses."

"I think he killed them all," I said, patting Akela's head.

"Good," Carnon replied. "Then he bought us a little time."

※ ※ ※

I spent the day babying Akela and feeding him slices of raw steak while I sat curled up with him on the couch in our room. Artemis refused to leave his side either, so she perched on the mantle like a giant feathery statue while he napped on me.

I passed the time stroking his head and looking through my father's papers. I occasionally commented on my progress to Artemis, who usually responded with an aloof hoot. I didn't find anything else that seemed to be specifically for me, but he had some notes on the witches and the Crone that supported Agnes' story.

I reread his journal several times, hoping to trigger a vision of him and Mama with no luck. I knew that seeing them in a vision wasn't the same as being with them, but it was the closest I could get. I was thoroughly disappointed and irritated when Ceridwen flapped onto the balcony.

Akela whined when I tried to extricate myself from beneath him, and I rubbed his ears affectionately. "I'll be back soon. Carnon is right, you *are* a big baby."

Akela huffed as if to say, *but I'm a* cute *baby*, and I laughed as I scratched his head.

"Is he all right?" Cerridwen asked, looking at Artemis looming on the mantle with some trepidation. "Are you?"

"Just tired," I said, smiling up at her. The healing had, admittedly, taken more out of me than I would have liked. "What's up?"

"Tyr and Brigid have returned," she said. Her tone carried a note of unease that I couldn't quite put my finger on. "Something's up with them."

"We've known that for a while," I quipped, lifting Akela's head to a whine of protest so I could get my legs out from under him.

"Well it's worse," she said darkly. "Something happened between them out there. They are barely looking at each other."

I frowned. I had been rather hoping Brigid and Tyr would find an opportunity to confess their feelings on this trip. I wondered what happened between them to drive them further apart.

"I suppose it would be selfish for me to wish they'd figure out their relationship when we are in danger of imminent attack," I sighed, giving her a wry smile. Cerridwen returned the smile with a knowing look, and I laughed. "Where are they now?"

"In the dungeons with Carnon and Lucifer," she said, grimacing at the thought. "Dosing the prisoners to verify their stories."

"Do you think Scathanna coerced them?" I asked. We took the door and the internal hallways leading down to the lower floors.

"It wouldn't be the first time, although it's

admittedly more common in Blood where mind magics are well known," Cerridwen said thoughtfully, tucking her wings in tight so they wouldn't knock against the stone walls. "It's likely she did it through threats, rather than magic."

"And what's Carnon's plan?" I asked, rounding the corner to the main level of the palace and realizing I had no idea where the dungeons were.

"To wait for you, I think," Cerridwen said, giving me a nudge. "He values your input. So do I."

I smiled at my friend, taking her arm in mine. "You'd better lead the way then," I said, gesturing before us. "I have no idea where we are going."

Cerridwen squeezed my arm, leading me through so many hallways there was no way I could find my way back without her.

"Hopefully you don't have to come down here much," Cerridwen said as we descended into passages that were a dank contrast to the moonstone halls of the upper palace. This section was made from rough-cut stone and was clearly designed for function over beauty. I heard recognizable voices floating up to us as we headed deeper. "Ah, here we are."

She pushed open an unremarkable wooden door to get to another hallway, dark and lit with torches. It was so at odds with the moonstone palace above that I balked a bit, but I supposed prisoners didn't need luxury. Carnon was inside, discussing something with Lucifer as Tyr looked on. Brigid was nowhere to be seen.

"Where's Brigid?" I asked, taking a moment to study Tyr. He looked travel-worn, but not too bad. The cut on his temple had already healed.

"She went to clean up," Tyr replied darkly, clearly

remembering belatedly who I was to him now. "My Queen."

"And the prisoners?" I asked, turning to Carnon. He was looking over some documentation, and I peeked over his shoulder to see what looked to be written confessions.

"I want your approval on my judgment," Carnon sighed, looking haggard. "One acted on orders under duress. Scathanna has her daughter. I'm inclined to let her go free on the condition she stays inside the city while we send someone to retrieve the child."

"Agreed," I said, wondering where the predicament lay. "And the other two?"

Carnon sighed heavily again, signing one of the papers and handing it to Lucifer. "The other two are more complicated. Both claim to have no knowledge of how they got here or what they were doing. Both had the same story under the influence of bloodberry."

"But you don't believe them?" I asked, looking between my mate and Tyr, who had conducted the initial questioning.

"If they're telling the truth," Tyr drawled, his mask of cool disinterest slipping for a moment to show that he was furious, "then it means that Scathanna likely has a demon from the Court of Blood working for her."

"I didn't say I didn't trust you, Lord Tyr," Carnon hissed sharply, glancing at Tyr through lowered lids.

"No, but you're thinking it," Tyr spat out. "May I please be excused, if you have no further need of me?"

Carnon waved his hand imperiously and Tyr stormed out of the gloomy hallway.

"Do you want to test him again?" I asked, putting a hand on Carnon's arm.

"No," he sighed. "I want him watched every second though. What should we do about these two?"

I bit my bottom lip, trying to think of a fair consequence. "Bind them with a blood bargain to serve in your guard," I suggested. "If they're telling the truth, they can make amends by protecting Oneiros. If they're lying..." I shrugged, the rest going unsaid. If they were lying, it wouldn't take long for the blood bargain to claim their lives.

"Agreed," Carnon said, looking to Lucifer, who nodded.

"It will be done," he said in his deep, sonorous voice.

Carnon signed the documents and guided me out of the cells, Cerridwen walking behind us as if she anticipated an attack at any moment.

"We should meet with Brigid and Tyr," I suggested. "We need to debrief their mission and plan our next steps for the meeting with the witches."

"Tomorrow," Carnon said, cracking his neck and groaning. "I need a bath. And a shave. And food. And you, naked in my bed." Cerridwen coughed in embarrassment and I smacked my mate on the arm. "What?" he asked defensively. "It doesn't have to be in that order."

Chapter 23

As much as I wanted to know what was going on with my friend and her potential mate, we didn't actually have time to debrief as we had hoped.

Akela seemed to be back to normal, but he—and his new shadow, Artemis—stayed close by my side as I practiced magic with Carnon. Tyr joined us to provide praise or pointers and never once mentioned Brigid, despite my veiled attempts to talk about her.

I tried to get her to talk about it during our tasseography and tarot lesson, but she refused to be distracted by whatever was going on between Tyr and her.

"Elara, I love you, but can we please focus?" she asked in that quiet way of hers. "Thinking about him makes me confused and irritated, and I want to try to figure out how to help you focus your visions instead."

Brigid so rarely disagreed with anything that I couldn't find it in me to argue. By the time we were done, I had barely enough time to bathe, change, plan my mending spell, and meet the others in Carnon's office.

"I've hardly seen you today, my love," Carnon murmured when I entered. We were alone, the others scheduled to join us any moment, and I went to him to claim a quick kiss before whatever was about to happen next.

"You spent the morning draining me of my magic," I laughed, wrapping my arms around his torso as he tucked me into him. "I'm pretty sure that counts as seeing me."

"Tyr was there," Carnon grunted, lowering his voice as the others entered. "It doesn't count."

Akela huffed, reminding us that we now had an audience, and I stepped away, turning my attention to the mirror. I wasn't sure that breaking it after every trip was necessary, but I supposed it was better safe than sorry. I suspected that the Crone must be watching our movements, and I checked my belt for the vials of blood I had taken from Carnon just in case she ambushed us.

"Remind me why we are not coming with you as backup?" Tyr drawled, leaning against Carnon's desk as if he owned the place.

Carnon narrowed his eyes, but I took his hand and squeezed, answering before he could. "Carnon would have to lower the wards that guard the Darklands to let you through," I explained. "I can pass because of my father's blood, and it would be too dangerous to lower the wards with witches at the border."

"Artemis and Akela will be with us," Carnon added.

"But you and Artemis *won't* be with Elara," Herne said, raising a brow at us. "How exactly is that going to help?"

"Oh, ye of little faith," Carnon sighed, grinning at his friend. "You'll have to trust that we have this handled, Herne."

"If anything goes wrong, send word through the mirror, or send Artemis," Cerridwen said, nodding to my pocket where I had stashed the mirror Tyr and Brigid had taken to the border. Carnon had a second enchanted hand mirror so we could communicate with each other and with everyone here. "We will have someone in here at all times in case you need us."

I nodded, checking my belt and pockets one last time for all of my supplies. Blood, mirror, dagger, a crystal for good measure. I was ready.

Once again, I mended the large mirror, the spell coming almost without thought now, and said the incantation for travel. The mirror shimmered silver and fluid.

"I want you patrolling the city tonight," Carnon said as we prepared to step through. "Tonight would be a good night for Scathanna to attack. Let's not get caught unprepared."

As one, our friends nodded.

"Don't die," Herne grunted as I pictured Lilith's mirror in my mind and pulled Carnon through with me. We had decided to have Carnon wait there since I knew there was a working mirror, and I could easily get back to him if I needed him.

For the usual few moments, there was nothing, and then we stepped out onto dusty wooden floors and a darkened cottage, the red tinge to the sky outside confirming that we had arrived in the Bloodwood.

"Gods, it smells like death," Carnon said, grimacing as we stepped into Lilith's bedroom.

"The place is still standing," I noted. I had been half-worried that the mirror would be broken, but everything looked as it had been when we had last been here. "Do you think—"

"I doubt she survived, Red," Carnon said gently. "But I'll have a look around while you're gone. If I find her body, I'll take care of it."

"Goddess," I murmured, feeling a little nauseated. "What will you and Artemis do to distract the Crone?"

Carnon grinned, looking wild and wicked like he had in the early days of our acquaintance. He pulled me to him in a passionate kiss, a last embrace before we parted ways. "That is a surprise. Don't you worry about me, Red. Go get us this alliance."

I staggered a little as he released me, and he chuckled, looking down at Akela. "With your life, my friend."

The wolf huffed as if to say, *of course*. I scratched his ears as I said the incantation and tried to picture Vera's mirror.

"I love you," I said over my shoulder as Carnon and Artemis watched us prepare to leave. "Please don't die."

"You're as romantic as Herne," Carnon said with a tender smile. "Come back to me soon."

With a deep breath, I fisted my hand firmly in Akela's fur and stepped through the mirror again. We emerged in Vera's bedroom, just as dark and empty as it had been when I had last visited.

"Elara?" came a hesitant voice from the doorway.

I turned as Vera threw herself at me, wrapping her arms around me in a tight embrace. "Goddess above, when I heard about you and your mother and then *my* mother—"

"Vera," I said, interrupting her almost as capably as her mother. I smiled, taking in the sight of my childhood friend. Despite the fact that I had realized the friendship was somewhat one-sided, I still liked Vera, and I spoke true when I said, "I missed you."

"Are you alright?" Vera asked, patting my arms as if she could find some injury or damage. "The Demon King didn't—"

Akela growled at the suggestion, and Vera yelped, noticing the wolf for the first time. I put a soothing hand on his head, stroking him to show both him and Vera that everything was fine.

"I'm fine," I assured her, pushing her hands away gently. "And the demons aren't wicked or evil." I opted to gloss over the fact that a few most definitely were, figuring it could wait. "And the Demon King is…He's…" I hesitated, knowing Vera would struggle with the concept as much as I had when I first learned of it. "He's my mate," I finished with a shrug. "I love him."

"Your mate?" Vera asked in confusion, her eyes wide. "What does—"

"Later," I interrupted, enjoying this newfound firmness I had with my friend. "I promise I'll explain all of that later. But we need to go," I said, checking the position of the moon out the window and feeling anxious. Carnon had not given me the specifics of the distraction he and Artemis would be causing, but I didn't want to waste any time. "Where are we meeting?"

"Mother thought it best if we met here, actually,"

Vera answered, leading the way down the stairs. Akela padded next to me, keeping a watchful eye on the walls as if he feared Scathanna's spiders might be lurking. "The others are already here. I swear I had *no idea* that there were so many unhappy witches."

"I think we were kept very sheltered from it all," I said, remembering our innocence when sneaking into our first Coven meeting. The fact that we knew so little truth about the demons and that I had no idea our lands were failing without demon magic.

"Listen, Elara," Vera said, stopping me with a hand. "I want to..." She cleared her throat, searching for words. "I want to apologize. I believed all the stories the Crone told us when you disappeared. Long before that too. When my mother told me the truth, I felt like I was a terrible friend for not believing that you were innocent."

"It's fine, Vera," I said gently, patting her hand.

"It's not," she argued, shaking her head vehemently. "I was so wrapped up in my own life and desires that I realized, while you were gone, that I wasn't a very good friend to you. Anyway, I'm sorry."

My heart constricted at Vera's words, and since there was really nothing I could say to any of that without bursting into tears, I hugged her.

"I'll do better," Vera said quietly. "And you have support among us. Some of them are even Coven mothers."

"Really?" I asked, surprised that witches in the ranks of leadership would want to change anything about the system in which they lived.

"Really," came an elderly voice from the kitchen. "Hurry up, the tea is getting cold."

I raised my brows at Vera, who shrugged and shook her head. She must not recognize the voice of the witch either. We entered the kitchen where Agnes and four other witches of varying ages and appearances were waiting for us. Two I recognized to indeed be Coven mothers, one with black raven hair, and the other with warm chestnut brown. It meant we had some allies in power, and something in me sagged in relief.

I didn't recognize the other two witches, but they stood and bowed, raising their heads to look curiously at me, and casting wary looks at Akela. The youngest looking witch had golden hair, and reminded me a great deal of Brigid. The other was the oldest-looking of all of the assembled witches, with white hair the color of new snow, and she regarded me with beady black eyes.

"You look just like Circe," the golden-haired witch said. "Goddess keep her."

The other witches nodded and murmured condolences as we sat uncomfortably around the small kitchen table.

"The Crone will be coming," the black-haired Coven mother announced. "She watches the mirrors."

"How much time do we have?" The brown-haired mother asked at the same time a roar rent the quiet night.

"My mate has taken care of that," I said with a smile, imagining the havoc Artemis must be causing, and trying not to worry. "We have a little time."

"Your mate?" asked the white-haired witch, narrowing her eyes at me.

"The current Demon King, if I'm not mistaken," Agnes said, pouring tea as if she had merely mentioned the weather. The other witches murmured and looked at me with interest.

I nodded. "That's correct. How did you know?"

"The Goddess has a strange sense of humor," Agnes responded. She handed me a teacup which I accepted, although I didn't dare drink until I knew it wasn't poisoned or drugged. "She united your parents and similarly matched you to your father's successor," she explained, looking at the other witches.

Vera sat silently, biting her lip as she tried to take everything in. She took a sip of tea, which was enough to convince me that it was safe.

"Circe was right then," the golden-haired witch said seriously. "About the prophecy?"

"How did she know about that?" I asked, remembering that Lilith had said something about meeting her once.

"Your father," said the golden-haired witch again. She had dark, serious eyes, and she studied me in a way that told me she was much older than she looked. "He filled in a lot of the gaps for us about our history. The *real* history, I mean."

Vera looked like she was about to ask a question, but her mother silenced her. "Later dear, when there's more time. We need to talk quickly."

"Agreed," said the black-haired coven mother. "What is your plan, Elara?"

"Oh," I said, feeling suddenly very unprepared and nervous. Akela butted my leg as if to say, *you've got this*, and I tried to channel Carnon's confidence in me. "Well, we obviously need to be rid of the Crone, and eventually bring down the Bloodwood."

"Are you sure that's a good idea?" asked the white-haired witch. "The Bloodwood has stood for a millennia. It will not be so easy to merge two peoples who have so much hate between them. As much as I agree that the Crone must be replaced, why not simply continue on as we have with a new leader?"

Some debate broke out about this among the witches, and I steeled myself to advocate for my people. All of them. Demons and witches and mortals needed each other to thrive, and though I understood their fear of bringing down the Bloodwood, we couldn't go on as we had been.

"The Witchlands are dying," I protested, effectively cutting off the debate. "The realms were never intended to be separated. Do you not wonder why my powers are so much stronger than yours? Why so few witchlings are born, and why the mortals struggle to farm?" I paused, looking around at the witches to make sure I had their attention. "My father was a demon, and his blood strengthens my magic. Witches were born from demons and mortals, and we need the demons and their Horned God to remain strong."

There were some wide-eyed stares at this, but no one accused me of lying outright, so I went on. "Moreover, the mortals here are treated no better than cattle. But my mother believed, and I agree, that they deserve respect. Demons don't consume mortals to power their magic. They need mortal dreams to give them power, and so they are treated with respect in the Darklands." Now was not the time to add caveats about the Courts of Blood or Shadow, so I skipped past those and continued my appeal. "I have seen demons and mortals live together in peace, intermingle, even wed. And we are better and stronger for it."

I finished this speech to a mixture of nods and

frowns as the witches took in my words. I assumed these witches must agree with at least some of this to even be here, and I prayed to the Goddess and the Horned God alike that Agnes had spoken the truth about them.

"Which is why," I continued, latching on to the momentum of the moment, "we need to reveal the Crone's lies. In front of everyone."

There was a beat of silence, broken by Agnes taking a noisy sip from her teacup. She smiled warmly at me. "See," she said, "I told you, didn't I? Just like her mother."

"Show us this Goddess magic then," commanded the white-haired witch, still looking skeptical. Her voice was hoarse and cracked with age, and here eyes narrowed beadily in suspicion. "Your mother, Goddess bless her, told us before the Crone took her that she was right. That your demon powers emerged and you saved a child with Goddess-blessed magic granted only to the Demon Kings. A sign that you must be the one the prophecy foretold. Show us."

I felt a sudden flare of anger at this witch, demanding that I prove myself. "My presence here and my mother's word should be enough to convince you."

"It convinces me that you somehow escaped the Crone," the white-haired witch pressed. "And that you are allied with the Demon King."

"Fine," I gritted out, trying to sound diplomatic. "Agnes, do you have a piece of fruit?"

The witch raised her brows, turning to Vera, who nodded and fetched an apple from a bowl in the corner. I smiled as I took it, holding it before me and willing the dark snake of power in me to slither out and coil around its flesh. The apple blackened, withering as the witches gasped.

"Wait," I said, holding up a hand. I willed the bright magic out next, pouring life back into the fruit until it was red and crisp in my hands again. I let the healing magic show off a little as it bathed me in its silvery light. Carnon had taught me the importance of putting on a good show.

"Only the Goddess has the power to grant life," I intoned, trying to adopt my mother's way of speaking about our deity as the light shone around me. I let the magic work on the apple, shrinking it back to a small pink blossom like I had done once accidentally. "And she grants that power to the Demon Kings, who represent her will in the Darklands. Now, the power is mine. A Witch Queen, mated to and crowned by a Demon King a thousand years after the last such pairing was destroyed by the Crone."

I let the light fade as I finished my speech, placing the apple blossom on the table, hoping the whole performance had made me look a bit Goddess-blessed. It wasn't really lying if I *was* Goddess-blessed, after all.

The witches looked at me and then at each other in a mixture of awe and fear. I was just starting to worry I had gone too far when they nodded. Standing almost as one, all but the white-haired witch, bent to one knee before me. Agnes and Vera followed suit until only the white-haired witch was regarding me with hesitation.

"My Queen," said the golden-haired witch, smiling so brightly she reminded me again of Brigid. "We are honored to serve in the name of the Goddess."

Chapter 24

Coming up with a plan was not as simple as I had hoped. Not only did we need a way to convince the rest of the Coven of the Crone's lies, but we needed to bind her with a powerful truth spell and neutralize the mothers who would mobilize to defend her.

"With her blood magic, the Crone can escape any truth or binding spell," the golden-haired witch declared with frustration. "There's no way one of us can hold her."

"What if we all hold her?" I suggested, still thinking through the logistics. Agnes had produced maps and plans of Ostara, the Covenstead, and the Crone's manor, which were scattered across the table and somewhat stained with tea. I lifted the diagram of the Covenstead, examining the round room where Mama had died, "When is the next Coven meeting?"

"Not for three weeks," said the black-haired Coven mother. Before I could curse in irritation, a loud bang sounded from the direction of the forest causing Akela to growl and pace irritably. I took that as a sign that whatever my mate had planned was still going on, although I wasn't sure for how long.

"We have a few minutes left at most," I said, leaning forward to regard the witches. "Is there a way we can get the Coven to assemble sooner than that?"

"We could call an emergency quorum," the brown-haired Coven mother said thoughtfully. "If this distraction your King has orchestrated is as bad as it sounds, we could convince enough of the Coven mothers to request one. Attacks from the demons, and all that," she added, waving her hand to emphasize how ridiculous she knew the idea to be.

The thought that this could all be over in just one night was both thrilling and terrifying, and I squared my shoulders as my ideas solidified into a plan.

We quickly agreed upon how to proceed to make the best use of the witches we could rally to our cause. Each of the five representatives were in contact with a group of the other members, and each agreed to relay the plan to those who would ally with us.

"It seems we are in accord," said the golden-haired witch, smiling faintly. "What now?"

"Now I need you to bind your word," I said at last, "that none of you will betray us to the Crone. Or the mothers. Or anyone else who might try to thwart us."

"A witch's word is not enough?" asked the white-haired witch.

"Of course, we will bind our word," said Agnes, going to her cabinets and pulling out chalk, crystals, and candles.

"Not like that," I said, as Agnes brought the casting elements to the table. "With a blood bargain. Demon magic."

"Blood magic, you mean?" the golden-haired witch balked.

"All magic can be used for good or ill," I said, hearing myself parroting the same speech Tyr had given me. "Intention is key in casting, and yes," I added, looking at the young witch, "it's a form of blood magic. But I will not force anyone. If you don't wish to be bound, I will erase your memories of this night instead." It was something of a bluff. I hadn't practiced the memory-altering blood magic, since I never planned to use it, but I couldn't think of another way to make sure we weren't betrayed. "It is your choice, but I *will* protect my mate and my people, including you, if you are truly with me."

I had not practiced blood bargain magic either, aside from being on the receiving end of two blood bargains with Carnon. I should have asked him to teach me, since it was the only blood magic he willingly practiced. *The Blood Grimoire* said blood and intention were all that was needed to cast a blood bargain, and I hoped to the Goddess it worked as I retrieved my dagger from my belt.

"I'll do it," said Vera, the first to hold out her hand to me. "I was not always the best of friends to you, Elara, but I hope you know that I *am* with you."

"Thank you," I said. I smiled gratefully at her then turned back to the witches, who were looking warily at the dagger. "I want you to swear to me that you will harm no one present here, nor their loved ones, through word or deed that might betray us to the Crone." I hoped the part about loved ones was enough to protect Carnon, as well as my friends back in Oneiros. "A small cut is all that is needed," I told the witches as I sliced a line of red across my palm. I willed the healing magic down, needing the blood to complete the bargain. "My intention will bind the spell. If you do not wish to be bound, now is the time to speak."

Vera, in the first truly brave and non-reckless act of her life, took the dagger and winced as she sliced her palm. She grasped my hand as the magic flashed, sealing the bargain between us, and I breathed a silent sigh of relief that it had worked.

Vera pulled her hand back, studying the line of red that marked the bargain.

"When will this go away?" she asked, ever concerned with her vanity.

I smiled reassuringly. "Tomorrow night, once the plan is finished."

She nodded, cradling her hand as Agnes held hers out to me next. One by one, each witch agreed to the bargain, including—to my surprise—the skeptical, elderly witch.

"What will happen after?" the golden-haired witch asked, looking at me expectantly as she shook the pain from her hand. "Once the Crone falls and the Coven is free, I mean."

"I'm not entirely sure," I confessed. "We will need to find a way for witches and mortals and demons to all live and work together, and have everybody's interests heard. I hope you all will help me figure it out."

The two coven mothers left first. They would be

responsible for convincing the other mothers to call an emergency meeting, and they had to make a show of surprise when the commotion caused by Artemis was made known.

One by one, each witch left through Vera's mirror, each agreeing on which witches they would be in contact with over the next day to execute the plan. I grew increasingly nervous as the minutes passed, worried that the Crone would be coming for us, until finally only Agnes, Vera, and the white-haired witch still remained.

The white-haired witch grabbed my arm as she prepared to leave. "Your mother was right about you, child," she said, tilting her head to study me thoughtfully. "I think you will be a Queen to be reckoned with, and one worthy of the Goddess' blessing."

She dropped to her knee, rising with a nod before she stepped through the mirror. A strange thrill of victory went through me at the gesture.

"My turn," I said, turning back to Vera and Agnes. "Will you stay here?"

"Too risky," said Agnes, shaking her head. "Even with that rather admirable distraction, so many witches coming and going will attract the Crone's attention. After you depart, I'll smash the mirror. We will leave for the capital by horse tonight and stay in hiding until tomorrow."

I nodded, seeing the wisdom of this plan. "Until tomorrow then," I said, casting the incantation that would take me back to Lilith's cottage. The glass shimmered silver and liquid as the magical passageway opened.

"Smash the mirror and run," I said, turning to the back to Vera and Agnes. "Stay safe."

I put my hand on Akela's head and we stepped through the glass.

Carnon and Artemis were waiting, the strix perched on a bedpost while Carnon paced the tiny bedroom.

"Thank the gods," he said, crushing me to him.

"What happened to 'you are powerful' and 'believe in yourself'?" I joked as Carnon held me away from him to check for any injury.

"That doesn't mean I won't worry," he said, cupping my cheek. "You're well?"

"Yes," I said, rising on my toes to kiss him. "Ready to go?"

"Gladly," Carnon said. "The leshy were *not* happy to see us."

"The leshy?" I asked, whirling on him to gape. The wicked forest spirits had tried to lure me to my death and chased us up a tree my first time in the Bloodwood, not to mention the fact that they had killed Akela. I shuddered, remembering their skull-like faces and twisting horns. "*That* was your distraction?"

"Artemis led them on a little chase," Carnon said with a wry grin. "But I'll be happy to be back in Oneiros."

"Agreed," I said. "We move on the Crone tomorrow. There's a lot to do."

I quickly murmured the incantation for travel, picturing the mirror in Carnon's office.

Nothing happened.

"Red?" Carnon asked, his voice brimming with concern. "What's going on?"

"Hold on," I said, trying to clear my mind and carefully picture the mirror in Carnon's office. Every detail of the gilded frame. The glass that had been shattered many times. The etchings of the runes I had carved there myself. I spoke the incantation, pouring my intention to travel into it.

Still nothing.

"I think it's the mirror in Oneiros," I said, panic rising as I fished out the small mirror in my pocket. I tried the same incantation again, to the same effect. "It must be broken. It's just not there anymore."

"Fuck," Carnon said, running a hand agitatedly through his hair as I shook my head and tried again. "Somethings definitely wrong." He looked at Artemis and had a silent, intense conversation. She hooted her acknowledgment, flying out through the open window. "Artemis is going to fly to Oneiros tonight. We'll have to just sit tight and wait."

"You don't want to go now?" I asked in disbelief. I began to pace the small room, worry for our friends and the city and us combining into a knot of anxiety in my gut. "What if they were attacked? What if it's the Crone?"

"It will take us three days to reach Oneiros by horse, Elara," Carnon said. He grasped my shoulders firmly to stop my frantic pacing. "I can only travel short distances through shadows, and you just said that you need to face the Crone tomorrow night."

"But Cerridwen and Herne—"

"Can take care of themselves," Carnon assured me. "As can Brigid and Tyr. There's a whole host of guards in the city, and the Crone can't get into the Darklands, in case you have forgotten."

"Scathanna can," I said, my eyes meeting his as I saw the same realization coalesce there. "She's invaded the city."

"Probably," Carnon said, sounding altogether too calm and collected. "But we can't do anything about it here, Red, and I don't have a horse in my pocket, as much as I wish I could claim to. So we will stay here, and keep trying on the small mirror until we either get answers or until after tomorrow night. I think we should smash the large one, just in case the Crone gets ideas about following."

I nodded, casting a breaking charm so that Carnon wouldn't shatter glass all over the floor with his fists. The glass cracked neatly in two.

"Nice," Carnon murmured, smiling at me.

"How are you so calm?" I asked, feeling myself deflate into helplessness.

"Believe me, I'm not," Carnon answered, pulling me into his arms. "I will burn that bitch alive if she hurts our people or our friends. But I *have* to trust that they can defend themselves. They're strong and capable, and all of them knew the risks."

"The Crone probably knows too," I said, thinking through the logistics of whatever arrangement she and Scathanna must have. "They must have a faster way to communicate than just spiders."

"More mirrors, I'd guess," Carnon replied. He let me go and sat down on Lilith's careworn bed. "The Crone probably suspected my diversion was of demon origin and sent word to Scathanna to move on us."

"Or she saw us in the mirrors," I said. I sat down next to him, but the bed was too soft and sank low, with a spring digging uncomfortably into my hip. I wasn't sure how Lilith slept here for so many years. No wonder she was so cranky. "What are we going to do?"

"Tell me what you and the witches decided, and we'll go from there," he said.

Carnon listened intently as I described the meeting, and he laughed when I told him about the apple. "You're a fast learner," he praised, kissing my head. "And tomorrow night?" I explained our plan, how I was going to take out the Crone, and what the witches would do to support me. I also told him about the blood bargain I had sworn everyone to.

"And where do you want me in all this?" Carnon asked when I was done.

"You don't want to come with me?" I asked.

Carnon shrugged. "It's your call, Red. You know the witches. If I'm there, will the Crone twist it into the demons invading? Will it make the other witches doubt you?"

I pursed my lips, thinking. "Maybe," I conceded. "I want you with me, but you're right. The witches might interpret your presence as a threat. And if we are stuck here, you need to save your magic to get us out of the Bloodwood. There are no mortals to draw from if you drain yourself, and I can't travel through shadow."

"Yet," Carnon said, giving me a wry smile. "Knowing you, you'll start doing it before too long."

"Is this a terrible plan?" I asked. "We faced the Crone together last time, and we failed."

"You don't need me, Red," Carnon said, squeezing my hand. "Maybe if you didn't have a hundred witches, but you do. As much as I want to watch you destroy the Crone, and keep you safe from everything, this feels like something you need to do."

I nodded. "I feel it too," I sighed. "But I want you near the mirror, just in case," I said. "If we fail, or something goes wrong, I'll need you and Akela."

"Always," Carnon said with a nod. "Your plan is solid, Red. Best case scenario, the Crone doesn't suspect we would be reckless enough to walk into her seat of power, and everything goes as planned. Worst case—"

"Yes?" I pressed when he cut himself off with a sigh.

"Worst case," Carnon said seriously, "we improvise. And try not to die."

"Sterling advice," I said sarcastically. "Herne would be so proud."

Carnon grinned, despite the gravity of our circumstances, and I gave him a rueful smile in return. "I told you, my love, we are a formidable pair," he said, putting an arm around me. "I would not want to face either one of us in battle."

We sat there for a while, both lost in our own thoughts. Akela whined softly, resting his big head on my knee, and I stroked his ear absently.

"Thank you," I said finally, "for letting me figure out that meeting. For trusting me with this."

"You have literally nothing to thank me for, Red," Carnon said, looking at me with a lopsided smirk. "I know you can handle yourself. And if this is going to work, both our mating and the joining of our peoples, then you'll have to help me understand how the witches think and what they need. I'll need you to be a true queen."

He kissed my head, and I let myself lie against him before asking the question I had been dreading.

"Did you find her body?" I asked, nodding to the closed bedroom door.

"No," Carnon said darkly. "There's nothing in or around the cottage. It looks completely untouched."

We sat for another few minutes as the sky grew increasingly dark. It was peaceful, despite my anxiety for our friends and the aunt I never really got to know. If she was gone, then the last of my true family was really lost.

But I had Carnon and Cerridwen. And Herne and Brigid, of course. Even Tyr, although not exactly a friend yet, might eventually work his way into our little found family, if he and Brigid could figure themselves out.

My stomach rumbling loudly broke the spell. "Come on then," Carnon chuckled. "Let's see if there's anything edible here. You can't fight evil on an empty stomach."

We left the darkening room and opened the bedroom door with a loud squeak. I lit a small flame at the top of my finger until I found a lamp and some candles to light. The room looked just as we had left it, and Carnon went to the small kitchen and rummaged around the cabinets.

I took a seat at the small kitchen table, where the two bowls that had once held our blood still sat. "What's this?" I asked Carnon, reaching between the bowls. A small piece of parchment had been folded and stuck between them. I flipped it over to see what was written there and my eyes widened in surprise.

"That wasn't there earlier," Carnon said warily, coming to sit across from me. He watched me over clasped hands as he leaned his elbows on his knees.

I cleared my throat and read aloud:

> *I thought you'd be back here eventually. Don't go trying to bury me, I've taken care of all the particulars. There's no food, but there's tea in the drawers. Remember that fire destroys and also creates.*

"What does that mean?" I asked. I looked at my mate as I held the closed paper in my shaking hand.

"No idea," Carnon said, nodding to the note. "She can't have left. There's nowhere to go. And I doubt she survived the witches' attack."

I put the paper down, looking around the tiny cottage and wondering what my aunt had done. I sent a little prayer to the Goddess, asking her to guide Lilith's passage. I burned the note as an offering, a small gesture, but one I felt was needed.

It was silly, and probably just my overwrought brain playing tricks on me, but as Carnon prepared to hunt for our dinner, and I cleaned up the bowls of blood, I could swear I heard her cackle.

Chapter 25

It was one of the longest nights of my life—trying to sleep in the little hut that felt haunted by the memory of Lilith while worrying about our friends.

Carnon returned with a couple of rabbits that he set to work skinning and gutting outside. Akela padded inside to sit with me as I tried repeatedly to reach Oneiros through the small mirror. The spell failed each time, and I was so anxious that something was wrong with my witch magic, that I started casting scrying and locator spells just to make sure everyone was still in Oneiros.

"It's not you, my love," Carnon reassured me, sitting cross-legged beside me. I was sketching yet another pentagram into the floor using the ashes from the little note to draw it. He held a skewer of meat out to me, reminding me of our first trip through these woods. I took the skewer, sniffing at the meat. I plucked off a cube and tossed it to Akela, who caught it neatly between his teeth.

"Eat and come to bed, Red. You need to be rested for tomorrow," Carnon said, stroking a hand down my back. I looked outside, surprised to see that the moon was high in the sky and the fire had burned low. My eyes suddenly ached with tiredness.

"I can't sleep in that bed," I said, nodding toward Lilith's bedroom. "It feels haunted."

Carnon hummed, rising to his feet. "Fair enough. Give me two minutes."

I raised my brow in question but didn't follow as he left. He returned a moment later, pillows and blankets piled in his arms.

"Come on, Akela," he said, nodding to the wolf. "You can help with this."

"What are you doing?" I asked, rubbing the last of the ash from the floor. It probably wasn't necessary, since Lilith was gone, but it was still polite to clean up after casting. I rose, groaning a little as my knees cracked.

"Making us camp," Carnon said, laying out blankets and pillows on the floor in a somewhat haphazard nest. "It won't be as good as a mattress, but Akela makes a good pillow, as you know."

"I remember," I said, smiling at the wolf. Akela huffed in a superior sort of way, looking proud of his role as the official royal pillow. "What have I done to deserve you two?"

"Put up with a lot of lies and bossiness from me, for a start," Carnon sighed, flopping to the floor and patting the place next to him. "Come here."

"You *were* very bossy," I agreed. I dropped down next to him and let him settle me close. "And rather pushy."

"My sincerest apologies," he murmured, pressing a kiss behind my ear. "Sleep, Red. You need it. Akela will keep watch."

The wolf settled next to me and, snuggled between him and my mate, it wasn't long until I drifted off.

It was another fitful sleep, one in which visions of Lilith and my mother and my father wove in and out of each other with dizzying confusion. I tried to focus my dozing mind on Mama, willing her to answer my questions and tell me some grain of truth. I seemed to chase her in my dreams, winding through endless corridors of memory until at last I arrived in our cozy kitchen, Mama baking a pie in her floral apron, humming a tune as she worked.

"Why?" I croaked, crossing the room to grab at her sleeve. My hand went right through her, but she turned anyway, looking down at me with a sad smile.

"It was always going to end this way, my heart," she said, lifting a hand to pat my cheek. How she could touch me, I couldn't understand, and I choked back a sob at how real the moment felt. "And I don't regret anything, except leaving you without answers."

"But you loved him," I argued, trying to understand. "You could have gone to be with him."

"I did," she agreed, her sad smile turning a bit more joyous. "Why do you think I was so eager to be with him when I died?"

"I tried to save you," I sobbed, feeling both of Mama's hands on my cheeks as she soothed me.

"I know," she replied gently. "But I wanted to go. I

missed him."

"Circe!" shouted a male voice from outside the cottage. I gasped, eyes widening as I saw the distant form of my father striding up the garden path. The image fogged, and I clawed at it, trying to remain in the vision and see my father.

"We will see you again, my heart," Mama's voice said, her form drifting away from me in the haze of the fading vision. "We are always watching."

When I woke, I felt warm and safe and strangely light for the first time since Mama's death. Carnon's arms were around me and Akela was watching me with big, yellow eyes. I blinked, wiping away a tear as I tucked the vision into my heart. I would tell Carnon about it eventually, but for now I wanted to keep it just for me. My mother and my father, together finally in death.

The sky outside was lit in a dim red glow, the closest thing to morning the Bloodwood ever saw, and I wondered what it would look like when the wood came down. And how I would bring it down.

"Fire destroys and creates," I muttered, remembering Lilith's final message to me as I patted Akela's nose. He yawned, and I scratched his ear: "You can sleep now. I'm fine."

He huffed, dropping his head onto his front paws as he closed his eyes.

"When do you need to be ready today?" came a rough, sleepy voice from behind me. I turned toward my mate, who looked like he hadn't slept much better on the hard floor with anxiety riding him than I had.

"Sundown," I said. "I'm to arrive in the Covenstead. If Agnes is waiting for me, then it's happening. If she's not, I'll turn around and come back here."

"And then we figure out the next steps," Carnon finished, brushing a lock of hair out of my face. "Have I told you recently, Red, how gloriously beautiful you are?"

I smiled faintly. "A few times," I murmured, brushing a kiss over his lips. "You're very pretty too."

He chuckled, pulling me closer to him. "It's been a long time since I counted all of your perfect freckles," he said, his tone sending warmth tingling down my arms. "When this is all over, remind me to make sure they're all still there."

"Not now?" I teased, gesturing around us. "Is this not romantic enough for you?"

Carnon wrinkled his nose, but my anxiety about Oneiros had returned in full force, and I couldn't make myself laugh.

As if he knew what I was thinking, Carnon sighed. "They'll be able to hold out for a few days. Herne had the forces ready to defend the city in our absence."

"It will take longer than a few days for us to get back," I reminded him, wondering how close Artemis was to the city by now. "We should have planned a backup mirror."

"I can get us through the Bloodwood in a few hours moving through shadows," Carnon said, looking grim. "It will nearly drain me though, especially with no mortals around here to refill my magic. You'll have to protect us until we reach Oneiros. That will take another two days if we push ourselves and change horses every few hours."

"Scathanna could do a lot of damage by then," I said, flopping onto my back with a groan. "Will she kill them?"

"I don't think so," Carnon said, pushing himself up onto his elbow to look down at me. We had both slept in our clothes in case we needed to move at a moment's notice, and I had never wished more for his bare chest and tattoos. Something about them soothed me. "More likely she'll use them to get me to abdicate. If she kills them, she'll have multiple courts to quell."

"But not if you abdicate?" I asked, raising a brow. "I thought you couldn't abdicate?"

"It wouldn't be easy," he replied with a sigh. "And technically, I can't. But she'd used them to trap me into a bargain, then imprison me to keep them compliant."

"Let's not let it get that far then," I said, running my fingertips across the hard line of my mate's jaw. "There have to be a hundred ways to kill a spider."

"A thousand," Carnon agreed, turning his head to kiss my palm. His eyes flashed wholly green for a moment as he added, "but fire is the most satisfying."

※ ※ ※

"I'm starting to think I should go with you, Red," Carnon said as I checked my belt of supplies. I had the small hand mirror, which I would use to keep an open channel with Carnon in Lilith's mirror, my dagger, the silver athamé from the market in Oneiros, and a few vials of Carnon's blood.

We had spent the afternoon making sure Carnon could work the mirror, practicing the incantation over and over again until he could flawlessly reach me on the hand mirror every time. I also described the Covenstead hallway in detail, every single thing I could remember, so that if I needed him, he could reach me.

The mark of multiple blood bargains across my palm reminded me of what I was about to do, and I turned to my mate with my hands on my hips.

"Carnon," I said, using my best no-nonsense voice.

"I know, I know," he said, running a hand agitatedly through his hair. Akela whined in sympathy, also displeased that I was going alone. "I just...if something happened to you, Red, that would be it for me."

"I'll be fine," I reassured him, putting my hands on his face and pulling him down to me for a kiss. I tried not to let him see that the same anxiety ate at my soul too. "I had an excellent teacher."

"Gods, I love you so damn much," Carnon said, dropping his forehead to mine. The fact that my gentle teasing hadn't reassured him told me how anxious he truly was, and I stroked my fingers through his hair to soothe his nerves. "Please, Red, please be careful. If things go bad, promise me you'll run."

"I can't promise that, my love," I said. The agonized look he gave me almost made me waver, but I stayed firm. "But I'll find a way to get back to you, no matter what."

"You'd better," he growled, pulling me in for one last deep kiss. I felt him pour all of his love and fear and admiration into that kiss, and I held him tightly one last time. "I have freckles to count."

I smiled, pulling back and brushing the tear from his eye. If something happened—if I never saw my mate again—well, I didn't want to think about it. I smiled bravely, trying to hide my own terror at our parting. "Someone needs to be here if Artemis returns. Our family needs us, too."

Carnon nodded, still looking pained. He pulled his dagger from his belt and opened a small cut on his forearm. "Drink," he commanded. "If this is the best protection I can offer you now, I want you to take it."

"I have enough," I argued, indicating the vials.

Carnon just waited, so I rolled my eyes and took what he offered. His blood was warm and earthy and spicy, just like him, and I had to force myself to withdraw after a few mouthfuls, sealing his wound with a zap of magic and a kiss.

"My warrior Queen," Carnon murmured, wiping the blood from my lip. He tucked my cloak around me, lifting the hood over my head. "Give them hell."

"Remember, it's about intention," I said, gesturing to the mirror. "If you can't remember what the Covenstead looks like, think of me. That should work."

"If you need me, Red, I'll crash through every mirror to get to you," he said, watching me with crossed arms. "Just come back to me when it's done."

I nodded, feeling like no words would be enough at this point. My throat was rather thick anyway, so I gave my mate and my wolf one last long look before opening the mirror and stepping into the glass.

The moment I stepped into the paneled hallway of the Covenstead, I knew that the mission was happening. Witches hurried to and fro, and I pulled my hood down lower to cover my face.

Agnes saw me from across the hallway where I knew she would be waiting. I gave her a nod to indicate I was ready. We had very specific plans we had to follow to make this work, and I didn't have time to wonder which of the witches around me were on my side, and which were not. I followed the general crowd toward the open doors of the massive chamber that held the Coven meetings, scouring the floor for telltale signs of chalk.

I found the chalk circle quickly, shuffling into the row next to witches who I prayed to the Goddess would play their part. The night sky was darker than the last time I had been in this chamber, as the moon was still far from full. In the dim candlelight, I tried and failed to make out the hooded faces of the mothers on the dais. I hoped my allies were up there as a hush fell over the crowd.

"Sisters," came the icy voice of the Crone. "Let us begin."

With the practice of hundreds of meetings before this, the witches of the Coven began to intone as one:

> *In the name of the Lady of the Moon,*
> *Blessed be this place, and this time,*
> *and they who are now with us.*

I studied the Crone as I said the words with everyone else. Her missing hand was concealed by her long cloak, and it was impossible to tell if she was limping as she sat in an elegant chair, similar to a throne, that definitely hadn't been present before. The Coven mothers took their seats around her, and she cast a spell to amplify her voice and cast more light on herself.

She looked as young as ever, nowhere near the age of Lilith. I had refused to look at the anti-aging spell in *The Blood Grimoire*, but I strongly suspected it required a living sacrifice, based on the death I had witnessed here and the others that had no doubt occurred behind closed doors.

As she finished, I began casting the spell I would need in my mind. If everything had gone as planned, a hundred other witches would be doing the same.

"There has been a disturbance on our borders," the Crone intoned. "The Demon King attacked our lands at the edge of the eastern Bloodwood last night."

There were faint murmurs and gasps at this, but none from my near vicinity. I hoped and prayed this was because the witches near me already knew. I trusted that Agnes and the others had gotten our instructions to those loyal to my mother, but there was no way to be sure until the moment of truth.

I finished my incantation, prepared to use the spell when the moment was right. Agnes had said I would know it, but nothing had felt right to me yet.

"There is also a traitor in our midst," the Crone continued, ignorant of my silent casting. "A witch who we suspect to be colluding with the Demon King himself."

More mutterings erupted at this, and I had a sinking feeling that something was about to go terribly wrong.

"We have not been able to find the witch, as she fled in the night like a coward," the Crone added, as imperious as a queen holding court before the assembled witches. "I now ask that you, my sisters, find her and bring her forward. Where is Agnes?"

My heart sank to my toes as witches looked around for Agnes, whom I knew to be present. Was this the signal? The Crone must have seen the activity in her mirror.

"I'm here, you old bat," shouted a voice from across the hall.

Agnes stood, straight and tall and unflinching as the Crone pointed a finger at my mother's friend and shouted, "Seize her!"

"No!" I objected, rising from my place and closing the binding spell on the dais.

"Elara," snarled the Crone as I heard Agnes yell, "Now!"

A circle of witches rose from their chairs, all sitting around the line of chalk that the Coven mothers had drawn on the ground before the meeting. The dais was at the center of a massive pentagram etched on the stone floor, and we had just formed a closed circle around it.

At each point, a witch held up an element, a piece of the binding spell that the other witches would cast to hold the Crone in place as I wrestled the truth from her. One was Agnes herself, then Vera, standing tall at the point of the next arm of the pentagram, then two other witches, the blond and the white haired from our meeting. I was the fifth, and I held the athamé tightly as I felt it vibrate, connecting to the other elements at each point of the pentagram.

The whispered incantation of a hundred witches grew around me, a secret army closing the circle and binding everyone present to their seats.

"The spell is cast," I said with a smile almost as wicked as one of my mate's.

Chapter 26

"You," the Crone snarled, gritting her teeth as she wrestled with the binding spell.

I was sure she had consumed enough blood to do all manner of dark magic before attending tonight, so speed was of the essence.

But I had done the same. I felt it then, Carnon's blood pounding in my veins begging me to take her and tear her apart, my deadly serpent rising to steal the life from her.

Not yet, I told the writhing power inside me. We needed her truth first, or the rest of the Coven would never follow us. Vengeance had to wait a little longer.

"Good evening, Grandmother," I said, willing ice and steel into my voice as I spoke to the woman who had murdered my mother.

"Your magic cannot hold me," the Crone spat. "Release me and I may even let you return to your little dog and your snake."

"My mate sends his regards," I said, stepping onto the dais in the center of the witches. "Isn't witch magic marvelous?" I asked, gesturing around the circular hall. "I remain unbound because my friends will it, but with a single thought they could trap me like a fly in a web." The Crone twitched her pinky finger, a sign that she was fighting the magic and, terrifyingly, winning. I had to talk fast, but I worked to distract her as I built the mental altar for my next spell. "Speaking of spiders, how *is* Scathanna?"

"You must fight this demon magic, sisters," the Crone shouted to the bound witches. "She is using her mate's unnatural powers on you."

"Enough of that," I said, drawing on Carnon's blood to silence the Crone. The spell she had used on us was laughably easy, and her eyes widened in shock as she realized what I was doing. "They can plainly see that this is good old-fashioned witch magic, cast by a hundred witches who grow tired of your selfish lies and your murderous ways."

I cast the spell for truth, trying to find one of my own that would pay the cost for all of the Crone's lies. I settled on the one that brought me the most shame now, one that my childhood self would be loathe to admit.

"I used to want to be exactly like you," I said, feeding my truth into the spell that I wrapped as tightly around her with my will as I could. "And now I am eager to watch you die."

"Blood magic," spat the Crone as I released her from

the silencing spell. "See how she betrays the Goddess?"

"Like you, you mean?" I asked, praying the spells would hold a bit longer. Two fingers were twitching now, and I silently prayed to the Goddess for time. "How long have you been practicing blood magic against the Coven?"

The Crone opened her mouth, then closed it, realizing what I had done a moment too late to stop the truth from flowing out of her.

"A thousand years," she growled.

A gasp went up from the immobilized witches, who could do no more than widen their eyes in shock.

"A truth spell, Elara? Really?" the Crone chided. "You are wasting precious time. You should kill me before I break this pathetic binding spell and kill you all."

More mutterings from the crowd told me I was on the right track.

"Sisters," I intoned, softening my voice to try to sound more like my mother, warm and convincing and lovely. "The Crone has been lying to you. For a thousand years, she has used blood magic against you, and has worked to bring down the Bloodwood—not to fight an evil that longs to destroy you, but to wage war on innocent people."

"Tell them," I said, whirling on the Crone. "Tell them what the witches who confessed to betraying you really did. Tell them what you used their blood for."

The Crone's mouth twisted as she fought the truth again, and I poured a little more of my will into the spell to force the words from her, feeling the blood magic bleeding into witch magic.

"They did nothing," she said, her voice still magically amplified. "I accused them. Forced them to confess.

Used their blood to keep myself young." Each word sounded forced, and I hoped the gathered witches could feel the truth of them.

"My sister!" a voice from the crowd cried. "She was my sister and you killed her!"

More murmurings and cries grew, but I ignored them as I focused on the Crone.

"And why do you want to bring down the Bloodwood?" I asked, anxiety rising as I watched four fingers twitching now. "Why attack the Darklands?"

"We are not attacking them!" one of the immobilized mothers cried in shock. "Are we?"

"Answer her," I commanded, willing the Crone to obey. I felt Carnon's blood begin to ebb, and I tried to hold out for the final spell I would need.

"We are," the Crone choked out, words coming between tightly clenched teeth. "I want their lands. Their power. It should be mine!"

This last word was shouted as the Crone freed an arm, which she used to magically throw me to the ground. I managed to hold my point of the pentagram and pulled a vial from my belt, drinking it quickly. I felt power flood my veins, and I let the blood and my will do my bidding as I clenched my fist in the air, binding her once more.

"And who killed my mother?" I asked, voice cracking on a sob as I rose to my feet, athamé still in hand. "Who murdered her on this dais, slitting her throat for a blood spell?"

"I did," rasped the Crone, gasping in the clutches of my spell. I loosened my grip, just enough so she could speak.

It was a mistake.

With a roar, the Crone threw her power into the crowd. I cast my own magic out, uncertain what the Crone's goal was and trying to protect as many witches as I could. I sent both a shield of air powered by Carnon's blood to stand between the Crone and the witches and a wave of healing magic that crashed over the immobilized crowd. I couldn't tell if the screams were of pain or surprise or awe, but I held the shield in place and continued sending waves of healing out as the Crone threw her power at me.

"You will *not* harm these witches!" I shouted, gritting my teeth as I held the spell. The witches in the circle chanted the binding incantation louder, and I swore I *felt* the Goddess there, flowing around us and strengthening our magic. "And you will *not* harm me."

> *Maiden, grant me patience,*
> *Mother, grant me life.*
> *Crone, grant me wisdom,*
> *And lead me in the light.*

The words poured from me unbidden as I fought with all of my will and strength to hold back the Crone. I had felt the hand mirror shatter when I fell, and Carnon wouldn't be here in time. I had to do this, and I had to do it now.

The witches that formed the circle took up the chant with me, each glowing a faint gold in the darkness.

> *Maiden, grant me patience,*
> *Mother, grant me life.*
> *Crone, grant me wisdom,*
> *And lead me in the light.*

I repeated the incantation to the Goddess again and

again, until the faint golden glow that graced every Coven member's first official spell was a bright golden light that shone around me. It twined with the life magic, waves of white and gold washing over everything as I held the Crone back from my people.

"How…?" the Crone rasped, looking at me in horror as the witches throughout the hall began to chant in unison the same words over and over again.

> *Maiden, grant me patience,*
> *Mother, grant me life.*
> *Crone, grant me wisdom,*
> *And lead me in the light.*

Soon the room was awash with gold, and the Crone looked on in what I could only describe as awestruck terror, although I had no idea what she saw in me that changed her face.

She wouldn't live long enough to tell me, anyway.

I had wanted her to slit her own throat, to command her to end her life in the way she had stolen my mother's. But at that moment, surrounded by the light of the Goddess and the chanting of my Coven, I did not think a quick death was much of a mercy in the end.

"Goodbye, Grandmother," I said, as I tore the life from her with my father's Goddess-blessed power of death. His final vengeance for his mate.

Her face and skin withered first, the youth falling away to reveal rotting teeth and sunken skin and protruding bones as she screamed. Her skin blackened as she shriveled, until the last of her life drained away to nothing.

Her body hit the floor of the dais in a soft thud, and I dropped the magic, exhaustion washing over me as I spooled my power back into me and sank to my knees.

I expected screaming and terror and running in the aftermath of my magic. I did not expect a room of silent witches watching me, all stepping back to give me space, as I breathed heavily and tried to regain my footing in the wake of what I had just done.

"Please," I croaked, feeling hoarse and suddenly extremely vulnerable with so many eyes on me. Agnes and Vera reached me, the only witches moving in a sea of silent, shocked faces. "It had to be done."

"My lady," whispered one of the mothers from the dais. She was not one from our meeting, and her face was filled with awe and something else. Adoration, perhaps? She bent to one knee and added reverently, "My Queen."

As one, the chamber knelt, a great shuffling and scraping as every witch, including Vera and Agnes, took a knee.

"Why?" I asked, looking at Agnes and Vera for some explanation. Vera tried and failed to speak, looking as astonished as the other witches before me. I was still glowing faintly gold, and I wondered if that was the cause of everyone's awe.

"My lady," Agnes said, giving me a look that verged on warmth but was still very much consumed with awe and a little fear. "For a moment, just a moment, *she* was here. In you. Her three faces."

"Who was here?" I asked, my mind feeling sluggish and exhausted as I struggled to understand. "Who had three faces?"

"You," whispered Vera. "*Her*. The Triple Goddess."

❊ ❊ ❊

Becoming the Goddess, which all the witches swore up and down I had done, even though I had no knowledge it had happened, served to speed up the transition of power very efficiently.

Agnes took charge, announcing another meeting for the next day where everything would be fully explained. I didn't want to tell her that there was no way I could be there, but I hoped delegating was considered an appropriate action for a newly minted Goddess-Witch-Queen.

I had the wherewithal to fetch Carnon before I had to answer a hundred difficult questions, opening one of the many mirrors in the Covenstead hallway and shouting at him to step through. When he emerged, looking more like the hunter than the king, I burst into tears.

"It's over," Carnon murmured quietly, wrapping me in his arms and shadows, a cocoon of cooling darkness hiding us from view. "You're fine, my love. It's done."

"I know," I sobbed, drawing in wracking breaths as I tried to calm myself. I was exhausted, and the idea of having to do anything more than crawl into bed and sob made me weep harder. "I know."

Neither of us said anything for another moment as he held me, letting me gather my strength to face whatever came next.

"I am so fucking proud of you," he murmured, pressing a kiss to the top of my head. "And I'm never leaving your side ever again. I need you to protect me."

I laughed wetly, hugging him tightly once more before gently stepping away.

"Where's Akela?" I asked, noticing he hadn't brought my companion with him.

"Waiting for Artemis," Carnon replied, looking me over to double-check I was uninjured. "I thought a giant wolf might put your more flighty witches on edge. And he hates traveling by mirror."

"I don't blame him," I said with a light laugh. "Poor puppy. He gets all the steak."

"What do I get?" Carnon asked with a suggestive waggle of his brows.

"You get to be my supportive mate while I try and figure out how to be a Queen," I replied, squaring my shoulders. "I think I'm ready."

"Spoken like a true Queen," Carnon joked, offering me his arm as he swept away his shadows.

Agnes had efficiently ushered everyone away, except for the members of my mother's resistance, setting us up in a smaller meeting room to discuss what would happen next. There were, as Agnes had said, about a hundred witches present, and it was strangely more overwhelming seeing them crowded together than it had been seeing them stand to cast in front of the whole Coven.

Agnes handed me a cup of tea as Carnon and I entered the meeting room, bobbing in a deferential curtsy to us both.

I would definitely need to promote her.

"Order, please," called one of the Coven mothers, once I had worked my way to the front of the room. "We thank you, sisters, for the blessing of your trust and support. Blessed be."

"Blessed be," came the murmured reply of the witches, who turned to face me with a mixture of awe and fear and eagerness.

"My Queen," said the mother, nodding politely to me.

"How do you wish to proceed?"

I sighed, feeling completely wrecked. "Everyone here knows everything, yes?" I asked. "About the demons and the Bloodwood? About the prophecy?"

The mother, along with a hundred other witches nodded, still looking at me in a way that definitely suggested I had momentarily been the Goddess incarnate. Carnon shot me a bemused look.

"In that case," I said, handing my teacup to him as I stood, "you know what must be done next. The reunification of our realms," I said simply, nodding to my mate. "The Darklands and the Witchlands have been separated for a thousand years. It's time they were brought back together."

"And then?" asked one of the witches from somewhere in the middle of the room.

"And then," I laughed, feeling completely overwhelmed, "I have no idea. But I'm open to suggestions. I will need your help ruling, since my place will be with my mate much of the time."

There was some interested murmuring from the witches, and I looked to Agnes, who waved at me to go on.

"There is something else," I said, preparing them for the blow that I'd be leaving almost immediately. "We believe the Crone was working with one of the Daemon Lords. The Lady of Shadows seems to have been in communication with her, and we suspect that she has attacked the demon capital city, Oneiros. It's likely that she will try to take the Witchlands next if we can't stop her."

"So you must return to that city," Agnes guessed.

I nodded tiredly. "As soon as possible. I am

entrusting the witches in this room with three tasks. First, to explain everything to the rest of the Coven. There will likely be those who wish to leave, or who disagree with reuniting the realms. As long as they harm no one, let them leave."

"It will be done," said one of the Coven mothers.

"Second," I continued, "I need you all to decide together how you will govern yourselves without the Crone."

"But we have you," one of the witches said in confusion. "You are the Queen who was promised to us."

I quelled the following sounds of approval and chatter with a raise of my hands, scowling at Carnon's smirk of amusement.

"Yes," I agreed, trying to be patient, "but I can't always be in Ostara. My place will be to rule alongside my mate in Oneiros, like I said."

"Can I make a suggestion?" Carnon asked, raising the teacup to get my attention. The room went wide-eyed at his interruption, but I laughed at the ridiculousness of my fearsome, horned mate holding the tiny teacup.

"Please," I said, gesturing to the Coven.

"You did not choose me as your King," Carnon said, speaking more softly than he would to his own court in Oneiros. "And I will be the last to claim an understanding of Coven customs or laws. But in the Darklands, there are four courts led by lords that I entrust as stewards of my realm. They rule in my absence, manage matters of their court, and mete out justice for crimes against demons *or* mortals."

There was again some murmuring, this time perhaps because the idea of mortal justice was so foreign to the Coven, but he continued despite it. "The lords meet with me and answer to me, and in return, they have my trust and protection. My recommendation would be to create a fifth court, the Court of Witches, to preside over the Coven. That you choose someone to serve as its leader who will serve in this role for Queen Elara."

"And for King Carnon," I said, beaming at my mate and his use of my formal title. I turned back to the group, feeling more confident with his support. "You all must make the final decision about how it is done, but whatever you choose, your leader will swear fealty to *both* the Witch Queen *and* the Demon King. As will this court."

I noticed Agnes was taking notes on a piece of parchment, and I genuinely hoped the Coven chose her for the role.

"Finally," I said, "you must agree to share and abide by the laws of the Darklands. The demons treat mortals with respect. Practicing blood magic against another, or taking blood unwillingly, is forbidden. Mortals are not subservient or enslaved, and they may choose to live where they please. These rules will also apply to all of you, of course." I added this last bit as Agnes made a flourish with her pen, nodding as she looked expectantly at me.

"And the Bloodwood?" asked one of the mothers. "When will you return to destroy it? When exactly will our borders fall?"

I glanced at Carnon, who raised his eyebrows, letting me know the choice was completely mine.

"The King and I must return to Oneiros, tonight if possible," I announced, looking around the room for anyone who might complain or call me a fraud. No one did, and I went on. "Once the city is safe and we have dealt with Scathanna, I will return here to settle matters."

"Good," said Vera, smiling at me. I wondered at my friend, who was so similar to her mother. She seemed to have adjusted quickly to the new way of things, and I realized I might have misjudged her.

"In that case," Vera continued, glancing at her mother for permission to continue. Agnes nodded, and waved her daughter on, adding a few notes to her parchment. "In that case, you must go. We will meet again tomorrow, as you have asked, to explain and relay the new laws. We will discuss the leadership question tonight, and hopefully have a plan ready when you return."

"Thank you," I said, meaning it sincerely. "Thank you all, for your help and your trust, and for your loyalty to my mother."

The witches nodded, still watching me intently as Carnon took my hand and we made to leave. It felt strangely awkward and anti-climactic after everything, and I wondered if this was how Carnon felt after court.

"Wait," I said quietly, stopping to turn back to the room. Carnon stopped, too, squeezing my hand for support.

"I don't know what I'm doing," I admitted to the Coven, feeling like it wasn't a very queenly thing to admit. "But I want you all to know that I've seen how it could be, in the Darklands. I think we can do better. *Be* better. And I'm going to try my hardest to be a queen you can be proud of. A witch that my mother would be proud of."

"Thank you, my dear," Agnes said from the stage, standing to put her arm around Vera. "She already is."

Chapter 27

"I think I might be a little in love with Agnes," Carnon said as we crossed back into Lilith's cottage for what I hoped would be the last time. "Maybe I can convince her to come and work for me, and finally fire Lucifer."

"You can't fire Lucifer," I chastised, greeting Akela with scratches and pets as he nosed me to check for injury. "You mother hen," I murmured to him.

"Why can't I fire Lucifer?" Carnon asked, watching me greet the wolf with a long-suffering look on his face. "He's the surliest head of staff I've ever known, and I've known a lot of them."

"Firstly, because I want Agnes to be *my* representative in Ostara," I argued, giving him a wry smile. "For when we stay there, of course."

"Of course," Carnon agreed, as if he had already

determined which high holiday we would spend here. "Maybe for its namesake holiday."

I smiled, loving this male more than I could possibly have fathomed possible.

"Second," I continued, rising and catching Carnon's hand, "you can't fire him because he's in love with Pierre."

"What?" Carnon asked, giving me the most skeptical look I had ever seen on his handsome face.

"It's very obvious," I said, remembering the dessert incident. "Enemies to lovers. Classic."

"Had I known about this propensity for matchmaking, I would have seriously reconsidered plucking you out of the Bloodwood," Carnon grumbled as I wrapped my arms around his neck.

"No, you wouldn't have," I said confidently. "And it's not matchmaking. It's match-recognizing."

Carnon kissed me, a stolen moment between battles as I prepared myself for what we would have to do next.

"That's not a thing," Carnon said. "Are you ready to go?"

"No," I sighed, letting go to test the mirror one last time. I spoke the incantation, picturing Carnon's office so clearly I could almost smell the leather chair and the old books and the ink.

Nothing.

"Shadows then?" Carnon asked, holding out his arm. I let him fold me into him, putting a hand on Akela's neck to make sure he didn't get left behind.

"I can probably get us to Mithloria by dawn, but you'll need to be on guard duty. All my magic will be tied up in moving us."

"I'll do my best," I said, giving him a kiss on the cheek

for luck. "I have been told we make a formidable pair."

Carnon swept us into shadow with no more than an amused smirk at my joke. It took most of my concentration to not vomit all over him as he whirled us into shadows over and over, zipping us through the wood in less than half the time it would take to ride.

When we arrived at the edge of the wood, I barely had time to catch my breath before I heard an incantation.

I had forgotten about the witches at the border.

"Stop!" I shouted, throwing a ring of fire around the two witches who were preparing some offensive spell that would take far too long to cast. Both gasped, dropping their elements as Carnon slumped, exhausted, against a tree.

"The Crone is gone," I said, feeling very little sympathy for the witches attacking the border. They had a clear view of the quaint little village and could see the people meant no harm. "I suggest you run as fast as you can to escape the Bloodwood. I hear the leshy are hungry for witches."

The witches paled, sharing a panicked glance before running off into the woods.

"Wicked thing," Carnon groaned, pushing himself up as I bent over, trying not to be sick. "Are you alright?"

"I hate shadow travel," I groaned. Akela whined next to me in agreement and sympathy. "Are you alright?"

"Almost drained," Carnon rasped, still leaning on the tree for support. "The rest of my magic is holding the wards."

"We need to find some horses," I said, straightening, and pulling his arm over my shoulder as I tried to give him some of my healing magic. I didn't know if it would do anything, but he seemed to walk a little more steadily after. "We can go to the farrier in Mithloria."

"It will take us days to reach Oneiros," Carnon grunted, stumbling a bit as we moved.

"Then we ride hard," I huffed, struggling under his weight. "I need to kill a spider."

We weren't able to ride as hard as we wanted. We were both exhausted and drained of magic, and the short time we spent in each demon village wasn't enough to properly revive us.

Akela ran alongside us as we rode, barely stopping for a few hours here and there to rest or eat something. Carnon was growing increasingly worried that Artemis hadn't returned, keeping his eyes on the sky when he wasn't watching the horizon.

"I don't like this," Carnon murmured at one such stop. We had stopped in a small village to get some fresh bread and change horses, and he was scowling at the sky as we waited for them to be saddled. "She should have found us by now."

"If Scathanna has the city, it's possible Artemis has been caught," I said, stroking Akela's ears to soothe him. He was also anxious for his feathery friend, and I wasn't sure what would happen to either him or Carnon if Artemis was—well, I didn't really want to think about that.

"You look better," I commented to Carnon, trying to keep his mind off his bonded strix.

"You always know how to make a male feel special," he quipped, giving me a faint smile. "The sooner this is over, the sooner we can both sleep for a week."

"How long now?" I asked, watching the stablehand as he finished tacking the second horse.

"Maybe a day and a half," Carnon replied, knowing exactly what I was asking. "Then we need to take stock and plan."

Carnon tipped the stablehand, giving him an extra silver if he promised to alert the leaders of the village to have the people stay inside and keep their guard up.

"Scathanna's not likely to attack openly," he added, pinning the poor boy with a hard gaze. "But the people should be on guard until they have the all-clear from my soldiers."

"Yes, sir," squeaked the boy, running off to deliver his message.

"This is torture," Carnon groaned, mounting his steed as I climbed onto mine. "We are traveling too slowly. Damn me for not thinking of placing another witch mirror in Cerridwen's house."

"She could have destroyed that one too," I pointed out, also feeling chagrined at our lack of foresight. "All we can do is move as quickly as possible."

We took off again as fast as we could once we had cleared the village, riding so quickly that my legs and back and core were screaming in protest by the time we stopped for a few hours of rest.

As Carnon predicted, the mountains surrounding Oneiros came into view the following morning. As we neared, I expected to see smoke and carnage and fire, or at least something that warned us all was not well. But the mountains were quiet, the stone gate standing as a stalwart guardian as it had done for thousands of years.

"How did she cross the threshold of the city?" I asked, remembering the blood toll required of Oneiros' gates. "I thought the gate wouldn't let in anyone who intended harm?"

"Demon magic is tricky, Red," Carnon said as we slowed our pace so the horses could climb. "As long as she firmly believed she did not *intend* to do harm, she would be able to pass. The intention is everything. If she believed she were liberating the city, she'd have no problem passing."

"That seems like a useless piece of magic then," I scoffed.

"It's harder to trick the gate than I make it sound," Carnon argued. "You have to be *very* self-deluded or use powerful magic to convince the gate you are innocent. Simply telling yourself you intend no harm isn't enough. You have to feel it."

"Could anyone else trick the gates like that?" I asked as we neared the massive stone pillars that flanked the moonstone entrance to the city.

"Maybe me," Carnon said, "or perhaps the Crone. Otherwise, it's never been done."

"Gods," I groaned, slicing my hand and pressing it to the stone gate to pay the toll. "How can we combat something like that?"

Carnon grabbed my reins, pulling me to a stop before I could proceed into the tunnel.

"We leave the horses here," he said, dismounting and holding out his arms to help me down. "I have no idea what we are about to walk into, and they make too much noise. We go on foot and assess the situation first. No rushing in headlong."

"Are you calling me reckless?" I hissed, giving him an arch look as he helped me down.

"Your words, not mine, my love," Carnon said. "Now shhh."

He took my hand and we began the trek through

the tunnel, keeping our eyes and ears open in case Scathanna or her guards came looking for us.

Again, I strained to hear screaming or wailing or crashing, but there was only silence.

"It's too quiet," Carnon whispered as we continued to move to the end of the passageway. "I really don't like this."

A shuffling behind me was the only warning I had before a flash of pain crashed through my skull, and the world went dark.

※ ※ ※

The first thing I registered when I woke up was the pain in my head, which should have healed by now. The second thing was the stench.

It was hard to focus, and I instinctively reached for the healing magic in me, coaxing it awake. It responded sluggishly, easing the pain enough that I felt like I could maybe sit without vomiting.

Goddess, how stupid or egotistical were we that we hadn't expected an ambush? Of course, Scathanna had been waiting for us. I had no idea the state the city was in, or where I was.

"Ugh, it smells like a sewer," I groaned.

"It is a sewer, my lady," came a familiar voice.

"Pierre?" I asked, trying to see around me in the dark.

"The very same," he replied in hushed tones. "The King is here too, but we cannot wake him. Lucifer was perhaps a little too eager in his attack."

"In my defense, I had no idea who they were," the voice of Carnon's head of staff growled from the darkness. I could faintly make out his hulking shape and another crumpled one on the floor. A whine made me scramble to my knees.

I pushed myself to my hands and knees so I could crawl to my mate. The sewers were narrow and low, and the floor and walls were slick with slime that I didn't want to think about too much.

"Carnon," I said, shaking my mate's shoulder. "Gods above, Lucifer, he is certainly going to fire you for this." I poured my healing into my mate. It moved a little faster this time, which felt like a good sign. Our proximity to mortal dreams must be finally starting to replenish our weakened magic. "Why did you knock us out?"

"Because we didn't expect you on foot," Lucifer grumbled, sounding a little abashed. "And I had just finished taking out the shadow demons at that gate. I assumed you were hers."

"Scathanna's?" I asked. I cursed the Lady of Shadow's name to the Goddess when Lucifer nodded. We already suspected that she was here, but the confirmation made my stomach sink. Carnon would be devastated, and he'd blame himself for not staying. "When?"

"About an hour after you left," Lucifer said darkly. "It's like she knew."

"We think she did," I said, shaking Carnon's shoulder as I poured more healing magic into him. He groaned, and I shushed him with a gentle kiss. Akela attempted to help wake my mate by licking his face, which was quite effective.

"Gods," he groaned, reaching for me and pulling my body on top of his. "You smell terrible."

I let him kiss me once before pushing off, ignoring the insult. "We have an audience, my love," I said. "And you've taken a rather heavy blow to the head."

"Where—"

"The sewers, apparently," I said, anticipating his question. "Or so Pierre tells me. Lucifer is here too. He… uh," I looked at the hulking demon, who was clearly bracing himself for his forthcoming firing. "He saved us and dragged us down here," I finished, giving Lucifer a piercing look warning him not to contradict me.

"The Lords?" Carnon asked, groaning as he made to sit up. Pierre and I helped him, and he hissed in pain. "The city?"

"It's bad, Your Majesty," said Lucifer, clearly deciding deference was the best way to ensure he both lived and stayed employed. "The Daemon Lords are being held by Scathanna. The city has been damaged badly. Many have been killed or injured."

"Fuck," Carnon exhaled, gritting his teeth. "Why exactly are we down here?"

"Ambush," I responded quickly before Lucifer could contradict me. "We were ambushed."

"Some of the staff and people have been hiding in the sewers, my King," said Pierre, giving me a grateful look. When this is all over, I would insist that they thank me by confessing their feelings for each other. "Lucifer was helping some of the civilians escape and saw you…uh… approach."

I scowled at Pierre for this not-very-believable lie, but Carnon seemed too muddled still to notice.

"How many soldiers does she have?" he asked. "And where is the guard?"

"Fifty casters, my King," Lucifer said. "Your guards were forced to surrender. She was going to cut Lord Herne's throat."

"Fuck," Carnon swore again. "So she just walked in here and met no resistance."

"There *was* resistance," Lucifer corrected. "But she took us by surprise. Many of the guards were incapacitated by her shadow casters, and the rest were forced to submit quickly thereafter. She invaded through the palace. It was…unexpected."

"Through the palace?" I asked, confused by this phrasing until I realized how she had done it. "The mirror." I turned to Carnon, giving him a searching look. "How would she know what it looked like? You can't travel to an unknown mirror."

"Not sure," Carnon grunted, sitting with his back against the slimy wall. He shuddered a little. "Her spiders can go anywhere. It would only take one, and the knowledge of how to use them. I'm assuming we can thank your grandmother for that."

"She died too quickly," I said, feeling the dark ball of anger rise for just a moment until Carnon squeezed my hand and brought me back to myself. "What is the status of the city, Lucifer, as far as you know?"

"There are no guards at the nearest city entrance," he answered, sounding rather smug for someone who had just attacked his boss. "I took care of them. But there are five on the other gate, twenty patrolling the city, and the rest guarding Lady Scathanna and the lords."

"I shouldn't have left," Carnon sighed, letting his head fall back against the sewer wall. "You did fine without me there," he added, turning to me. "I should have stayed here and let you handle the witches."

"I needed your distraction," I pointed out. "And there's no use lamenting our choices now. Who's to say she wouldn't have you at knifepoint too? The only thing we can do now is decide how to act."

"How many did you get out?" Carnon asked. "Are there any soldiers down here with you?"

Lucifer exchanged a dark look with Pierre. "No, my King," he said. "Most of the kitchen staff, some of the household, and a few of the gardeners escaped the castle. The city is under lockdown. No one is permitted to leave their homes after sunset."

"And she hasn't sent anyone out of the city to hunt for us?" Carnon asked.

"Not that we've seen or heard," Lucifer said.

"She must think the Crone has us," I murmured.

Carnon nodded in agreement. "Probably trying to reach her to confirm as we speak."

"Excuse me, your Majesties," Pierre interrupted. The chef had been quiet, letting Lucifer handle the explanations, and I had almost forgotten he was there. "But what exactly are we going to *do*?"

"*We* are going to take our city back," Carnon said, looking at his chef seriously. "You and Lucifer are going to go to as many people as you can and organize them. We need the civilians to take down the shadow casters in the city. One by one, and as silently as possible. Arm them with whatever you can find."

"And you?" Lucifer asked, raising his brows at Carnon.

My mate gave him one of his typical smirks. "We are going to do something reckless."

Chapter 28

"This is the opposite of a plan," I hissed as Carnon and I crawled through the sewers. "Beyond reckless."

"I did say it would be," Carnon whispered back.

We had parted ways with Lucifer and Pierre just before dawn. They headed in the direction of the market to start planning the incapacitation of the sentries, while Carnon and I crawled toward the palace at the city center. Akela followed us, growling every time the sewer dripped on his muzzle.

"We need manpower," Carnon murmured, his voice muffled and distorted by the sewer walls. "Getting our friends out first will give us a better chance of taking out the Spider. And we can't exactly march in the front doors of the palace, can we?"

"What if they aren't in the dungeons?" I asked,

panting as I struggled to keep up.

"Then we will improvise," Carnon said simply, craning his neck to look back at me. "And hope that we are not too late."

"Goddess, I hope they're alright," I muttered, giving Akela a grateful pat on the nose when he whined in sympathy.

"If Pierre and Lucifer are successful, then the city guards will be off the streets by nightfall," he continued, taking a confident turn as if he knew the map of the sewers by heart. "And we will have had enough time to fully recover our magic. Then we should be able to break into the dungeon and—with my brilliant, reckless scheme underway—into the throne room."

"There are about a thousand ways this could go wrong," I mumbled, thinking through my inventory of spells for anything that might be useful.

"Ever the optimist, my love. Ah," Carnon said, stopping below a grate in the middle of the tunnel. "We're here."

"Where?" I asked, frowning as Carnon heaved the grate aside and stood to his full height.

A glint of his teeth in the dim light told me he was grinning at me. "Somewhere we can bathe."

"Really?" I hissed. "How is that a priority right now? We are just going to end up right back in the sewers."

"Have you smelled yourself?" Carnon joked. I poked him in the side, and he stifled a laugh. "We need to eat and sleep, Red, or we will be useless tonight. I'm going to climb up first, and then pull you up after me."

"What about Akela?" I pressed, turning to see that the wolf was gone.

"He already figured out where we are going and took

the less disgusting route," Carnon replied with a smirk.

Before I could ask again where we were, Carnon was shimmying up a dank tunnel above the grate. After a brief moment of scuffling, he reached his arms down for me.

"Remind me to add climbing to our training plan after all of this is over," he joked, grabbing my hands and pulling me up. "I'd forgotten how terrible you are at it."

"I hate you," I replied as I kicked off the wall to assist my ascent, and he pulled me through the opening and on top of him.

"No, you don't," he huffed, kissing me soundly despite the filth and slime. I made a face of disgust and he laughed loudly, so I assumed he was not concerned about being overheard anymore.

"Where exactly are we?" I asked, scrambling off him and looking around the dark room. We were in some kind of underground room or basement, if the outline of stairs against the wall was any indication.

"I'll show you," Carnon said, replacing the grate quietly and lighting a tiny flame in his hand. He guided me up the stairs confidently, and I wondered if this was yet another secret home he owned.

When he pushed open the door at the top of the stairs, I found myself squinting in the bright sunlight of Cerridwen's kitchen. A scratching at the door that led to the back garden told me that Akela had found us too. Carnon let him in, and he huffed at us happily. I was relieved that he was safe.

"Alaunus made me memorize the sewers as a child," he explained, holding the door open for me to enter. The kitchen was just like I remembered, if a little dusty, and I felt a small pang of guilt at the mess we were about to track through the tidy little home.

"Why?" I asked, raising my brows as Carnon looked at his hands, grimaced, then went to the sink.

He began scrubbing as he replied, "He made me memorize every inch of this city. I snuck out quite often as a boy, and he decided that if he couldn't prevent it, then he'd force me to learn how to get back without him knowing I'd left."

I smiled a little sadly, glad that my father had been able to raise one child as his own. Happy to have these stories passed down to me from my mate, even if it ached a little.

"He would have been an excellent father to you, Red," Carnon said, sensing my shifting mood. "He was to me. And I wasn't even his."

"You were a bit, though," I sighed, taking his place to wash my hands as he rummaged through cabinets for food. My stomach rumbled loudly, and I realized it had been a full day since I'd eaten anything.

"I'm sorry you didn't get to know him," Carnon said gently, producing bread that was a bit stale, but not moldy, and some cheese. "We eat and we sleep," Carnon added, dropping the food on the table, "and then we finish this war."

※ ※ ※

We didn't bother bathing in the end, knowing we'd be climbing right back into the sewers to get to the dungeons, but I had used one of the cleaning spells my mother had favored to get most of the slime off us and Cerridwen's floors. I didn't think my friend would thank us for tracking sewer muck around her house, even if she was grateful for the rescue.

The trek to the dungeons was longer and somehow even more disgusting. I had no idea how long it took us to get there, but the flashes of sky I glimpsed from the open grates above showed that it was full night by the time we reached the palace.

"This is going to be unpleasant, Red," Carnon warned, hefting a grate from the tunnel before us.

"Oh good, I was wondering when it would *start* to be unpleasant," I said sarcastically, giving him my most disdainful look, which he probably couldn't even see in the dark.

"And it will require some climbing," he chuckled. "All of your favorite things."

"Prick," I hissed.

"No time right now, my love," he murmured suggestively. "I think you'd better go first so I can give you a push if necessary."

"Please don't try to seduce me in a sewer," I groaned, entering the passage first and bracing myself against the walls as it sloped upward. "There's a line. That's it."

Carnon chuckled again behind me, and I knew that we were both distracting ourselves from our anxiety for our friends. And from this terrible plan Carnon had come up with. I also wasn't convinced it would actually work, but he seemed to have more of a grasp on how Scathanna's mind worked than I did.

"I can't believe you ever slept with her," I hissed, shuddering at the rancid water trickling past me. I tried not to think about what I was touching as I added, "Your standards were appalling."

"No argument there," Carnon huffed behind me,

grunting as he gave my backside a nudge. "As much as I'm enjoying this view, Red, I'll need you to climb a little faster."

"Can't you just spin us into shadow and shoot up this tunnel?" I asked, wondering how Akela was managing. Carnon had sent him on a separate mission to find Artemis, telling him to stay out of sight until they were both needed. He had whined and protested, but I had assured him we would be fine.

"I *could*," Carnon said, breathing heavily under me. "If you don't mind us falling and breaking our necks when I try to land vertically."

"Fair point," I said, groaning as my arms and legs strained to pull me up the increasingly steep shaft. "When does this thing end?"

"A few more yards I think," Carnon whispered. "Time for silence, Red."

We crawled and struggled the rest of the way in relative silence, with the occasional quiet grunt or snarl or curse, until the tunnel curved upward almost vertically. A grate blocked off the opening, and Carnon sent his shadows past me to remove it since all of my strength was focused on not slipping.

"Go," he hissed, pushing me from behind to help me up the final few feet. It was very undignified, and I crawled out of the tunnel vowing never to climb anything ever again.

"Well done," Carnon whispered, looking around for a sign of guards. There should be at least a few down here, guarding our friends, but I couldn't see anyone lurking as we checked our surroundings.

The room we had emerged in seemed to be the very end of one of the long, dark, stone hallways I had seen when I came down to the dungeons once before. Carnon gestured at me to stay quiet, taking my hand, and heading silently down the passageway. The hall was dimly lit by braziers, rather than the soothing ambient glow of moonstone, and I had to shuffle to make sure I didn't trip over anything as we hurried along.

One moment there was stone at my back, and the next there was nothing as Carnon turned us to shadow and darkness. A guard walked past, and I held my breath as I willed him not to look too closely at us.

"One," Carnon whispered, once the guard was far enough away that we wouldn't be overheard. "I'm guessing this is the right way."

He kept us in shadow, flitting down the hallway between the beams of light. He held in his whine of discomfort and I tried to breathe through the building nausea of shadow travel. Finally, after passing two more guards, we found a promising hallway.

This one was better lit, and a guard stood at attention before the door. It was iron, which meant we couldn't slip past it, and Carnon dematerialized before I had time to ask him what his plan was.

In seconds, the guard was gone, withered to a blackened husk by Carnon's death magic.

"Four. That one couldn't be helped," he whispered, clearly feeling the need to justify the death. "Can you unlock the door, Red?"

"Are you going to count every guard we pass?" I hissed, building the altar in my mind as I began to cast. I had used the unlocking spell on iron when the Crone had taken us. It had been the first time I had tried casting without elements. The lock clicked softly as my magic took hold.

"Sixteen to go," Carnon replied in answer, pushing the door open on a soft creak.

"You bloody fool," Herne growled from the corner of the dark room, yellow eyes glaring at Carnon with characteristic annoyance.

"Good to see you too," Carnon hissed, shutting the door behind us. "The cuffs, Red."

I went to work unlocking the iron cuffs that chained our friends to the walls as Herne cursed our stupidity. I thought I heard Cerridwen chime in, but I was focusing on getting Brigid free. The place reeked, and I tried not to imagine what had happened down here to make it so putrid so quickly.

"You came," Brigid whispered, eyes shining in the dim light of the room. "That was reckless."

"I believe recklessness was the whole point," I replied, giving her a tight smile. "Carnon has a plan."

"Of course he does," drawled Tyr. He watched as I unlocked Brigid's cuffs and met my gaze. I nodded, understanding his silent request as I pushed my healing magic into her.

She sighed with relief. "Don't waste your magic on me. I'm fine," she said. Her face was pained, despite her reassurance, so I pushed a little more.

"Your ribs are broken," Tyr reminded her. "You are *not* fine."

Brigid didn't reply, shooting him a hard glare as I moved to work on his cuffs. Clearly, they hadn't repaired whatever rift had come between them yet, but I didn't have time to worry about it.

"Any other injuries?" I asked as I unlocked the cuffs.

"I'm fine," Tyr said. "Cerridwen's leg is likely broken though."

I nodded, finishing his cuffs and moving to my other friend, who greeted me with a weak smile. "Welcome home."

I laughed weakly as I set to work on her cuffs. I couldn't heal her leg until the iron was gone, and my healing magic was already starting to feel sluggish again.

"Some welcome," I said, removing the cuffs and turning my attention to her leg, which was definitely broken. "How did this happen?"

She winced, then sighed as my magic began to work. "Oh you know," she said, attempting for levity. "Spider squishing."

"I've got this," Carnon said, squeezing my arm as he took my place. "I need you to do Herne's cuffs."

I nodded, going to the Lord of Beasts to work on unlocking the iron. "This was a terrible plan," he growled by way of greeting. "You couldn't convince him to be smart about this?"

"Have you ever known Carnon to change his mind once he has set it?" I asked, giving Herne a fond smile as I worked on his cuffs. "He says he has a plan."

"It's not much of a plan if we all die in the process," Herne grumbled, rubbing his wrists as I freed his ankles. "Scathanna lured you right into her web."

"It *is* convenient that you're all here in one place," Carnon quipped as he settled Cerridwen's leg. "Much easier to stage a half-baked rescue."

"Almost like someone planned it," I muttered, catching Carnon's eye. I raised my brows at my mate, and he responded with a nod and a smirk.

A faint popping noise was our only warning as several guards materialized from the shadows around us. Brigid cried out in surprise, and Tyr and Herne cursed as bands of shadow wrapped around us all.

I met my mate's gaze once again, and he mouthed the word, "showtime."

Chapter 29

"Well, well," said Scathanna with wicked delight as we were dragged before her. She was sitting on Carnon's throne, the once beautiful room now covered in webs and shadows. "What a lovely surprise. I hope you don't mind that I redecorated."

Carnon, who had been too focused on counting guards to pay much attention to the room up until this point, smiled blandly. "I preferred it without the spiders."

The whole plan, Carnon had told me in the sewers when I had argued that this was a terrible idea, was to make it seem like our plan was a terrible idea.

If we had walked in the front doors of the palace blazing fire and death magic, Scathanna would have captured us eventually, kept us separated from our friends, and bent us to her will. The dungeons were the farthest point in the castle from the throne room, and by falling into her rather obvious trap, we ensured that every guard in the palace, along with our powerful allies, joined us for the final spectacle.

Carnon's subtle nod assured me that he had been right and that, if Lucifer's count had been accurate, every one of Scathanna's guards, minus the ones Carnon had killed, were now in this room.

I hadn't been sure that Scathanna was vain or shortsighted enough to let us have such an advantage. It turned out that she was both.

"Pity," Scathanna drawled, pouting her lips in a way that was both pretty and sinister. "I was hoping to convince you to make the change permanent."

Carnon laughed, and I began running through my mental inventory. All of us were bound in iron to stop us from using our magic. Clearly, the guards didn't think I could unlock the cuffs if my own hands were bound, assuming incorrectly that iron worked on witches the same way it worked on demons. They were keeping me away from the others as an extra precaution, so I couldn't get to any of their cuffs easily.

Tyr and Herne had struggled against the iron bonds, but Brigid and Cerridwen were still, saving their strength and conserving their magic. Whoever said males were the better battle strategists were clearly mistaken.

"Believe me, Scathanna," Carnon drawled, giving me time to plan my moves, "I would sooner mate the Crone herself than make you my Queen."

"I assume you killed her?" Scathanna asked, her tight-lipped smile hinting at displeasure. Carnon shrugged, and she sighed. "The fool. She thought she could meet the Demon King in battle and walk away. But no matter. That makes getting rid of her much easier for me. You've done half of my work for me."

"And the other half?" Carnon asked, carefully not glancing my way as I tried to think. Witch magic would unlock the cuffs, and then I could either strike with my own demon magic or go for my friends. If I struck, I would likely burn out before I had finished the job. Better to go for my friends' cuffs then before I tried withering the room. But the moment I unlocked myself, the guards would restrain me. I needed a way to move quickly and remain free long enough to unlock all of our cuffs again.

"Why, that half is up to you, Carnon dear," said Scathanna. Her voice grated on me, and I felt strangely inferior, clad in iron and smelling like a sewer; while she sat on our throne in all of her glittering finery. I was sure that was her goal. "The Horned God made a mistake choosing you as the leader of these lands. It's high time we had a Demon Queen, and returned to the old ways. The Crone was a means to an end, but you've fallen so neatly into my trap here, it appears I gave her too much credit." Scathanna paused, preening at her own cleverness. "Now, Carnon dear, you can either make me your queen by marriage and get rid of your little inconvenience," she said, nodding toward me. I snarled at her and she rolled her eyes. "Or, you can abdicate to me and consent to remain in the dungeons for the rest of your days. I'll even consider sparing your little mate," she spat the word like it was a foul thing, "and leave her down there with you."

"Touch him, or any of my family, and I will tear your

spine from your body and choke you with it," I growled, throwing all of my vitriol into the threat. Scathanna crowed disdainfully, as if I were nothing more than a nuisance.

"Gods, I love you, my violent little witch," Carnon laughed, grinning wickedly as I bared my teeth like a wild animal. He turned back to Scathanna, still looking and sounding completely unconcerned about the threats to all of our lives. "You heard my mate. Let us go, or I'll let her end you."

How could I get to our friends quickly without being caught? Obviously stepping through shadow would be a handy trick. There was no witch or blood magic like it, save for mirrors. But I couldn't do that without Carnon, and the time it would take to free him would get me recaptured.

Unless...

I tried to think rapidly as Carnon stalled. My father had gifted me with fire magic and the power of sight from his own court, but I also had the powers of a Demon King. Life and death...but what of the others? I could wield blood magic. I could understand Akela. What if I could harness the power of one more court?

"Please," Scathanna said as if supremely bored. "Spare me the theatrics. One last chance to surrender like a good boy, or I start plucking out eyeballs."

I dug deep within myself, feeling for my magic. There was life and death, always coiling in my gut, and fire slithering around it. I felt my blood like another serpent wending its way through my veins, and a fifth snake, this one golden and shimmering, coiled around my mind.

I dug a little more until something black raised its

head, darker than my death magic and more intangible. It was this power I gripped onto, coaxing it awake as I began casting the unlocking spell around my wrists.

Carnon looked to me for less than a second, and I nodded imperceptibly. "If those are my options, then I suppose I choose violence."

"Fine," Scathanna said, waving her hand as if she had known she would have to call his bluff all along. "Kill them all."

The Goddess was in me. She was the moon and the night sky. The light and the darkness. The beginning and the end.

And so was I.

The spell is cast, I thought as I spun into shadow, the iron dropping from my wrists as I became nothing and darkness. The world seemed to slow and tilt as I moved through its shadows, going to Carnon first and unlocking his cuffs as I spun immediately away to the others.

Scathanna let out a roar as Carnon struck, taking out the guards holding him with a wave of death and fire that burned black, disintegrating flesh and bone and singeing the webs from the walls.

Akela and Artemis took this as their cue, both entering the room with animalistic roars and screeches as they began attacking the guards at the door, Akela with teeth and claws, and Artemis with beak and talons.

Herne was next, pulling the sword from his guard's scabbard and plunging it into his gut as I moved to release Cerridwen. She leaped into the air, grabbing the spear that Herne tossed her as she made for Brigid's guards.

Brigid and Tyr whirled into action as I freed them,

still consumed by shadows. Brigid became a pillar of flame, incinerating the guards in her path, and Tyr's eyes flashed red as he tore into the nearest male's throat.

The room was fire and blood and chaos as I spun into shadow one last time, making for Scathanna. Her shadows were spooling out around the room haphazardly, as if uncertain where to go, and I dispelled them with a thought, that dark, black thing inside me roaring with approval.

"You little bitch," Scathanna screamed, plunging her dagger into my gut as I materialized beside her.

"Elara!" Carnon roared, watching in horror and whirling into shadows of his own.

But I wasn't concerned. The Goddess was in me, and her magic filled me, sealing the wound shut within seconds as I pulled the dagger from my ribs and smiled at the spider bitch.

"Long live the Queen," I hissed, as I plunged the dagger between her ribs, the same spot Carnon had been forced to kill his lover for mercy.

Scathanna's eyes widened in surprise, but she didn't have time to respond as I took her life, sucking it from her and casting it into the air.

She had lived for far too long.

Carnon appeared at my side as she fell, his severely weakened magic reaching out to heal the wound that I had already closed.

"I'm fine, my love," I said, handing him the dagger I had used on the Lady of Shadows. "As you said, we are a formidable pair."

* * *

The whole thing was over rather quickly, and I mulled over how the battle had ended as I helped Carnon and Brigid purge the webs from the throne room. Tyr and Cerridwen were hauling bodies from the room, while Herne had gone to free the rest of Carnon's guard and send reinforcements to purge Scathanna's forces from the city.

Akela followed me dutifully, enjoying a head scratch every so often while Artemis watched all of us imperiously from her perch on the back of Carnon's throne. She gave a self-important hoot every now and then, and Carnon raised a brow at her in wry amusement.

"This felt too simple," I told Akela as I finished burning away the webs behind the thrones and pushing mine back into place next to my mate's.

"Simple?" Carnon laughed, coming over to join me, his own section of the throne room cleared. He kissed my head and pulled me down to sit with him on the steps of the dais. "My love. We crawled through sewers, staged a daring rescue mission, killed quite a lot of guards, escaped iron cuffs, not once but twice, *and* you harnessed yet another new magic that I'll have to train you to use. I wouldn't call this simple."

"But it was over so quickly," I said, frowning up at him.

"So hard to please," Carnon joked, kissing me again. "Take the win, my love. Sometimes the Goddess favors us. I believe this was one of those times."

"Plus," said Cerridwen, who slumped down in front of me, alongside Tyr. They were both covered in sweat and blood and grime and smelled absolutely terrible. "There's now a lot of boring bureaucratic work that has to be done."

"Like what?" I asked, trying not to grin as she shot Tyr a hateful look. Cerridwen was clearly on Brigid's side of their rift.

"Like finding the next Lord of Shadows," Brigid said, joining us to sit daintily next to me. "And rebuilding the damaged part of Oneiros and the Court of Sun."

"And bringing down the Bloodwood," Carnon added, nudging my shoulder, "reuniting the realms, figuring out a new political system for the witches, and convincing everyone to play nicely together. Believe me, Red, this was the *easy* part."

I smiled faintly, the weight of all there was left to do finally hitting me. Maybe it wasn't so terrible that, in the end, Scathanna had fallen easily. After all, it hadn't just been me doing any of it. I'd had the witches to help me with the Crone, and the most powerful demons in the kingdom to take out the spider bitch, as we were now all calling her.

Herne came clattering through the doors of the throne room, covered in just as much filth and blood as the rest of us, scowling thunderously.

"What in the damned depths of hell are you all just sitting around for?" he bellowed, eyes blazing as he took us in. "There's work to do!"

Chapter 30

It had taken a month to repair the damage that had been done to both our city and the Court of Sun. I had spent that time jumping back and forth between the Darklands and the Witchlands, which we would have to rename to something more inclusive, trying to make sure everything was ready for the moment when we officially joined our realms.

To my delight, Agnes had been chosen as the regent over the witches, and she had begun to train Vera as a possible successor. I supposed the witches would vote when the time came, but I hoped with enough time and practice, Vera would rise to the occasion. She was thrilled to be working in the capital and had taken to politics far more quickly than she had to healing or growing.

"Everything is ready for Mabon," she said, running through the final checklist with me before I departed through the mirror for Oneiros.

We had set up a small network of mirrors between the major courts in the past month, and they were becoming extremely popular amongst demonkind. I hoped a piece of popular witch magic would help ease the transition when we joined the realms.

All of the newly-elected Coven mothers, who would serve under Agnes, had been to Oneiros by this point. And they had relayed the wonders of the demon city to as many as they could in hopes of spurring friendly relations. With the Bloodwood still standing, no one but Carnon and I could travel into the Witchlands, but he had been able to drop the wards to allow the witches passage, under my supervision.

"Good," I said, tying my cloak. There was a chill to the air now, and I was buzzing with excitement for the fall. It was my favorite season, and this Mabon would hopefully be the first of many that Carnon and I celebrated in the Witchlands. "Are you happy, Vera?"

"What?" she asked, so surprised she nearly dropped her list. "What do you mean, my Queen?"

"Elara," I corrected, frowning at her. "You've known me since we were tiny. And I mean do you feel more content now, than you did when we were witchlings?"

"Yes," she said, hesitating slightly.

"But?" I pressed, smiling encouragingly. I had been working hard to rebuild a true friendship with her over this month, and while I had not yet thought her ready to meet Brigid and Cerridwen, we were getting there.

"Well," she said, suddenly sounding abashed. "I've been thinking."

I waited for her to continue, but she seemed to struggle with the words.

"You don't have to—"

"No, it's nothing serious," she said in a rush. "Just that, well..." her cheeks flushed very pink, and I raised my eyebrows. "Just that your Demon King...well he's very handsome. And I wondered if maybe I might have a mate out there too, somewhere. Maybe."

I grinned, both pleased and surprised that Vera had been considering this. "Would you *want* to settle down?" I asked, casting the incantation to open the mirror. "I always thought you liked being a bit wild."

"I do," she agreed. "I did. But...maybe change is good."

"Maybe it is," I said, smiling at her. "We will be back tomorrow at noon. Please tell your mother to have her official announcement ready."

"Of course," Vera said, slipping back into her diplomatic role. "And Elara," she added, still hesitant. "Maybe don't tell your king I called him handsome?"

I grinned, laughing as I stepped through the mirror and into our bedroom. It was much easier to have access to travel in multiple spots around the castle, and I enchanted several more mirrors, since frequent trips to the witches were necessary. Shadow travel was still tricky and nauseating, and I preferred mirrors anyway.

"You're late," Carnon drawled from the armchair, a glass of amber liquid in his hand as he waited for me in his finery.

"I know," I said, pecking him on the cheek as I ran to get changed. "I just need five minutes."

"That's what you always say," Carnon sighed, doing his best to sound like he was truly suffering. "And it's always at least ten."

"I promise, I'll be worth the wait," I called, teasing out my hair and brushing powder across my cheeks. The gown I'd commissioned for today was hanging on the armoire, and I spent a long moment just admiring it before I put it on. It was gray satin, with rose gold embellishments in the shapes of moons and flowers that flowed down the skirt and gathered in a pool of rose gold at the hem. The sleeves fluttered gently over my shoulders, and the neckline scooped low to reveal an expanse of breast that Carnon would certainly delight in. I smiled, reaching into the pockets that I had insisted be included.

A witch should always be prepared, especially if she was also a queen.

"You know," Carnon said behind me as I laced up the dress. I turned to see him watching me like a predator eyeing a particularly juicy gazelle. "We could possibly afford to be a little later."

"It's our party," I argued, laughing as he rose and prowled toward me. I ignored him, turning to pin the beautiful crown he had designed for me into place. My necklace hummed happily as he placed his hands on my hips and pressed a kiss to my neck.

"They'll wait for us," he purred, sending bolts of lightning down to my core as his hands worked to undo my progress on the dress. His lips trailed down my shoulder before he moved to the other side of my neck. "Just five minutes, like you said. We *still* haven't tried all of the things I want to do in that armchair."

"What exactly is it that you think we can do in an armchair in just five minutes that will make it worth being late to our own mating celebration?" I asked, giving up the fight over the laces and letting him undo my hard work.

He chuckled, kissing down my spine as a reward for my submission. "Lots of things," Carnon suggested, drawing the sleeves of the lovely gown down my arms and reaching around me to cup my breasts. He pressed against me, already hard, and I gasped a little as he played with a pebbled nipple. "Do you remember when I took you to that tavern? With the clams?"

"Vaguely," I lied, reaching back to grip his thighs as he continued to tease me. I remembered that dinner *very* clearly, and the idea that he wanted to replicate what we had seen the demon patrons doing that night was intriguing. Exciting.

"Liar," Carnon teased, sliding a hand down the front of the dress, which was bunched around my waist, and through the curls between my legs. He growled at the wetness he found there. "I think you remember just fine."

"Don't wrinkle the dress," I gasped as he pushed it further down my hips and slid a finger into me.

I moaned, thrusting against his hand as he tutted. "Let it wrinkle," he rumbled, lips trailing down my neck as one hand teased my nipple and the other parted my legs. "Then they'll all know what we did. How I claimed you." He nipped gently at my throat with his sharp canines and I melted, feeling warmth pool in all the places he was touching. He pressed harder against me, painfully hard beneath the trousers.

"Step out of the dress," he ordered, still holding me flush to his front. I tried to wriggle, to turn so I could feel him and tease him the way he was teasing me, but his grip was iron around me. "And then step backwards."

I obeyed, letting him walk me backward until I landed heavily in his lap. He hissed, thrusting his pelvis against my backside a little.

"Gods above, Red," he groaned. "You're going to make me finish before I've properly started."

"I'm still waiting for this to start," I challenged. He growled, rewarding my insolence with a second finger.

"Oh!" I cried out, falling back against his chest as he began to thrust his fingers in me, slowly at first. He continued to play with my nipples and taste my neck, all the while working to thoroughly unravel me. My feet struggled for purchase on the floor, but I was too far from the floor to brace myself with him sitting beneath me. I lifted my legs to rest on the arms of the chair instead.

"That's it, Red," Carnon growled, pressing into me from above and below me as I began to ride his hand. "Take what you're owed."

His hand left my nipple, sliding up to cup my throat as he continued working me with the other hand until the pressure and tension was too much. I shattered as I ground against his hand, heedless of the moans of abandon I was making that any servant in the hallway might hear.

"We're going to be late," I panted as I shuddered against him, his fingers slowly easing their way out of me. He brought them to his mouth and licked.

"Very," he agreed, turning my head to kiss me as he worked at the laces of his trousers. I shifted so he could get to them more easily, and he growled in protest, holding me close. "Don't you dare move, Red."

"But how will you—"

"I'll fucking manage," he said, cutting off my protest with another consuming kiss. "Curse the gods who invented trousers."

He finally worked himself free, which was made more challenging by the fact that he wouldn't let me stand up, shifting me slightly so he could free his length from beneath me.

"Now ride, Red," he growled, lifting my hips so I was sliding down onto him in a gloriously slow stroke.

"Gods," I moaned, throwing my head back as he palmed my breast again. The other hand returned to my center as he teased where we joined, and I wedged my knees into the sides of the chair so I could move properly above him. "This is..." I trailed off, words feeling too difficult and foreign with him filling me so completely.

"Interesting?" Carnon joked, letting out a soft groan as I moved up and down his length. He let his own head drop back on the armchair as he began thrusting up into me, meeting my hips with every move.

"Something like that," I teased right back breathily, letting out a cry of pleasure as he pinched my nipple in retribution. "Don't stop."

"Never," Carnon vowed, rolling his hips faster now as my second orgasm began to spiral out from me. "Gods!"

He groaned into my neck as he crushed me to him, my own release shattering through me in waves. We fell back into the armchair, spent and boneless as a knock sounded at the door.

"They're all waiting, your Majesties," Lucifer called through the door.

"Tell them they can keep fucking waiting, then," Carnon called back, his tone one that brooked no argument and sent Lucifer back down the hall without further discussion.

He squeezed his arm around me as I turned my face to his, capturing his lips with mine. "Five more minutes?" I asked, toes curling as I felt him harden against me again.

"Five more minutes," he agreed with a growl, kissing me deeply and reminding me exactly of all the things we had seen in that tavern.

We were, of course, more than five minutes late when we finally arrived downstairs, both a little wrinkled and disheveled from our tryst. Cerridwen looked harried as she waited for us by the big double doors of the throne room, Artemis and Akela waiting with her for their grand entrance.

"You're late," she admonished, narrowing her eyes at me.

"Don't look at me," I said, proclaiming innocence. "It was all *his* fault."

Akela huffed as if to say, *of course it was*, and Artemis ruffled her feathers in annoyance at being kept waiting.

"I'm sure it was," Cerridwen said acerbically, narrowing her eyes at her brother as he flashed her a grin.

"Totally worth it," he said shamelessly. "I won't even pretend to apologize."

Cerridwen grimaced and I laughed, finding it very difficult to be annoyed with my mate after what we had just done. I was feeling very warm and loving toward him at that particular moment, and I wondered if there might be time to sneak off part way through the party and defile some more furniture.

"Whatever you're thinking, Red," Carnon murmured

as Cerridwen arranged us for our grand entrance, "you need to stop." He twisted the black ring on his thumb and I felt my necklace hum in response. "Work now, play later."

"Promise?" I asked, giving him a seductive little smirk.

He laughed, kissing my nose. "Promise," he said. "Now behave."

The party had been planned for the people of Oneiros, a way to celebrate our mating and rebuilding as one, and it looked like the whole city had shown up. People cheered and laughed and danced and drank, and even Tyr and Brigid softened their icy treatment of each other in honor of the occasion. They were still only formal with each other, and I frowned.

Brigid had finally confessed what had happened between them to me and Cerridwen one night. We had decided to have a girls night and take a well-deserved break from rebuilding, and we got horrifically drunk on bloodberry wine and macarons.

"I wanted to," she said, confessing a moment they'd had while in Mithloria. "He kissed me and told me he was feeling the Pull, and I asked him to my bed."

"And then?" Cerridwen asked, clearly living vicariously as she had been a happily mated female for almost fifty years.

"He refused," Brigid said, choosing anger over despair, which I was always supportive of. "The bastard refused. He told me I deserved better. That I shouldn't want him."

"He told you what you wanted?" I asked, the bloodberry making me far too honest for my own good. "Rookie mistake."

"Ugh, I hate him," she said, throwing a pillow in anger. It exploded into a fiery ball of feathers, and she winced. "Sorry."

"Destroy as many pillows as you want," I said, handing her another.

"I hate him, I hate him, I hate him," she growled, each pillow exploding in feathery plumes of flame. "And I don't," she added, the anger fizzling to sadness. "Gods, I want him so badly."

"Then just seduce him," Cerridwen suggested. "Insist that you know what you want. It worked for me and Herne."

"No," Brigid growled. "He needs to come groveling back to me." She exploded one more pillow for good measure.

I sighed at the memory, watching her and Tyr awkwardly navigate around each other with polite but distant smiles. I would have to think of a way to force their hands, if neither saw reason soon.

"A dance, my love?" Carnon asked, drawing me from our friends and guests with a strong hand on my back. He added in a low voice, "I can still taste you, and it's driving me mad."

"More reason to leave this party early, then," I teased, taking his hand and letting him lead me around the floor. "Even if it *is* a lovely affair."

"Not so lovely as a private room with you, my mate," Carnon said, nuzzling my ear as he pulled me close. "What do you say to us escaping this infernal party in our honor and making violent love to each other for the next five or six years?"

I thought it was a very good idea.

※ ※ ※

Mabon was a celebration of the second harvest, and one that was typically celebrated with feasting and apple picking and, of course, prayers to the Goddess.

We had decided to spend the holiday in the Witchlands to celebrate the union of our realms and the official announcement of the new Court of Witches. I had spent a lot of the past month researching how to undo blood magic and difficult enchantments, and nothing had given me a very clear picture of how to destroy the Bloodwood. After weeks of searching, it was a passage in *The Blood Grimoire* about the effect of fire magic on blood magic, and Lilith's final cryptic note, that had given me an idea of what to do.

Agnes and the other witches had set up the fair at the edge of the Bloodwood in the small village ten miles from my old cottage. The irony that my journey would end in the same place it had started was not lost on me.

"The Goddess is a cyclical being," Agnes reminded me when I commented on her choice of location. "She appreciates the convergence of beginnings and endings. And she has a wicked sense of humor."

The Coven mothers were present for the celebration, along with Agnes and Vera, several witches from important families around the realm, and several important human families as well. I was pleased to see Agnes taking my requests to heart and inviting them.

"It was all Vera's idea, actually," she confessed, nodding to her daughter, who was flirting shamelessly with Sebastian, the farmer's son. Clearly, her interest in a potential mate had not dampened her interest in extracurricular pursuits yet, and I supposed it wouldn't until she found her true match. "She suggested we form two courts, if it pleases you. One for the witches and one for the humans. So that they feel they have an equal voice."

"I think it's brilliant," I said, smiling at my friend from a distance. "What will you be called?"

"The witches have agreed upon the Court of Moon, in honor of the Goddess," she replied.

"And the mortals?" I asked, smiling at the newly minted Lady of Moon.

"The Court of Earth," Agnes replied with a scoff. "I suppose it's because they are mostly farmers."

I smiled. "Earth and Moon, Sun and Shadow, Beasts and Blood," I intoned, mulling over the names of the courts. "It fits."

"If you say so," Agnes said skeptically. "They still have to appoint a lord, but you know how humans are about power. It could be a while."

"That's two courts without lords," I said with a frown. "No one from Shadow has claimed the title yet either. There's a great deal of infighting."

"Not so different from mortals after all, I suppose," Agnes joked. "Go enjoy the feast, girl. Be a witch for a while, instead of a queen."

I took her suggestion, congratulating Vera on her success and trying to make conversation with as many of the assorted mortals and witches as I could. Our family couldn't be with us, since they couldn't pass through the Bloodwood, but Carnon was here. He was engaged in animated conversation with the Coven mothers about some kind of trade plan, and children ran all around us, bobbing for apples and collecting fall leaves for wreaths.

Before long the sun had begun to set, turning the sky a crimson orange.

"It's time," Carnon said quietly as he joined my side. "Akela and Artemis just returned. The lands should be clear."

"The leshy?" I asked, turning to my mate. "The rusalka?"

"Despite my arguments against it, they warned all of the living creatures," Carnon said, giving me a rueful smirk. "If any are left, it's not because we didn't try."

"I suppose it really is time then," I said, taking a fortifying swig of wine. "You'll stand up there with me?"

"Always, my love," Carnon said, smiling down at me. He gave me a surreptitious smack on my rear as I made my way toward the small platform that had been built for the occasion, and I scowled at him playfully.

He shrugged, looking unapologetically wicked. My demon.

"Friends," I said, casting a quick spell to amplify my voice for the crowd. "For a month now, you have all been working hard to prepare for the union of our realms. The Court of Moon," I nodded to Agnes, "and the Court of Earth," I nodded to the mortal representatives who had yet to select a lord, "will join the four demon courts to become one united realm."

I paused for dramatic effect, letting a little of what Carnon had taught me about showmanship out to play.

"There is one final step in the process, and it currently stands before us." I gestured to the Bloodwood, the trees black and gnarled and the sky tinged red, as it had been for as long as anyone present remembered. "For a thousand years, the Bloodwood has separated our lands. It is time to drop that barrier and become one people once more."

I turned my back to the crowd, steeling myself for the magic I was about to expend. It wasn't complex, but it would be draining. Carnon joined me on the platform, as did Agnes, ready to ceremoniously join me in the destruction, even if they couldn't partake in it.

Lilith had left me the answer to destroying the Bloodwood, although it had taken me an embarrassing amount of time to figure out the meaning of her final note.

Remember that fire destroys, and also creates.

Magic was all about intention. The Bloodwood had been sustained by her magic for nearly a thousand years. It had been sustained by my father's sacrifice for another ten. And now, his power and my will would destroy it.

I thrust my hands toward the wood, letting that fiery snake grow and expand until a column of red-orange flame was skittering across the ground toward the wood. I blended it with my healing magic, willing the two to dance together in the remains of the old world, burning it down and growing it anew. The trees nearest to us caught, their branches burning brightly as I willed the Bloodwood to burn. To heal.

Carnon cast his fire out next, and the Lady of Moon cast a witch fire to add to my blaze, an inferno that turned the sky black and orange as it burned away a thousand years of betrayal and hatred.

The people cheered, a feat in and of itself considering how worried I had been about everyone accepting this new arrangement. Carnon put his arm around me as we watched the final barrier between our realms burn to nothing.

Mortals, I had learned, were industrious. In their short, bright lives they could do incredible things. Agnes had assured me that they would spread and farm and build roads, and that in another hundred years, no evidence of the Bloodwood would remain.

I prayed to the Goddess that she was right.

"You are a surprise and a delight, Red," Carnon murmured, kissing my head as we watched the world burn, just as he had told me we would. "And I'm honestly not sure I deserve you."

I looked up at my mate, at the beloved planes of his face, at his horns that glowed a faint orange in the light of the blaze, and then at our friends and new subjects, who watched as he and I forged a new world in the flames of the old.

I smiled up at him, hoping he could see the love and devotion I felt for him with every breath as I said, "You do."

Epilogue

Carnon

"Honestly," my mate said, chastising my chef in a very queenly manner. "You shouldn't be getting distracted like this around hot ovens."

I watched, still awed by the fact that someone shared my magic, as she healed Pierre's burned arm. Lucifer looked on like an irritable stone statue as he watched my mate heal his own.

It turned out that Elara was right, as usual, about their connection. I supposed that becoming fugitives together had made the two demons realize that their passion was less fury and more—well—passion.

"There," Elara said, the skin of Pierre's arm back to

normal. "No more distracting him while he is working," she added, wagging an admonishing finger at my head of staff.

"I make no promises," Lucifer replied in his characteristic, emotionless way. He looked stoically at Pierre, who raised a bushy brow at his mate, a smirk curving his lips.

"Take the evening off, if you can't focus on your work," I said, feeling strangely indulgent to the newly mated couple. "Elara and I can dine out tonight."

"But the soufflé!" cried Pierre, distracted momentarily from his lust by his other great love—baking. "I must rescue it before it falls."

I laughed as Elara shook her head at them, closing up her clinic for the day. Her idea to offer healing to others had been a good one and one that she had pursued with enthusiasm once the Bloodwood fell. It had only been open for a week, an unused section of the servant's quarters repurposed for her use, and already she had a line of injured and ill demons and witches and mortals out the door each day.

"I think I may have to recruit some help," she admitted, tidying up her books and herbs and general clutter that accumulated throughout her day. "Maybe some witches who are gifted in healing, to help with the less dire cases. And maybe we should move to a larger location in the city, since so many witches and mortals are pouring into Oneiros. These rooms have been fine, but I'm already outgrowing them."

"You can have anything you want, Red," I said, smiling at my beautiful, courageous mate as she tidied. I had tried to argue that this was a task she could leave to the servants, now that she was Queen, but she argued that a witch should take pride in her workspace, insisting on doing it all herself. "Have I told you lately how much you amaze and awe me?"

"Only five or six times every day," she laughed, wiping her hands on her apron as she hung it on a hook, and coming to me. She wrapped her arms around my neck, rising on her toes to kiss me. I fucking loved how she fit in my arms, against my body and lips, and it was very hard to stay focused on the reasons I had come to find her in the first place.

"Mmm, Red," I groaned, feeling myself stiffen as she kissed me. Gods above, this mating bond made me no better than an adolescent boy. "I can't think if you keep kissing me."

"Then stop thinking," she purred, catching my lower lip between her teeth. I groaned again as I caressed her, all soft curves and warmth and glorious freckles.

"In a minute," I promised, holding her away from me so I could get my head on straight. "I've had word from Tyr."

"Did they find the heir?" she asked, immediately snapping into the persona of the concerned Queen. "They only just got there."

"No," I said, sighing at the difficulty the Court of Shadows was causing us. Even the Court of Earth had figured out their plan for succession before Shadow had identified a new heir. It had been a month, and Samhain was quickly approaching. "But they hope to by the time we arrive. Do you still want to go?"

"Of course," Elara said, as if the thought of canceling hadn't even occurred to her. "It's tradition to spend Samhain in Shadow. I intend to honor your traditions, just as you have agreed to honor mine."

"The people in Shadow may not be the most welcoming, Red," I reminded her. "You killed their Daemon Lord, and now there's a battle raging over succession. And Tyr still hasn't figured out who was helping Scathanna with blood magic against his orders."

It had been a point of contention between us, the unknown source who had helped Scathanna warp minds. I argued that Tyr must know who it was, and Tyr argued that he had no idea. In the end, we dealt with the disagreement the same way Herne and I worked out our differences: we beat each other to a bloody pulp until we both relented. I agreed that Tyr was probably not to blame, and he agreed to root out the traitor,

"Tyr and Brigid will figure it out," she said confidently, a gleam of something a little mischievous in her eye. "Hopefully they figure out their nonsense, too."

"It will be another complication," I pointed out, "having Blood and Sun mated to each other. What if they don't have children? Or what if they only have one?"

"We will figure out succession in the future," Elara said confidently, leaning against me and resting her head on my chest. It fit perfectly in the space below my chin, and it was impossible not to relax into her when she made herself soft and warm against me. "I just want them to be happy."

"Tyr is a fucking idiot," I scoffed, remembering his drunken rant about the difficulties of females the night he and Herne and I had decided to go out drinking while our mates took over my bedroom to drink too much Bloodberry wine. Tyr was desperately, hopelessly in love, and also believed he wasn't worth the love of his mate. He refused to complete the bond with Brigid, arguing that she deserved better. Frankly, I was starting to agree. "He needs to get over himself and *let* himself be happy."

"Hmm," Elara mused, looking up at me. Her golden eyes and coppery hair lit her face like the sun, and my breath caught a little as it occurred to me that she was *mine*. After everything I did and every lie I told, she was still mine. I was Goddess-damned blessed. "Who does that remind me of?"

I chuckled, kissing the top of her head and steering her out of her little clinic and back through the castle.

"So, my love," I said, feeling like the luckiest demon in the Darklands. "Since our chef has the rest of the day off, what do you want to do about dinner?"

"I was thinking," she said, an adorable blush creeping up her cheeks, "that we could go back to that tavern."

"The one with the clams?" I asked, surprised after she was so scandalized by the place. "I doubt they'll have any today. The conflict brewing in the seas has led to a shortage, and the sirens are shipping less than half the supply they used to. I hope that their war doesn't touch us here, so far from the sea."

"Not for the clams," she said, her face turning an even brighter shade of pink. The ring I wore to symbolize our bond hummed, recognizing something in her that made me feel suddenly needy and feral. "I was thinking we might try something *new* there."

"Indeed," I drawled, pretending not to notice her rising arousal or the blush or the way my cock was currently straining against my trousers. "Salmon perhaps? Shrimp?"

"You are an ass," she said, face flushing crimson as I grinned at her discomfort.

"And you love it," I said, pausing in the hallway to kiss her soundly. She melted into me, and I had half a mind to forget entirely about dinner and sweep her through the shadows up to our room. "Tell me you love it."

"I love it," she confessed, speaking against my lips. "Now why are we still standing here talking?"

I grinned, kissing her again as I obeyed my Queen and swept her away to show her exactly how much I adored her.

And it involved very little talking.

COMING OCTOBER 13

After he rejected their mating bond, Brigid is resigned to working with Tyr as no more than a colleague. But when events conspire to throw them together in order to select an heir to the Court of Shadow, the pair are faced with the difficulty of their ignored bond and the reality that the Pull between them is stronger than ever.

To Sway a Demon Heart is an epilogue novella in the King and Coven series following the second chance romance between Brigid and Tyr begun in book 3. This book should be read after To Wear a Demon Crown in the series.

ACKNOWLEDGEMENTS

It feels very odd to be writing the final acknowledgement page in this series. It feels like far more than seven months in the making, and represents such a huge part of my identity this year.

First, my biggest thanks has to go to the amazing team of alpha readers, who are more like my developmental editors and had a huge hand in the creation of this series. To Aurora Culver, A. Linda Farmer, Kelsey McCullar, Jenessa Ren, Kimberly Sathmary, Lindsey Staton, Heidi Torr, and E.F. Watson: thank you all for every comment and edit and idea. I hope you see yourselves in this book as much as me, becuase it truly couldn't exist without your love, devotion, time, and ability to talk me off any number of ledges.

To those of you who served as therapists, idea bouncers, and emotional support buddies, this process definitely could not have happened without you. May Mama smile down upon you from a pillar of heavenly peen.

A huge thank you to my beta team, who serves as the greatest proofreaders, copyeditors, and comma catchers: Megan Brown, Brook McNabb, Maggie Miller, Cait Millrod, Abigail Myles, Christina Routhier, Dakshayani Shankar, Caressa Slater, Jess White, and Brenda Vann. Your dedication, willingness to nitpick, and time have made this book so much better than it would have been without you.

To my ARC teams, I am so blessed to have such amazing people both hyping and supporting me, and reading and reviewing my books. I know I'm a lot, and being part of my team means never getting a very long reading break. Please know how much I appreciate it and you.

To Kaya, thank you for continuing to be one of the best damn artists on instagram, and for bringing my characters and work to life so beautifully.

To my friends, family, husband, and everyone else who has supported this journey, thank you for your time and patience and support. It truly means the world.

And to you, dear reader, if you are still reading this now. Thank you for sticking with me this far. I hope you love what I have in store for you next.

ABOUT THE AUTHOR

Madeleine Eliot

Madeleine Eliot loves to read and write spicy romantasy with all of the best tropes. Dubbed the "Queen of Cozy" by her readers, Madeleine enjoys writing romantasy that is all vibes and spice, with a dash of adventure and world-building. She is always working on her next book, which is probably another spicy romantasy. Follow her adventures and latest works at instagram.com/madeleineeliotwrites

MORE BOOKS BY MADELEINE ELIOT

Queen Of All Fae Main Series

A Dream of Stars and Darkness
A Dream of Earth and Ash
A Dream of Frost and Fury

Queen Of All Fae Novellas

A Dream of Sun and Solstice

King And Coven Main Series

To Hunt a Demon King
To Break a Demon Curse
To Wear a Demon Crown

King And Coven Novellas

To Claim a Daemon Lord
To Sway a Demon Heart

Made in United States
Troutdale, OR
09/20/2023

13061414R00217